A Thorn in the Saddle

D1041852

By Rebekah Weatherspoon

A Thorn in the Saddle

If the Boot Fits

A Cowboy to Remember

A Thorn in the Saddle

REBEKAH WEATHERSPOON

DAFINA

Kensington Publishing Corp.

www.kensingtonbooks.com

Dedication

In Loving Memory of Jordan Roberge

This book is a work of fiction. Names, characters, businesses, organizations, places, events, and incidents either are the product of the author's imagination or are used fictitiously. Any resemblance to actual persons, living or dead, events, or locales is entirely coincidental.

To the extent that the image or images on the cover of this book depict a person or persons, such person or persons are merely models, and are not intended to portray any character or characters featured in the book.

DAFINA BOOKS are published by

Kensington Publishing Corp.
119 West 40th Street
New York, NY 10018

Copyright © 2021 by Rebekah Weatherspoon

All rights reserved. No part of this book may be reproduced in any form or by any means without the prior written consent of the Publisher, excepting brief quotes used in reviews.

If you purchased this book without a cover, you should be aware that this book is stolen property. It was reported as "unsold and destroyed" to the Publisher and neither the Author nor the Publisher has received any payment for this "stripped book."

All Kensington Titles, Imprints, and Distributed Lines are available at special quantity discounts for bulk purchases for sales promotions, premiums, fund-raising, and educational or institutional use. Special book excerpts or customized printings can also be created to fit specific needs. For details, write or phone the office of the Kensington special sales manager: Kensington Publishing Corp., 119 West 40th Street, New York, NY 10018, attn: Special Sales Department, Phone: 1-800-221-2647.

The DAFINA logo is a trademark of Kensington Publishing Corp.

ISBN: 978-1-4967-2542-4

First Kensington Mass Market Edition: November 2021

ISBN: 978-1-4967-2545-5 (ebook)

10 9 8 7 6 5 4 3 2 1

Printed in the United States of America

Acknowledgments

Well. Here we are. Our final ride through Charming, California. I never thought I would fall so in love with Zach, Sam, and Jesse Pleasant, but the brothers, their family, friends, dogs, and of course their lady loves are now a huge part of me. I really hope you enjoyed spending time with them.

I need to thank my agent, Holly Root, for her amazing support. You are the ultimate cheerleader, the visionary of the century. My editors Esi Sogah and Norma Perez-Hernandez, and the team at Kensington for their enthusiasm, especially when it comes to Jesse. Yes, I know he's my favorite too. Valerie Woods for seeing exactly what I see in these handsome men and beyond. You brought an expanded vision to what I put on paper that helped me get over this final hump.

My parents and my family who continue to lift me up and tell everyone who will listen that I'm a romance writer. I appreciate that more than you'll ever know. To my friends, writerly and not, thank you for encouraging me and celebrating me when dragging myself to my laptop felt absolutely impossible. A big Fenty thank you to Alyssa, Leona and Sarah. Oh you, know. YOU KNOW.

To Beverly Jenkins and Brenda Jackson. Your cowboys are the blueprint in my eyes. Thank you to the mountain tops and back.

A big thank you to Compton Cowboys, photographer Ivan McClellan, and the hundreds of Black equestrians who have let the world know that they are still here, riding high and proud in the saddle. I have to give a special thank you to Miss Alison and the crew at Moms Country Orchards. Our conversation has sparked six books now. I can't wait to come out to visit again sometimes soon.

And finally to the readers. Cowboys of California was something new for me. I was scared, I won't lie, but the love you've shown for the Pleasant brothers, especially Jesse (I GET EVERYONE LOVES JESSE), let me know I'd made the right decision to bring these fairytales to life, my way. Your kind words and amazing social media posts mean the world to me. For you, I write on! Yeehaw, baby.

Chapter 1

Jesse Pleasant's flight from Vegas to Ontario, California, touched down right on time. He'd managed to hold off the hangover he was positive would be waiting for him; still, leaving his brother and his soon-to-be sister-in-law's weekend of fun on the strip a little early was the right move. He needed to pace himself for the week ahead. The whole extended Pleasant crew, currently spread far and wide, would gather in Malibu to celebrate the union of Zachariah Pleasant and renowned celebrity chef Yvonne "Evie" Buchanan.

Jesse had to admit, it was strange to be on the personal side of things this time around. Long before his father, Jesse Senior, relinquished control of their family business Big Rock Ranch to Jesse and his brother Zach, Jesse knew how important weddings had been to their profit margins. Fifty-two weeks a year, and nearly every one of those weekends since Jesse had been a kid had been booked with a wedding. He knew all the ins and outs of seating arrangements, menus, floral arrangements, rehearsal dinners, receptions—all with a clinical eye for the cost. This time though, he could sit back and enjoy the duties of best man and people wrangler.

Zach wasn't the first Pleasant grandchild to get married, but thanks to Evie's celebrity status, this wedding was definitely going to be the biggest, the most lavish, the most over-the-top. The photos had already been sold to *People* magazine. Jesse needed to be present and prepared for every minute of it. On hand to keep his play-cousin Corie in check. Eyes open just in case his actual cousin Lilah decided sometime during the reception was the right moment to cuss out her estranged father, who had assured Jesse several times he was in fact coming, even if Lilah didn't want him there.

He'd keep an eye on his grandmother, Miss Leona, make sure she was comfortable. Keep his mother from trying to set him up with any single women in attendance, and if there was time he might hit the dance floor. It was a celebration after all, and if the week went well, maybe he'd be in the mood to celebrate by the time Evie walked down the aisle.

Jesse let out a deep breath and looked out the cabin window, waiting for the crew to give him the go-ahead to disembark. There was something about weddings, or knowing you have to give a best man speech for your own brother and a woman who was already close enough to be family, that had Jesse trying to shift through certain thoughts, certain memories. Picking out the good, for quality wedding toast's sake, while avoiding the bad, mostly 'cause there was nothing he could do about it.

He never imagined he and his brothers,—hell, he and whole his *family*—would be where they are now. When his grandfather Justice, once a Hollywood animal trainer, and his young wife, film actress Leona Lovell, had secured the deed to Big Rock Ranch in the scenic valley town of Charming, California, there had been one goal, one plan. Build the ranch up as a source of wealth for their Black family. Their three sons had their own plans, though. Their oldest son moved to Chicago, where he was now a successful surgeon. Another son went off to wine country to build up a vineyard of his own, and Jesse Senior went on to claim a record number of champion buckles on the rodeo circuit.

When they were old enough, Zach and their youngest brother Sam had set out on the rodeo circuit with him. Senior and Sam had been scouted as stunt performers and that led to both of them pursuing their dreams of acting, unexpectedly following in Miss Leona's footsteps.

Jesse was proud of them. Senior and their mom had relocated to London so Senior could work on a police drama, officially giving up the ranch to Jesse and Zach. They'd been living over there ever since. Sam was exactly where he belonged, one Oscar win under his belt and Jesse had no doubt there were more to come. He was dating a great young woman named Amanda McQueen, who was making her way as a screenwriter.

Evie had been along for almost the whole ride. After her parents had passed away, she moved to Big Rock to live with her grandmother Amelia Buchanan, the ranch's lead trainer and Miss Leona's oldest friend. Evie had fit right in, always out on the trails with Zach and Sam or in the kitchen learning to cook with Jesse and

Miss Leona. Somewhere along the way she and Zach had fallen in love, even if Zach didn't realize it.

Life and a little bit of stubbornness on Evie's part and a lot of foolishness on Zach's had sent them their separate ways after Amelia passed away too, but fate brought them back together. Sure, a piece of that fate involved Evie suffering a pretty nasty blow to the head at the hands of her former costar and losing her memory. But she was back in the fold now and the restaurant she'd just opened in Manhattan was doing great. She and Zach split their time between Charming and New York, and would keep that back and forth going after they were married.

Jesse sniffed and fought the urge to sigh again. The flight had only been forty-five minutes, but he needed to move and stretch his legs. First class on these tiny commercial jets didn't provide the legroom Jesse needed for his six-foot-seven frame. He let out another deep breath, keeping his eyes on the window as he heard the sounds of the Jetway locking into place. His seatmate was already on her feet, shuffling and shimmying so she could get off the plane first.

She'd been antsy the whole damn flight, but lucky for him she wasn't the chatty type. Jesse didn't want to slip up and make eye contact with her, just in case she suddenly had some last-minute things to get off her chest. He turned off the airplane mode function on his phone and checked the text messages that popped up on his screen: a picture from his cousin Lilah, holding up a plate with a waffle the size of her head.

You definitely should have stayed for this.

He held his thumb on the message and sent her two exclamation points of excitement back. He did enjoy a good waffle, but not enough to spend another minute in Vegas with his brothers and cousins and their significant others. Yeah, Lilah was single, but she seemed to enjoy all the girl time she got with Evie, Corie, Amanda and Vega, formerly Evie's private nurse following her incident, currently Corie's girlfriend. Jesse liked hanging out with his brothers. He loved them, but for some reason this weekend he just wasn't feeling it and instead of letting his emotions get the best of him, he used his early morning meeting as an excuse to skip out on the remaining hours of their bachelor/ette weekend.

He switched over to the message waiting for him from Bruce, one of the drivers from the ranch.

Waiting at pickup site B.
Let me know when you land, boss.

Landed.
Out in a few.

The cabin door opened and his seatmate was off, damn near plowing over the flight attendant to power walk up the Jetway. Jesse followed, Stetson in one hand, his carry-on in the other. He politely thanked the flight crew before he ducked his head and exited the plane. He waited till he cleared the enclosed bridge before he slid his Stetson on his bald head. The airport wasn't too full, but he could feel several pairs of eyes on him as he made his way toward the exit. He knew what he looked like, dark brown skin, tall as fuck, wide as fuck, legs the size of tree trunks, well-dressed with a cowboy hat on his head, a manicured goatee that maybe one in a few thousand men could pull off.

He attracted attention wherever he went. Some of it good, some of it not. With his long strides it wasn't long before he caught up with his seatmate, just before she darted into the women's restroom. Probably explained her two-stepping to get the hell off the plane. Jesse continued on, past baggage claim and out into the warm desert sun. Bruce was waiting right at the curb in one of the ranch's navy blue SUVs. He hopped out as soon as he spotted Jesse and rushed around to open the trunk for his carry-on.

"Welcome back."

"Thank you. Had enough Vegas to last me the rest of the year."

Bruce laughed and clapped him on the shoulder. "Let's get you back to the comforts of home."

Jesse climbed in the front seat, glad to see Bruce had already pushed the seat back as far as it would go, not that it was the amount of legroom that Jesse liked or needed, but it would do for their short ride back to his house on Pleasant Lane.

"So, you have a good time?" Bruce asked as they pulled out of the airport loop.

"I think so."

"Not sure? You were there, right?"

"Well, it wasn't my weekend. I enjoyed myself, but it's more important that Zach and Evie enjoyed themselves."

"I'm sure they did. Especially with Corie tagging along."

Jesse held back a shudder. It only made sense for his grandmother, thee Leona Lovell, star of stage and screen, to have a personal assistant. And that assistant had been like family before she was officially hired, but Corie had her doctorate in fuckery and bullshit. If there was trouble with a side of drama to be had, Corie would find it. Luckily, Evie wasn't afraid to tell her no.

"I'll swing back with the pass van at seven to pick up Zach and the rest of the gang."

"Thank you." Bruce knew Jesse well enough to know that was enough conversation for today. He turned the country music he had streaming through the car's speakers back up and let Jesse enjoy the rest of the ride back to his home at Pleasant Lane in silence, the way he preferred it. His own brain produced enough ambient noise most hours of the day. Jesse pulled out his phone and checked his emails.

His meeting with A New Way Forward or ANWF, was locked in for ten a.m. the following morning in the big conference room at the ranch. The Democratic action committee had reached out to him a few weeks before, hoping to convince him to run for Congress. Paul Cogger would be vacating the seat and there was a push to fill it with young, progressive blood who would do well across generational demographics.

While Jesse was an older millennial who'd spent 90 percent of his free time in service to the elderly folks in their community of Charming, he was convinced they had to have the wrong Pleasant. When they pressed him on the opportunities this could provide for himself and his district, he'd resolved to hear them out.

He and Zach had been running their family's luxury dude ranch for over ten years now. Things were going well, great if he was being honest. Most weeks they were booked to capacity. The calendar was filled with weddings, reunions, corporate retreats all year long, thanks to the changes he and his brother had made when they took over from the former manager. Jesse had set out to make his parents and his grandmother proud, honor what his grandparents had intended and so far, he and Zach had pretty much nailed it.

The ranch was in good hands with Zach as the face of the business and Lilah there to support him. It might be time for Jesse to step away and, for once, look toward a future for himself. Only Lilah knew he was meeting the folks at ANWF. Zach thought he was meeting with some new vendor, and would only step in to smile and grease the deal if Jesse wanted to go ahead with a contract. He'd tell Zach after, depending how things went. After Zach returned from his honeymoon.

Jesse looked up as Bruce pulled up to the gates of Pleasant Lane, the private cul-de-sac he shared with his brothers, cousins, and his grandmother on the outskirts of Charming. Miss Leona was still acting regularly on a primetime medical drama called *Rory's War* and doing guest spots on other shows and cameos in the occasional film, but she always spent her weekends at home. She was probably out, spending the afternoon with her girlfriends. No doubt bragging about the grandchildren she hoped Zach and Evie would unleash on the world as soon as possible.

The gates swung open and Jesse tried to ignore the way his nerves reacted. He knew the drill, the way his body switched gears when it was time to switch tasks. He had his to-do list for the afternoon and the evening. Several dozen laps in his pool followed by a large dinner. He planned to be in bed no later than ten p.m. As they got closer to the head of the cul-de-sac, something felt off. There was a red Buick SUV parked in Miss Leona's driveway.

"Pull up to Miss Leona's," Jesse said.

"Sure thing."

A mysterious lack of dogs caught his attention too. His black Lab, Clementine, was usually waiting for him on his front steps or his grandmother's porch; and their other dogs—Poppy, Euca, and Sugarplum—rushed any car that drove up the lane. He assumed they were all inside his grandmother's house, which was the center of their sprawling property.

Bruce pulled to a stop beside the red Buick. Jesse thanked him and climbed out of the truck. He grabbed his stuff before he walked up the front steps. He stopped as he took in the calm and eerie silence. Not a single bark or whine. Fear gripped his throat. For a split second he considered going back outside to catch Bruce in case he needed backup, but his feet were already walking him deeper into this house. Where was his grandmother and where the fuck were the dogs? He heard a noise when he stepped into the kitchen, but it wasn't until later that he realized what that noise had been.

He rounded the large kitchen island and caught sight of a tall man sprawled out on top of Miss Leona's sectional. Underneath him was Miss Leona. Jesse knew what he was seeing, knew he couldn't *unsee* it. There was no doubt as to the consensual nature of it all because, well, just because, but that didn't make a damn difference. No way this shit was happening, not on his watch. The wall between his temper and the rest of the world was paper-thin, on a good day. In that moment when he saw this elderly man tongue kissing his grandmother, his brain lit a match and that wall was incinerated in seconds.

"Get the fuck off of her!" Jesse didn't yell. He roared, trying to take the man's head clear off his shoulders with the power of his baritone. The man's head popped up, his eyes flashing wide with horror. Jesse recognized him as the man stood and stumbled backward. August LeRoux, a prominent accountant in town, tripped over the edge of the coffee table and fell right on his ass on the Spanish tile floor. The fly on his slacks was down and he was wearing about 40 percent of Miss Leona's red lipstick on his wrinkled, freckled face. That about did it for Jesse. He charged forward, ready to Uncle Phil the man right out the front fucking door, but Miss Leona was quicker, popping off the couch and shoving Jesse right in the center of the chest.

"Now what in the hell is wrong with you?" she yelled back at him.

"What is he doing here? What are the two of you doing?"

"No way! No sir! You back that trolley right up. This is my house and you are not going to come in here speaking to me or my guests like that."

Jesse knew she was right, but he was too focused on

the way her usually pristine wig was cocked a little to the left. This was not fucking happening.

"You need to leave right now," Jesse said over the top of her head. Miss Leona looked back and forth between them before she rushed over to Mr. LeRoux's side. She knelt down, lightly touching his shoulder. Mr. LeRoux was holding his wrist, pain spread all over his face.

"Yeah, I'm alright. Something's wrong with my wrist."

The flames burning through all of Jesse's control dulled themselves for just a moment. Mr. LeRoux was hurt. "Here, let me—"

"Get out," Miss Leona said.

"Miss Le—"

"I said get out."

"I—where are the dogs?"

"Up at the ranch. Chris came and got them for me this morning. Four dogs is three dogs too many sometimes. But it doesn't matter, I said get out."

"Let me at least—"

She turned on him, the same temper that ran through his veins setting her eyes ablaze. "If you don't get out of my damn house."

Jesse's teeth ground together as he turned and stormed out of the room. He could hear Miss Leona saying sweet, soothing things to the old man and he wondered if he should go back and punch him for good measure. He walked over to his own house instead. He didn't mean to throw his carry-on bag, but all intentions went to shit went it smashed against the wall and left a black mark. He took a deep breath, knowing he'd regret that later, then grabbed the keys to his truck. He needed to go get the dogs.

The lights came on as he walked into his garage. He stepped into his pickup truck and forced himself to wait until the lift door was completely open before he slammed into reverse. What the hell was Miss Leona thinking, making out with that man like some teenager? What the fuck was Mr. LeRoux thinking? Jesse knew exactly what he was thinking. Sick pervert with his fly down. When he got back, when Jesse had calmed down, he and Mr. LeRoux were definitely going to have a chat.

The garage door finally opened and Jesse started to back out, stopping as he saw the red Buick barreling down the driveway. And that was the moment Jesse knew he'd fucked up. Miss Leona hated to drive, but it was her behind the wheel, Mr. LeRoux beside her, clutching his wrist to his chest.

Jesse sat beside his pool, taking his time with the now room temperature beer in his hand. The sun had long set and the only things breaking up the darkness of his backyard were the blue lights coming from beneath the water's surface, and the stars overhead. He'd tried to get ahold of his grandmother, but she never responded. Hours later, when his brothers and cousins returned from Vegas, he got a single text from Corie.

What the fuck did you do?

He didn't reply, just let the dogs out so they could rush back over to his grandmother's house to greet their other humans. That was his proof of life, the signal that he was at home, but he knew it would be better if he lay low.

Hours later, even after he'd scrubbed the black mark from his suitcase off the wall, he still hadn't heard from anyone else in his family and it was just as well. He knew exactly what they were going to say. They'd tell him to check his temper. Give him some lecture about Miss Leona's right to booty calls and then go back to their own business without a care in the world.

He still had that meeting with the Democratic action committee to prepare for, but at the moment staring at his pool seemed like a better idea. He had to figure out what to say to his grandmother to get her to understand where he was coming from. He had to figure out what to say to his brothers, and Corie, to get them to shut the hell up about it.

He was about to reach for his phone, when Clementine hopped up from her spot beside his deck chair and wandered over to the back door. The door opened and Zach stepped into the backyard. He crossed the pool deck and took a seat in the open chair beside Jesse. His brother was usually all jokes and all smiles, but his jaw was set and he refused to look Jesse in the eye. A rare sight. An angry Zach Pleasant.

"Didn't bring Sam with you? I know you two love an intervention."

Zach didn't respond, he just leaned forward and rubbed at a scuff on the tip of his boot. Clementine took that as her cue to shove her head under his hand.

"Fine. Let me have it. I deserve it."

"I'm not gonna *let you have* shit." He scratched Clem behind the ear before he finally looked up. "Mr. LeRoux has a hairline fracture in his wrist. He's gonna be okay, but you could have really hurt him. Or worse, you could have given him a heart attack."

Jesse knew his brother was right, but for some reason he felt his temper rising again. Zach didn't fucking get it. "You didn't see what I walked in on."

"I didn't, but Miss Leona told me what happened. And as much as I don't even want to think about our grandmother mugging down, you cannot scream at old people. Like I don't know how else to make that clear. What if you had given Miss Leona a heart attack, or what if she'd gotten hurt? She's eighty-three, Jess. She's not falling apart, but she is still eighty-three."

Jesse sighed and leaned back into the deck chair. "Yeah, okay."

"I thought we talked about this." They had, over a year ago, but that was before Jesse walked in on what he walked in on. "I understand that you don't want Miss Leona dating—"

"That's not what I said. I don't want someone trying to take advantage of her."

"Okay, but don't you think she gets to make that call? Did you even try to talk to her?"

"Yes, but she kicked me out."

Zach let out a sigh of his own, then leaned forward. Jesse looked up and forced himself to make eye contact with his brother. "She's been seeing Mr. LeRoux for almost a year."

"Did you know?"

"No, she didn't want to tell me or Sam because she didn't want us to tell *you*. Do you see how that's a problem? Our grandmother, who trusts you with pretty much everything, didn't trust you with this, and it turns out she was right."

Jesse's gaze dropped back to the bottle in his hand. He didn't trust himself to say anything else.

"I think you need to give Miss Leona some space until she's ready to talk to you again. And I think you should apologize to Evie."

"What did I do to Evie?"

"Well, we're getting married in six days, and instead of yamming it up with the girls, talking about how much fun she had this weekend and how she can't wait for our very X-rated honeymoon, she's over at the house consoling our grandmother and praying you get your shit together so we don't have to spend our whole wedding day wondering if you're gonna start something. We already have the looming threat of Lilah versus Uncle Gerald to worry about, and now this."

"You're right," Jesse said, his tone gruff. "I messed up."

"And if I'm being real with you, you pissed me off too."

"I hear you." And he did, but Zach still didn't understand where Jesse was coming from. He didn't understand the pressure Jesse was under and he never would, so there was no use in arguing, even if Jesse wanted to lay it all out there. And he couldn't get up and leave this conversation. It was his house.

"Give Miss Leona a few days, and if you feel yourself about to explode again, at least fucking walk away or something, man. You should really see a damn therapist."

That stung, but Jesse kept that to himself too. He didn't need a therapist. He needed someone in his family, someone besides him, to step up and give a shit. But he knew that wasn't going to happen. Somehow, after his father, Jesse Senior, left to pursue his acting career, leaving Zach and Jesse in charge of the ranch, the roles in their family had shifted and then set themselves in stone. And that left Jesse as the rock. Sam and Zach could come and go as they pleased. Lilah had all the room she needed to learn and grow and be angry at her father, judgment-free, all because Jesse was holding it down. None of them wanted to hear that.

"I'll give Miss Leona her space. And I'll be on my best behavior for your wedding. I promise."

"I don't believe you, but at least Mom and Dad will be here to check you if you start tripping again."

Zach stood and started back inside, leaving Jesse alone with his thoughts and a few sad truths. The man he was gave his brothers the space they needed to live their lives, fall in love, all that shit. And even though Miss Leona was angry with him, they both knew he was the only one stepping up to take care of this place and their family. Maybe heading to Washington was the right thing to do. They didn't have to agree with his methods or understand why he was so pissed off, but maybe it was time for Zach and Lilah and maybe even Miss Leona to see how things worked around here without him.

Jesse went back inside and started to prepare for his meeting with A New Way Forward.

Chapter 2

Lily-Grace LeRoux was sick of men. She'd had it up to her damn eyebrows with the misogynistic posturing and outright shittiness.

Jesse Pleasant had picked the wrong day and he'd definitely picked the wrong one. Lily-Grace had left her job, left her man, and now she had nothing but time on her hands. So if some pig-headed, hot-tempered rancher wanted to pick on her seventy-five-year-old father? Well, Lily-Grace had nothing but time to mix it up. She hadn't been in a fistfight in years, but she was willing to come out of retirement. Fighting dirty never got old.

All of this was just so damn typical. She hadn't seen Jesse Pleasant since the final days of eighth grade. He'd rushed to her rescue when some high school boys had been making fun of her vitiligo. He must have been six-three at that point and only fourteen years old. Scary enough to get some seniors to leave her alone with just a look and few choice words. He'd walked her to her father's old office on Main Street, and that was the last time she'd seen him.

A few months later she was on a plane to boarding

school in New Hampshire. She thought about him every once in a while, but he hadn't crossed her mind in any serious way in years. What a way to reintroduce yourself, by sending an elderly man to the hospital. Jesse Pleasant could have really made a difference, put all that money and extra height to good use. Played charity basketball for a living or something. He could have been someone who looked out for the little guy, but no. The dickhead rancher truly lived up to his full dickhead potential, and now here she was, helping her father get settled for bed.

She held the armhole of his crisp white undershirt and helped him slide his arm with its fancy new wrist brace through it. He shimmied his head through the proper hole and pulled it the rest of the way down with his other hand.

"Thank you. I got the rest from here."

"You sure?"

"I'm sure. It's just a fracture. I'll survive."

Lily-Grace stepped back and eyed her father's phone. If she moved fast enough she could dart past him and snag it off its charger. Would it be weird if she texted Miss Lovell pretending to be her dad just so she could find Jesse's location? Yes. Did she care at the moment? She sure didn't. But she knew it would make her father upset, going behind his back. Maybe he'd approve of the ass whooping Jesse had coming his way if she was upfront about it.

She leaned against the doorway instead, and waited for her father to step into his slippers.

"Daddy, just give me his address. I just want to go over there and talk to him. I just want to talk. I promise I won't cut him."

Her father laughed. "Absolutely not. I'm not angry with Jesse and you shouldn't be either."

"He broke your wrist!"

"He didn't break my wrist. Lilybug, listen. He's just very protective over his grandmother, which I think you can understand. Look at you. Already got your knuckles all lined up and ready for a night out on the town."

"Boxing has been helping a lot with my pent-up emotions."

"I'm glad to hear it."

"Maybe I'll find a gym here in town. If you want me to stick around. You finally got the place to yourself. I don't want to cramp your style with your new girlfriend."

Her father gingerly slipped on his house sweater before he crossed the room and kissed her on the cheek. "I don't think anything can cramp my style."

"Whooa-ho! Not even those seven-hundred-year-old slippers?"

"These were a gift from my daughter."

"I'm aware. And I was twelve and I can afford to get you new ones."

"Me and my slippers are hanging on just fine." He gave her shoulder a squeeze before he slid past her and started down the hall.

"You're not going to bed?" she asked.

"It's only ten o'clock."

Lily-Grace rolled her eyes. He'd be dead asleep on the couch in fifteen minutes. "Well, I'll be in my room. I mean the guest room," she teased. It was good to be home. Home was where she needed to be right now. Where she wanted to be, but it was still a shock to find that all of her NSYNC and Tyson Beckford posters had been replaced with artful black-and-whites of their desert valley. At least her glow-in-the-dark stars were still stuck to the ceiling, and in a feat of scientific achievement that could not be good for humans, some of them were still glowing.

"Your stuff is all packed up. I didn't throw anything away."

"I know. I'm just giving you a hard time. I'm not going to sleep, I'll just be in bed. Let me know if you need anything. And don't try to lift anything with that wrist. The doctor said be easy with it."

"I had some late-night roof repairs I wanted to get to, but I guess it could wait."

"Try it," she said, pointing a finger at him.

He kissed her on the forehead again and made for the direction of his comfy chair. Lily-Grace let out a deep breath as she watched him walk down the hall. They'd been home from the hospital for a few hours, but she felt like she was still coming down from the adrenaline rush that had hit her when Miss Lovell called her from her father's phone.

She made her way back upstairs, stopping in the doorway of her old room. She looked around at the freshly made bed and her suitcase that was still tucked in the corner, half unpacked.

She'd come back to Charming for some peace and calm, to get the hell away from her job that had imploded in her face and her ex, who turned out to be less than supportive. She thought she'd finally built a life for herself in the Bay Area. A home and career, and now she felt betrayed by her own decisions, even though absolutely none of it was her fault.

Seriously, what was it with some men? Bad tempers, controlling behavior, straight-up harassers. She knew *all* men weren't like that. Her father was practically a saint. Loving and kind. To hear her aunt tell it, her mother had been so happy with him, their love was the stuff of legends. And even though they'd only spoken a few times, Miss Lovell had made it clear that her father was wonderful to her. Lily-Grace had made a few male friends over the years, but geez, was it fair to make them work triple time to compensate for the jackasses of the world, hell-bent on making her miserable? And now Jesse Pleasant was another name she could add to her list. She wasn't sure a boxing class down at the Charming rec center would do the trick this time.

The moment she realized how naïve she was? It was tough for Lily-Grace. She didn't have any misgivings about the way the world looked at her. She was brash and outspoken, and her intelligence and skill at sharp, quick observations made some people uncomfortable. She was also a six-foot-two Black woman with vitiligo. People were already staring at her before she set foot in any interview or meeting and dazzled/scared the shit out of the whole room with her knowledge for numbers.

She was what most millennials dreamed they could be: somewhat rich as hell, thanks to being in the right place at the right time, in the early days of Clutch, a social media app that survived long enough to make its creators a lot of money. She'd been the only woman, the only Black person on that team. And she'd walked away with her own sackful of money before the first sexual harassment allegation trickled in from the first round of female new hires. Allegations which she absolutely believed because while he was intimidated by her, Tim Cross, their dev lead, had been a total pig.

She bounced around until she landed at Ulway, the rideshare app that was doing phenomenally well, but was struggling in its own ways. They'd brought her in because she was a Black woman. She wasn't naïve about that, but she'd been foolish to think that Ulway wanted to actually pay their drivers more. She'd found a way to make her proposed compensation structure work. The pay increase and a move to a small but essential benefits package. It was absolutely doable, and frankly it would be a good look for the company. Drivers would be happy and safer, users would be happy, putting their dollars in a company that cared about their people.

But that didn't happen. And while she and her small team were trying to restructure her plan to convince the powers that be that this was the right move, their director of marketing decided she would be the next target of his foul mouth and grabby hands. She regretted not punching Aaron Genicks in the face, but all of her what-ifs and I-shouldas were drowned out by how poorly the company handled her formal complaint. She knew she had options, and all of them were unpleasant and none of them involved a time machine that would allow her to go back and convince Mr. and Mrs. Genicks to use protection.

And all of it, every single moment, was made ten thousand times worse by the way Dane reacted. There's something so uniquely painful about being betrayed by the man she thought was her soulmate. Dane knew Aaron from their fraternity days, but Lily-Grace had never considered them friends. Which shouldn't have mattered.

When your partner comes to you and tells you she was harassed at work, the only response should be outrage immediately followed by comfort and assistance.

Dane's words still burned inside her heart. Her own response had been swift and appropriate. She'd walked out of his apartment and left her copy of his key with the doorman. She'd also left the necklace he'd given her, the symbol of their arrangement and commitment, behind. It still hurt to think about them a few weeks later.

She lay down on her bed, staring at the plastic stars. Was there a planet free of men? What would it be like to go there? No. That wouldn't solve her problems.

Her phone picked that perfect moment to vibrate in her hand. She looked at the screen, her heart jumping when she saw Dane's name and a preview of a text. She knew she should delete it, but she unlocked her phone and read the whole thing instead.

I want you to come back.

She knew she definitely shouldn't respond, but she did it anyway.

I wanted you to support me, but here we are.

Lily-Grace hit send, then she tossed her phone on the beige armchair that had replaced her bright blue papasan chair. She thought about turning off the lights just so she could look at the stars, but she didn't feel like getting up. Her body was finally starting to crash. Her dad was okay. His wrist would heal. In a few days she'd figure out her next move and get her life back on track. Start something of her own, free of Aarons and Tims and Danes.

A fat tear ran down the side of her face. She didn't brush it away until it started to cool in the shell of her ear. In the morning, she was gonna fight Jesse Pleasant.

Lily-Grace pulled her father's red Buick up to the gates of Big Rock Ranch. She'd been there exactly once, back in the third grade. Jesse was supposed to bring something for show-and-tell, and somehow he'd convinced their teacher, Mrs. Lyons, to let him show the whole class the ranch. She remembered how warm it was that day and how she couldn't stop smiling. She got to pet a beautiful brown horse named Hazelnut or something to that effect. It had been the best field trip of her young life. And she wasn't going to let what she was about to do taint that memory.

She kept her eyes forward, focusing on the long, wide driveway that brought you up to the main visitor center. She saw a small group of people spilling out of a black SUV in front of the valet stand and some young kid with a plaid shirt pointed the driver off to where they were probably going to wait for their important people to be done with their important ranch-related business. She checked herself. They weren't the issue right now. Plus she had been one of those important business people up until recently.

There was no question of whether or not her plan was good or bad. It was the plan she'd decided on and she was following through with it. She'd talked to her friend Jenny Yang before she'd finally gone to bed. Jenny had stayed local and ran into the Pleasants all over town. She had no issue telling Lily-Grace that Jesse and his younger brother Zach spent most of their days right there on the ranch. She also promised to be on standby with bail money if this blew up in her face. Which it wouldn't. Lily-Grace had a few things she had to get off her chest and then she'd be on her way.

She slowed down and pulled up to the front of the lodge, lowering her window as that same young kid jogged around to open her door.

"Good morning. Welcome to Big Rock Ranch."

"Good morning."

"Checking in?"

"Oh no, just visiting an old friend for a moment."

"I'll be happy to park your car for—"

"I'm just running in real quick to speak to Jesse Pleasant. I won't be more than five minutes."

"Oh, well if you want to leave the keys with us, we'll have your car waiting."

"Uh, sure. Thank you."

"Right this way."

She let the young man open the car door for her. She stepped out of the car and handed the kid a twenty before she smoothed down her pencil skirt. She finished the look with her favorite black heels and a white ruffled blouse that made her breasts look amazing. Not that she was trying to look good for Jesse. She just knew it would be harder to make her point if she showed up in her pajamas with her hair still wrapped.

She left her purse but grabbed her phone, gripping it

tight in her hand. This was only going to take a minute. The other young person at the valet stand wasted no time opening one of the large doors to the lodge for her. She marched right in, her heels clicking on the pristine floor.

"Good morning, and welcome to Big Rock Ranch. Are you checking in?" the woman behind the reception desk said. As she got closer, Lily-Grace saw the name Naomi on her name badge.

"Hi, Naomi. Not checking in. I'm here to see Jesse Pleasant," she said, nice and calm, even though her heart was slamming into her throat.

"Oh sure. Are you here for the meeting? They just went back. They haven't started yet."

"Oh yes. I was just running a little behind."

"Excellent. You're just going to take a right at the fireplace and head straight down the hall. They are in the Sycamore conference room."

"Thank you so much." Lily-Grace smiled, then turned in the direction of the conference room. She had a feeling they might have this out in front of a staff member or two, but she could handle an audience of strangers. Hopefully it was an important vendor that would reconsider giving the ranch their business, thanks to Jesse's screwup.

She took the right and headed down a brightly lit hallway. Another staff member came out of one of the doors and just smiled at her as she slipped by. Ten steps later she arrived at the closed door to the Sycamore conference room. She could hear voices inside, but she couldn't make out exactly what was being said. Not that it mattered. She let out a deep breath before she gripped the door handle and whipped it open. Sure enough, she busted in on a meeting. Jesse was seated with two white men and a Black woman. All eyes shot to her, Jesse's practically bugging out of his head.

"Sorry to interrupt."

"Lily-Grace," Jesse said, the shock in his voice clear. He stood, immediately adjusting the front of his suit jacket. The words on the tip of her tongue died in her mouth as she took him in, towering over the far end of the conference table. He'd been tall when they were kids, but now he was enormous, a full head taller than her, which said a lot. He was wide too. Everything about him was wide. His shoulders, his chest, his arms. His thighs. Good Lord, those thighs. She couldn't imagine how much he paid for that navy blue suit to fit him so well.

"Excuse me. Jonathan, Cynthia, Michael, this is Lily-Grace LeRoux. One of my former classmates." She'd think about how they hadn't seen each other in over twenty years and he remembered her instantly.

"Nice to meet you," Cynthia said.

She swallowed, giving Cynthia a polite nod, while ignoring all the ways Jesse had somehow morphed into her exact type since the last time she'd seen him. There were maybe four men on Earth who could pull off an honest-to-goodness goatee, and Jesse Pleasant was one of them.

"I didn't come here to take up too much of your time. I just wanted to tell you something."

"Uh, sure. Please." He motioned toward an open chair, like she hadn't just barged in on an important meeting.

"I'm not going to sit. I'm not staying. I just wanted to let you know you will be paying my father's medical bills and any necessary rehab bills. I'd ask who the hell raised you, but I remember your parents and I know your grandmother, and I know she had nothing to do with the way you acted. If you come near my father again, I will own this whole fucking ranch. You got that?"

Jesse blinked, just staring at her. His guests looked between the two of them, probably wondering how hard it would be to disappear under the conference table.

"Lily, I—"

"It's Lily-Grace. You know that."

"Lily-Grace. I—think we should talk. I didn't—"

"I know exactly what you did, and I know just how badly you overreacted to something that is absolutely none of your business. All of it was a bit too much if you ask me. Get your temper the fuck under control and stay away from my father. And maybe show your grandmother the respect she deserves." She turned on her heels and quickly left the room, closing the door behind her.

She was hot all over and she felt like she was vibrating as she power walked back down to the lobby.

"Lily-Grace!" she heard Jesse call after her. She didn't stop though, even with the deep baritone of his voice sending shivers all over her body. She walked a little faster, her heels clicking across the floor as she gave the girl behind the desk a brisk thanks. The valets had her car waiting right where she left it.

"Thanks so much." She quickly hopped back behind the wheel just as Jesse came rushing through the lodge doors. He called out her name, trying to get her to wait. No chance of that happening. She looked carefully up and down the drive before she pulled back out toward the exit. If things went her way, she'd never see Jesse Pleasant again.

Chapter 3

Jesse sat at his desk, staring at his closed door. His meeting with the team from ANWF had gone surprisingly well. Especially after the unexpected appearance from Lily-Grace LeRoux. He'd given them the brief rundown of why she'd been so upset, and they couldn't seem to care less. They were worried about real scandals hiding in his closet. Not an argument between him and his grandmother's lover's daughter.

They seemed more concerned with the fact that he was single than that fact that a woman had stormed in before they could really get started, and threatened to own his whole ass if he didn't get it together. Jesse believed her. There was no doubt in his mind that Lily-Grace would find some way to sue the ranch right out from under him, all over a minor fracture.

Okay, maybe it wasn't fair to downplay Mr. LeRoux's injury. Jesse had had no intention of actually hurting him. And even though he didn't actually lay a finger on the man, he loved his own grandmother enough to know that he'd considered choking an old man to death for kissing her. Barging into a meeting would have been a mild response to Miss Leona actually being hurt.

Lily-Grace LeRoux. Jesse couldn't believe it was actually her. He wasn't surprised when she'd left town to go to a prestigious boarding school. She'd always been smart, and while Jesse had had his own issues with growth spurts, middle school hadn't been kind to Lily-Grace in other ways. Jesse's size had been seen as an asset to coaches across the state. Lily-Grace had also been tall for her age, but she was terrible at sports and her vitiligo made her a target for everyone with something shitty to say. He wasn't surprised she'd left town at all. He was shocked she was back.

Jesse let out a deep breath and fought the urge to loosen his tie. He had a lot to consider. Cynthia and her team liked what they saw in him, and pending a more intensive vetting process, they really wanted him to consider running for the soon-to-be-vacant seat for the eighth district of California. Jesse had a lot to consider, but ever since he'd sent them on their way, all he could think about was the fiery look in Lily-Grace's eyes when she came bursting through the conference room door.

He had to see her.

Jesse sprang up from his desk and started gathering his things, including his black Stetson from its hook on the wall. He cut off the light and stepped out into the small reception area between his and Zach's offices. Erin, their new receptionist, looked up at him with a bright smile as Clementine army-crawled out from under the accent table against the wall.

"More wedding stuff?" Erin asked.

He left at the same time every day, 5:37 p.m. on the dot, but this week he'd told Erin to expect his schedule to be a little irregular.

"Actually, I have to go meet a friend," Jesse lied. Erin's smile widened with unease as her eyebrows crept up. Everyone knew Jesse had no friends. Not really.

"Well, have fun with your friend. You have a ten a.m. tomorrow with Dr. Vasquez."

"I will be there. Thanks, Erin. Come on, Clem." He snapped his fingers once, and his trusty sidekick fell into step right beside him. He let Clementine lead the way down the stairs. People loved Clementine. Maybe he should bring her with him when he went to sort things out with Lily-Grace.

He rounded the corner and almost walked right into Delfi Hernandez, the ranch's GM.

"Jesse Pleasant. Just the man I was looking for. Hey, Clem." She gave the dog a playful scratch behind the ear before she looked back up at Jesse with a deep sigh.

He wasted no time waving her off. He knew exactly what she was going to say. "Tell Naomi it's okay. Seriously." The poor girl had burst into tears the second she realized that Lily-Grace wasn't a part of the group from ANWF. Normally Jesse would have been annoyed. All the employees had been well versed in ranch security and procedure, but this one was all on Lily-Grace. She knew exactly what she was doing. Naomi got a pass on this one.

"Oh, she's a wreck. I sent her home. I've never seen anyone more disappointed in themselves."

Jesse fought the urge to roll his eyes. "It was an honest mistake. She's on the schedule tomorrow, right?"

"Yes."

"Great, I'll talk to her. I gotta go."

"Wait, Jesse. I just got a little bug in my ear about Dr. Vasquez."

"He's coming by tomorrow at ten. What's going on?"

"Word on the farm is he's retiring."

"Fuck." Jesse let his head fall forward.

"Yeah."

Dr. Vasquez had been working with the animals at Big Rock since Jesse was a kid. He had a great rapport with the whole staff, and Jesse had never seen anyone with such a gentle hand when it came to the horses and dozens of other animals they kept on the ranch. The man was punctual and thorough, and most of all Jesse knew he could trust him. Finding someone new was not something Jesse was looking forward to.

"Does Felix know?" he asked. Their ranch foreman would have feelings about this.

"Not sure."

"Okay." Jesse squinted, thinking as he looked down at Delfi's black high heels. Of course they would need to find another vet to work with, but he couldn't put out feelers until he heard the word from the doctor himself. His gaze snapped back up to Delfi's patient expression. She'd worked with Jesse long enough, and knew him years before that. She knew how his thought process worked. "Let me talk to him first. And then we'll talk with Felix."

"Just say the word. You know I got you, boss."

"Thanks. And don't call me boss."

"Sure thing, boss." Delfi shot him a sarcastic wink before she disappeared back around the corner. She made it clear why she and Zach got along so well. Annoying Jesse was a fun hobby for the two of them. Jesse added talking to Naomi and making sure he got all the information he needed from Dr. Vasquez to his mental list of things to do the next day as he strode out to his truck. The sun was lower in the sky, but still bright and hot. He slid his Stetson on, shading his eyes from it. He waited until Clementine was comfortable in the flatbed before he climbed behind the wheel of his pickup truck and backed out of his reserved space in the rear of the lodge.

If he remembered correctly, Lily-Grace's father lived out on Wildwood Canyon Road. Of course the man could have moved, but Charming was small enough he would have heard at some point if the large farmhouse was on the market. Jesse stopped at the end of the road, just inside the exit to the ranch. Maybe he should change. He'd been wearing the same suit all day, and maybe showing up at her house unannounced, not looking as . . . He didn't finish the thought. Just put on his blinker and waited for an eighteen-wheeler to pass before he took a left and drove back toward his own place on Pleasant Lane.

Jesse made room for Clementine to squeeze by him before he locked the front door to his home. It had taken a few moments going through his sizable custom wardrobe before he changed into something appropriate for a drop-by and the dinner his family had scheduled in a couple hours. His mother would approve of the dress pants and light sweater he was wearing, and Lily-Grace . . .

Jesse focused on remembering the way to her father's house instead of the look on her face when she'd burst into the conference room that morning or what she might think of his current outfit.

He grabbed the bottle of Pleasant Gold Label wine from under his arm and headed out to his truck. Just as he opened the back door to the extended cab for the dog, he spotted his youngest brother, Sam, and Sam's girlfriend, Amanda, stepping out of Miss Leona's house, hand in hand.

They were both in between projects which gave them more time to spend in Charming. They were staying together up at the ranch until they left as family for the wedding in Malibu, but Amanda couldn't get enough of their grandmother, and he was sure Miss Leona felt the same way about the sweet, charming woman. She was a good match for Sam.

"Hey, Jesse," she said with a bright smile.

"Amanda."

"Where you going?" Sam asked.

"Just into town for a second. Dropping this off for Mrs. Donatelli."

"You know we have dinner with Mom and Dad, right?" Jesse didn't miss the warning in Sam's voice. Jesse had never been late for anything in his whole life, but he had already fucked up once this week. As a matter of fact, being early had been what led him to seeing things he wished he could forget. Still, he knew being late for their first family get-together in almost a year, a celebration for his brother and Evie, wouldn't be a good look.

He double-checked his smart watch. "Forty minutes, max. I'll be back."

"K. Text if you're running late. You know we all have to be in formation for Captain von Mom."

"I will." This might be Zach and Evie's special day, but their mother, Regina, had been waiting decades for her sons to get married. With the passing of Evie's mom, their mother felt it was her time to really shine, as mother of the groom and stand-in mother of the bride. When she made her appearance as Thee Mother of this occasion, he knew what she expected of him and his brothers. He knew better than to be late for dinner.

At Sam's nod, Jesse got behind the wheel of his truck and drove off to Wildwood Canyon Road. He spotted Mr. LeRoux's red Buick in the driveway as soon as the house came into view. Almost thirty years and the place looked exactly the same. Jesse wasn't shocked that he remembered it. He remembered strange things from his childhood, including the day his grandfather, Gerald Senior, had dropped him off at the LeRouxs' house for Lily-Grace's birthday party in the fourth grade.

Miss Leona had been away on a film and his parents were off on the rodeo circuit. His grandfather had teased him, asking Jesse if Lily-Grace was someone he thought he could have a crush on. Jesse shut down that line of questioning immediately, making it clear that none of the girls in his class had crushes on him.

"That's not what I asked you," his grandfather had said. Jesse remembered the way his grandfather smiled at him and the embarrassment that heated his cheeks in the moment. He'd bought Lily-Grace a pink cowboy hat with glitter all over it. He had no idea if she ever tried it on.

Jesse pulled up behind the red Buick, then cut the engine of his truck. Before he could cross the driveway, the front door opened and Lily-Grace stepped out. She'd changed out of the sleek outfit she'd been wearing that morning. Now she was wearing an oversized adult onesie with little Baby Yodas on it. Jesse pushed the thought of how good she still looked to the back of his mind.

"Daddy?" she called over her shoulder before she sucked her teeth and leaned against the doorjamb.

"Yes, Lilybug?" Jesse heard Mr. LeRoux call back. "How can I help you?"

"Can you grab my gun?"

"What—oh, Jesse. How are you?" Mr. LeRoux said as he stepped from behind his daughter. His tone was polite, but he didn't smile. Not that Jesse expected him to. His wrist was still wrapped.

"Good Evening, Lily-Grace. Mr. LeRoux. I—uh. I came by to apologize. I was out of line yesterday and I had no right to react that way," he said, just the way he'd rehearsed in his truck. Jesse held up the bottle of wine, proof of his sincerity. He didn't get a chance to hand it to Mr. LeRoux before Lily-Grace snatched the bottle out of his grasp. Jesse watched her face carefully as she glared at the label.

"Pathetic olive branch, Pleasant. It's your own brand. You know you should at least have sprung for a mix-and-match box from BevMo! and not some free shit from your own pantry."

Mr. LeRoux almost held back a loud snort. Almost. "Nice to see you, Jesse. And happy to accept a heartfelt apology and some Pleasant label wine. Come on in."

Jesse stepped up onto the porch, but Lily-Grace's arm shot out, blocking the doorway. "No, you can stay right there." She handed the bottle to her father, then stepped closer to Jesse, like he was going to have to tackle her to get inside. Mr. LeRoux apparently thought the whole thing was hilarious and not bizarre and kind of rude.

"Thank you for this. I'll let you two talk." Mr. LeRoux stepped back inside and closed the door.

"Well?" Lily-Grace asked, her eyebrow arching up.

"Well, what?"

"That was your whole apology? Free wine and a mumble mumble something, my bad I'm sorry?"

"I didn't mumble and I suppose I could have bought something at the store, but I thought something made by a member of my family would be a more meaningful gesture."

"Mm-hmm, I bet. Did your grandmother put you up to it? I'm sure she had more of an earful for you than I did."

"Actually she's not speaking to me right now."

"Ooh, icy. I like it. So you came over here with your cheap wine all on your own."

"Okay, I may have had it sitting in my kitchen, but nothing the family produces is cheap."

"I had a scorching *your mama* joke at the ready, but I always admired your mom. She's a goddess."

"You remember my mom?"

"Ah yeah. It's not every day you get to sell Girl Scout cookies to a former Miss California."

"Hmm."

"Anyway, it was a weak apology, and if I can verify the wine isn't poisoned, I'm sure my father and I will enjoy it. Hope I didn't mess up your meeting too badly this morning."

"Actually, you didn't. The meeting went very well, and

when I explained what happened, they said they admired my dedication to my family."

"Who is *they*?"

"Just a new vendor we're in talks with."

Lily-Grace's eyes narrowed like she knew he was lying. "I should leave a scathing Yelp review just in case they are still on the fence about working with you."

"So what brings you back to Charming?" Jesse asked. For some reason he didn't want this conversation to go down the road it was headed, but he didn't want it to end either. Which made no sense, considering Lily-Grace was set on giving him a hard time. She was just so easy to talk to.

"As you may notice"—she motioned over her head with a flourish—"we are standing in front of Chateau LeRoux. Last I checked I didn't know I needed a reason to visit my father."

"You don't. I just haven't seen you in a while." Jesse regretted the words as soon as they were out. "I mean—"

"I know what you mean."

"It's fresh into a new fiscal quarter and I figure Ulway would have you watching every dime after they squashed the benefits package the drivers were after."

Lily-Grace cut him a smirk that could shatter knee-caps. He could just picture how ruthless she was in a boardroom. It was probably her idea to keep workers comp and health care from ever coming anywhere near the table. Smart for Ulway. Bullshit for their employees, but that was her business. Jesse swallowed, ready for whatever brutal remark she had coming next. Instead, she cocked her head to the side and stepped around him.

"Is that your dog?"

"Yes." Jesse followed her to his truck and unlocked the door. Lily-Grace wasted no time opening the rear cabin door and Clementine wasted even less time sticking her big head out to receive some pets.

"She's so cute." Lily-Grace turned, and looked him up and down. "She deserves better."

That, Jesse took offense to. He'd never met a dog more loved and more cared for. "You want to give her a home? She'll outsmart you every day. And she likes her steaks cooked a certain way or she'll send them back."

Lily-Grace's eyes narrowed before she turned back to Clementine. "So what changed your mind?"

"What do you mean?"

"Well, from the way my dad and your grandmother tell it, you define stubborn these days. And bossy. Maybe a little controlling."

"I definitely wouldn't say I'm controlling. I'll give you bossy and stubborn, though."

"Right. Not controlling, but you never thought to consider why your grandmother might be hiding a whole healthy relationship from you. Specifically."

Another sting to the center of his chest. "She said that?"

"Yeah, she said that. So what changed in the last twelve hours? Threat of a lawsuit actually do the trick?"

"Actually, no. It was something my brother said."

"Sam or Zach?"

"Zach." It was jarring to hear her talk about his family in such a casual way. It had been so long and he was still a little shocked to be having this conversation right now. He never thought he'd see her again. He never thought she'd grow up to look like this, this beautiful. Even in a Baby Yoda onesie.

"And what did your wise younger brother have to say?"

"It's not so much what he said, more what he made me realize. I'm taking on too much, and that includes looking after my grandmother. Maybe it's time for me to step back. Let my family see how things play out when I'm not so vigilant. Or controlling, as you like to call it."

Lily-Grace rolled her eyes. "How do you confess to having so many complexes in one sentence? Have they gotten your size for your martyr robes yet?"

"I don't expect you to understand."

"Good, cause you still sound ridiculous and you're not the only person on Earth who loves their family. Luckily for you, I have my own problems, so as long as you chill the hell out and keep your hands and your temper away from my father, we'll be fine. Come on, Clementine."

Like the perfectly trained dog she was, Clementine jumped down from the cab and dropped her butt down on the driveway, looking up between them, waiting for her next command.

"Look at this polite little lady. So unlike her doggy dad. Let's go, Clementine. I have four episodes of *Ted Lasso* to catch up on." Jesse watched Lily-Grace as she walked back up her front steps. His traitorous dog actually followed her. "What does she eat?" she called over her shoulder.

"Uh, nothing store-bought. I make her her food."

"Oh wow. A spoiled good girl. I think we can swing

that. Later, Pleasant." She opened the front door and
Clementine just trotted right inside.

"Uh, what are you doing?" Jesse asked, trying to keep
his voice calm, even though he could feel the blood starting to race to the veins in his forehead.

"The wine was alright, but I still haven't forgiven you
yet. My father is all I have, but I think we could handle
another addition to the family. I think I'll keep your dog
for a while. I think that's penance enough. Byeeee."

Jesse blinked as she slammed the door behind her.
His mouth dropped open and then closed again. She had
to be joking, right? With a sigh he settled on his heels
and waited for her stupid prank to come to an end. Five
minutes later, though, she still hadn't returned with his
dog. Jesse took a deep breath, then gently pressed the
doorbell.

"Who is it?" Lily-Grace called out.

"Give me my dog back."

"*That's* a weird name!"

"Lily-Grace, you made your point. I have to meet my
family for dinner soon. Can you please send my dog out?
I have to go."

"Say it again?"

"What? Please?"

"No. Say *I'm a hotheaded jerk who needs to maybe
see a therapist for my temper and control issues.*"

"Lily-Grace!"

"Lower your voice! You're scaring my dog!"

Jesse's head fell forward and he pulled in two deep
breaths before he started quietly counting to five. Mr.

LeRoux was really inside, letting his daughter act like this.

"Just say it out loud, Pleasant. The first step is admitting you have a problem."

"Fine," Jesse said through gritted teeth. "I'm a hotheaded jerk who needs to see a therapist."

"For?"

"For my temper and control issues."

The door swung open and Lily-Grace greeted him with a bright smile. "See, that wasn't so hard. You should see your face right now. You're about to blow."

"Where's my dog?"

"She's watching TV with my dad."

Jesse stuck his fingers between his lips and let out an ear-splitting wolf whistle.

"Jesus Christ!" Lily-Grace winced, then jumped to the side when Clementine came sprinting past her. She ran right for the truck and jumped in the flatbed. "I guess I couldn't compete with that. Geez."

"Please tell your father I'm sorry again."

"I will, but I seriously hope you get your shit together."

"You've made your point."

Lily-Grace just shook her head. "Goodbye, Jesse."

He turned and headed back to his truck. When he had Clementine safely in the back seat he hopped behind the wheel and headed toward home. He tried to not make anything of the fact that Lily-Grace was still standing in the doorway, watching him go.

Chapter 4

Lily-Grace realized a moment too late she was actually watching Jesse Pleasant drive away like she was some young wife watching her menfolk head off to war. She shook herself, praying to God he didn't catch a glimpse of her in his rearview mirror. Heading back inside, she was suddenly hot all over. The weather was nice, but maybe a little too warm for her onesie. She needed to change and cool down with a nice glass of water, or maybe a cold shower. And then she would lock up the way Jesse Pleasant made her feel in a tiny, yet secure vault.

What was wrong with her? She'd just gotten out of a relationship that ended under less than optimal conditions. She was still extremely pissed at Dane, but it wasn't like she was in the midst of some unbearable sex drought. Her hand was keeping her company just fine. Still, at some point during Jesse's apology tour, all she could do was think about ways to annoy him. For some silly reason she wanted to get under his skin. She wanted to see him react, and then . . . Well, then she wanted to see if he brought that level of heat and passion between the sheets.

Lily-Grace closed her eyes, then let herself back into the house. Maybe she was the one who needed help. Her life was in shambles and she saw Jesse Pleasant as a viable distraction, even though everything about him screamed red flags. He needed therapy, but she needed to get a grip. Something about the whistle though . . . God, she was pathetic.

She figured out early on that her sex drive was extremely high and in need of her constant attention. It took her years to finally find what she thought was the perfect partner in Dane. And now her imagination was picturing all the ways Jesse could fill Dane's shoes. Not those exact shoes. She had no desire to repeat what she'd had with Dane. She loved being involved with a skilled, attentive Dominant, but she'd been oblivious to the ways his domineering side in the bedroom had been due to his lack of empathy in every other area of his life. She'd been so strong and so independent in so many other ways, she hadn't noticed that he was failing her in all the ways she would need a partner to show up for her.

"You done harassing that poor young man?" Blinking, Lily-Grace turned and looked at her dad. She'd walked into the middle of the living room and just stood there, still thinking about Jesse.

"Poor young man, my ass. He'll be fine. More than fine. His grandmother will forgive him. You've already forgiven him."

"No, I haven't."

Lily-Grace stared back at her father, cocking her head

in his direction. "Really, Dad? Really? You're just gonna sit there and lie to my face like you're not the most kind, forgiving person I've ever met? We're really doing this?"

"Okay, so I'm not one to hold a grudge. I haven't forgiven him just yet."

"Well. Making him uncomfortable for five whole minutes will not derail the life path of Jesse Pleasant. This time tomorrow he'll be right back to his old self, having learned absolutely nothing. That said. We should get a dog," she announced before she flopped back down on the couch.

"Are you staying long enough to take care of a dog? I know you got taking-care-of-a-dog money, but—"

"Hey, I ask the questions around here," she grumbled.

"Honey, I'm not trying to rush you out of here. You know I love having you around, but—"

"I know. I cope best when I have a plan, and I have not presented you with such a plan." Which was the truth. It had been the way her father had taught her to tackle all her fears, any setback: Come up with a plan. Figure out what you need to do, if you need help and where to find it and go from there. Usually by now she'd have something figured out. Plans to go back to work, plans to find a new place and no plan to tell Dane her new address, but after everything that had happened, for the first time in years she truly felt off-kilter. She had no idea what to do, no idea what she wanted to do. So for now, watching t.v. shows in her pajamas and driving Jesse Pleasant to the brink of insanity seemed like the best thing to do.

"You don't have to share the plan with me, but you usually mention when you have one."

"As soon as I know, Daddio, you'll know."

"And until then. No dog."

"A horse maybe?"

"Hmm, yes. Much more practical." He turned his attention back to the television. "I love you, Lilybug. You're gonna get through this."

"Thank you." Lily-Grace pulled out her phone and tried not to make it too obvious that she was trying to catch the fat tears that had just welled up in her eyes. Fucking Dane. There was another text from him.

Please call me.

He could have called her, but that wasn't how he operated. She could have deleted the whole text thread and blocked his number, but she didn't. She sent him a middle finger emoji, then she switched over to the conversation she'd been having with her friend Jenny Yang. She sent her the selfies she'd taken with Jesse's dog while she was making him sweat in the driveway. Clementine really was a beautiful dog and so sweet. Lily-Grace should have stolen her for real. A few moments later, her phone vibrated in her hand with Jenny's reply.

OhMGee! What is happening?

For a few fleeting moments,
I kidnapped Jesse Pleasant's dog.

I love it.

Did you give her back?
He loves that dog.

                              Unfortunately yes.
                    I should have kept her though.

You have to tell me how you came into possession
of this dog. Let's get dinner tonight!

Immediately the Dane-shaped storm cloud cleared
from her mind. "Dad, do you mind if I sup with Jenny
this eve?"

"One of my favorite people. I'd be disappointed if you
didn't."

"You okay on your own for dinner?"

He turned and smiled at her. "I think I'll manage."

Okay, yeah. He'd been taking care of himself—the
both of them—her whole life. It didn't hurt to check
though. "I'm thinking of your injured wing."

"I'll just pour that Pleasant label wine in a sippy cup."

"Ha. Ha."

                                   Let's do it.

Okay let's meet at the Marriott.
We can get fucked up at the bar
And I can silently judge their menu.

The brand-spanking-new hotel had gone up on the
edge of town, right near the new medical center. Charming still had that small town feel she'd loved as a kid, but
a lot of things had changed in the years she'd been away.

She still had to check out the SuperTarget on the way out
to the airport.

I mean you have to check out the competition.

No doubt. Those fuckers.

7 sound good?

I'll see you then.

Lily-Grace climbed out of Jenny's Subaru and followed her friend into the Charming Inn. Thanks to some
ear-nose-and-throat conference they were having at the
medical center, the Marriott was booked to the brim, and
when they tried to get two menus and two seats at the bar,
battling a crowd of doctors didn't seem like a laid-back
way for besties to catch up. The inn was an old-school
special occasions spot with the best appetizers in the
whole desert. Lily-Grace looked forward to stuffing herself silly.

"They've changed up the menu a bit, but you're not
gonna regret this. Their truffle risotto slaps."

"It slaps, does it?" Lily-Grace said with a smirk before
she greeted the hostess who happily grabbed two menus
for their perusal. Just as they fell into step behind the
older woman, Lily-Grace looked over her shoulder to
see who had just entered the Charming Inn behind them.
She spotted Mrs. Pleasant and her husband a split second
before Jesse's impressive build filled the frame. He did
a double take, before his gaze locked on hers as he held
the door for the rest of the Pleasant crew.

"Is that Lily?!?" his mother practically screeched, snapping Lily-Grace out of whatever bizarre trance was drawing her to the woman's oldest son.

"Mrs. Pleasant! It's so nice to see you." Lily-Grace stepped into the woman's open arms and then stepped aside so Jenny could receive the same treatment. Soon they were surrounded by the whole family, Zach and his fiancée, Evie, who Lily-Grace recognized from television; Sam, who Lily-Grace knew when they were kids but who she definitely knew now from the big screen, and the plus-size girl holding his hand who he introduced as Amanda; and of course Miss Leona, who had her own hug and kiss on the cheek for Lily-Grace and Jenny.

Miss Leona introduced them to her granddaughters Lilah and Corie, and Corie's girlfriend, Vega. The hostess waited patiently as they all exchanged hellos. Jesse hung back, of course, suddenly too calm and too cool. Or too embarrassed to even come near her now, after what had happened between them earlier in the day. Eventually he offered them both a quiet hello and tight nod, probably because his mother and his grandmother would call him out later for being rude.

"What brings you beautiful girls out this evening?" Mrs. Pleasant asked.

"Just catching up. It's nice to have this one back," Jenny said, bumping Lily-Grace's shoulder.

"How long are you in town?"

"I'm not sure at the moment," she replied, doing her best to ignore the way Jesse was looking at her. "But I'm glad I got to see Zach and Evie in person to offer my congratulations. When's the big day?"

"This weekend," they both said in unison.

"Already in sync. I think that bodes well for a happy marriage," Lily-Grace replied with a smile. Out of the corner of her eye she noticed the way Mr. Pleasant touched his wife's elbow.

Mrs. Pleasant took that as her cue. "Well, we're gonna get this dinner party started, but I hope I see you girls again before this trip is over."

"Likewise."

The two parties followed their respective servers to their respective tables. Lily-Grace almost asked the hostess for a new table when she dropped their menus on a four-top in the middle of the dining room. There was nothing wrong with the table, of course, but where they were sitting gave her a perfect view of the Pleasants' large reserved table along the windows that gave you a view of the inn's garden. She eyed the chairs, trying to decide if putting her back to a certain Pleasant brother was the right move.

"What's wrong?" Jenny asked.

"Nothing." She pulled off her jacket and made herself comfortable. Of course a few moments later, after he'd done his gentlemanly duty of pulling out chairs for his grandmother and his younger cousin, Jesse took his own seat facing their table. Their eyes connected again and this time Jesse frowned a bit. Lily-Grace didn't know what to make of it. Not that she should make anything of it. She'd given Jesse her terms. As long as he stayed out of her way and was kind to her father, there was no reason for them to speak again.

"You know he had a crush on me in high school?" Jenny said, opening her menu.

"Who?"

"Oh, okay. Now you want to play dumb."

"Why didn't you hit that?"

"No way." Jenny laughed. "He was so shy. I think I scared the shit out of him. That would have been too much work."

Lily-Grace thought of the look on his face when she closed the door on him, leaving him outside, alone and dogless. She thought of the way he'd chased after her. He wasn't shy anymore.

"He's not booed up now."

"No. Honestly, I'm shocked-not-shocked that Zach and Evie are headed to the altar. The whole town thought he and Jesse had taken some sort of vow of celibacy so they could focus on the ranch."

"Really? He hasn't been dating at all?"

"Nope. And you know my mom would find out."

"True." Mrs. Yang always had the good gossip.

"Who knows, maybe he's just waiting for the right woman to turn his head. A woman like you." Jenny offered up a dramatic wink that made Lily-Grace snort.

"I have a feeling he's still too much work, even if it's a different kind of work. I'm exhausted."

"You're telling me."

Lily-Grace held back the thought bubbling to the surface. Jenny had been in a decades-long entanglement with one of the maintenance supervisors who worked over at the ranch—Vinny Avila. Currently they were in an off period that they both knew would only last so long.

She wanted to tell Jenny to throw down the gauntlet and make things official with the man once and for all, but she knew how Jenny's mind worked. She'd make the move when she was good and ready, and apparently she wasn't ready.

"You talk to Vinny today?" she asked, though, just to test the water, just to be sure.

"I sent him a picture of my tits and then told him to leave me alone."

"Very mature. I like it."

"Whatever, he can bite me." Jenny closed her menu then rested her chin on her hands. "So tell me what happened with McHottie."

"Ugh." The pain flashed in the middle of her chest. "You know I hate being wrong."

"I do."

"I was really wrong about him and now I'm just trying to figure out if I saw the red flags and just ignored them or if I finally found the secret to his shittiness. I don't know. I told him, ya know. I said this bad thing happened to me. It hurt. It made me feel unsure and that was on top of other not great stuff going on at Ulway. And he just— he dismissed it."

"Can we go like, key his private jet or something?"

"His boat. He's a boat guy."

"I'm sorry, babe. I'm sorry all that shit happened and I'm sorry he didn't show up to support you. Let's go key his boat."

Lily-Grace couldn't help but smile, because she knew Jenny was serious. She'd take that road trip in a heartbeat.

"Not worth it. He'll just have to suffer without me in his life."

"Well, good. You deserve so much better. You deserve the best."

"Thank you, love."

"So are you going back?"

"Honestly, I don't know." She didn't know how to say out loud that she didn't want to go back. Since she'd been home, it had become more and more clear just how much she'd missed her father. When she was thirteen, she wanted to go away to school. Charming Middle had been an absolute nightmare. There was no way in hell she was going to take her chances at Charming High, especially when her father told her he had more than enough money to cover her tuition at Phillips Exeter.

She remembered how light she'd felt after she'd walked out of her final interview, knowing she'd nailed it, knowing she was finally getting the hell away from Charming. But boarding school hadn't been everything she thought it would be. She missed her dad like crazy, and if she thought the kids in Charming were cruel, there was nothing like being asked about your vitiligo by rich white kids.

It took some time, but she finally found her place, made some friends, connected with teachers who wanted her to do well. She made it through, but the experience changed her. She shut parts of herself away, and in some ways that prepared her for the future. There was no way to be an open, vulnerable Black woman in tech. No way. But here she was, years later, proud of what she'd done for herself, and no clue of what she should do next. God willing, she had more than half of her life ahead of her. Maybe the next round, she wouldn't spend her time or her brain cells making rich white guys even richer.

"Too bad there aren't any booming tech companies here in Charming," Jenny said.

"Yeah, I might be done with that."

"Well, if anyone can career hop, it's you. What are you thinking?"

"I might . . . I might retire."

"Bitch, what?" Jenny hissed, leaning across the table.

Lily-Grace winced as she offered up the truth. "I can retire. Like right now."

"Jesus. Why didn't I help start an app worth a gazillion dollars? Stupid family business."

"Awesome family business is more like it."

Right then a server made his way over and presented Lily-Grace with a bottle of pinot. "Excuse me, Ms. LeRoux. The gentleman, Mr. Pleasant, sent this over with a message."

"Oh God," Lily-Grace groaned as Jenny covered her mouth to laugh. "What did he say?"

"With his compliments and he wanted you to be sure it's the most expensive bottle in the house."

"How expensive are we talking?"

"Lily!" Jenny burst out laughing, just as Lily-Grace took the bottle and made a show of looking at every detail of the label. She looked over at Pleasant's table, where Jesse was suddenly very interested in his own menu.

"Never mind. Thank you so much. You can just leave the bottle."

"Absolutely."

"How messed up would it be if I sent back a glass of

lukewarm tap water?" Lily-Grace said as soon as the server was out of earshot.

"You've been back for like an hour. How do you have a whole feud going with Jesse?"

"Girl, I don't know, but I was starting to get bored sitting at home, so maybe torturing him will give me something to do."

"Send him a picture of your tits. That'll shake things up."

"Don't tempt me."

Chapter 5

Jesse couldn't sleep. His thoughts were too loud for the sounds of music or any TV show to calm him down. He'd spent the time his grandmother had spent ignoring him at dinner, filling his stomach with the best cuisine the Charming Inn had to offer. Baking always took his mind off things, but he was too full to eat a whole cake, and his family wasn't in the mood to accept late-night baked goods from him at the moment. He could take some laps in the pool, but he wasn't in the mood to get wet. He'd have to shower and lotion up again, and that seemed like too much work. He sat on the edge of his bed, thinking about how his brothers always turned to the stables in moments like this, taking their horses out on the trails to clear their heads. Solo rides, or together, always without him.

What had Lily-Grace said? Had he been fitted for his martyr robes yet? Maybe she was right. Sort of. He knew sometimes he overreacted, but sometimes he didn't. And always, it was always true that most people had no idea how he felt, what it was like to be him. They didn't understand the anger that simmered under the surface most of the time, and the completely reasonable places that anger came from.

Before he realized what he was doing, he walked over to his closet and put on a fresh sweatsuit and a pair of sneakers he'd only worn twice. Clementine watched him dress from her dog bed in the corner, but when he nodded toward the door, she ignored him and went back to sleep. Her brief kidnapping by Lily-Grace must have been enough excitement for one day. Jesse grabbed his keys and walked through his sprawling empty home. He'd offered his parents the larger of the guest rooms as a formality; he knew his mother would prefer the inn.

Outside, the night was cool and the sky was clear. This was what he needed, quiet *and* fresh air. He made it halfway down his driveway before he saw Evie walking up the road, bundled up in one of Zach's hoodies that was about three sizes too big for her. Sugar Plum was trotting a few feet in front of her. The dog ran toward Jesse as soon as she saw him. He stopped and scratched the dog on the head while he waited for Evie to catch up.

"Hey," she said, a sad smile lifting her cheeks. "Thanks for tonight."

"For what?"

She lifted her shoulder, shrugging. "I can tell you're trying."

"I don't follow."

Her expression blanked out. "Really, Jesse."

"I don't."

"Miss Leona is pissed at you. Zach is still kinda pissed at you, and I know all of that makes you want to grind your molars down to dust."

"To dust, eh. What brings you out here on this lovely evening? Where's your beau?"

"My beau."

"Well, since we're both talking like it's the 1880s."

"I told him I needed some me time. It was a long day."

"Hmmmm."

"Anyway. I know you're still upset, but I can see that you're trying to make this week good for us. One small glitch aside."

"I was caught off guard." Jesse almost said it wouldn't happen again, but he couldn't promise that.

"I—I uh, don't take this the wrong way, but I forgot what your mom was like. She's a lot."

Jesse nodded. He loved his mother. He admired her. But she had her mission and she never took her eyes off that focus. This week's focus was a perfect wedding. And she meant perfect. Jesse knew his role, and that's why he hadn't said a word during dinner. She already had her Jesse report. He was in good health. The ranch was doing well, better than everyone in their family expected it would do under Zach and Jesse's leadership. Since he had no news on the girlfriend front, there was nothing else she needed to hear. Mother of the Wedding Party mode activated. If all went well, she'd be bragging about it for at least the next year. She'd circle back to Jesse when he was ready to settle down. If that ever happened.

"She's great, but she is a lot."

"Hmmm."

Jesse watched Evie closely as she chewed the inside of her lip. "I miss my parents. I miss Nana."

"I miss her too."

Evie's heart belonged to Zach, it had from day one,

but the two of them had their own kind of connection. He remembered Miss Leona sitting him and his brothers down, telling them what had happened to Evie's parents, the accident that had taken them away. How she was coming to the ranch to live with her grandmother, Amelia, or Nana Buck as they all liked to call her. He remembered the heartbreak in her tone when she'd asked the boys to look after Evie, make her feel welcome and loved like she was a part of their family.

He remembered all the afternoons they'd spent baking with his grandmother when Zach and Sam were away at the rodeo with Senior, the moments when Evie would suddenly get quiet. Miss Leona would pull her close and let Evie cry. Jesse remembered the pain of losing his grandfather, but he couldn't imagine what it would be like to lose both his parents at once.

It was no surprise that Evie split for almost ten years after her nan Amelia passed. Sure, his brother had almost blown it by choosing that very moment to lie to Evie about his feelings for her, but Jesse knew what this town must have felt like for her. Full of sad memories and thoughts of people she'd lost. He was glad she and Zach had made up. Jesse was glad to have Evie back.

"You know we got you, right," he said as she wiped away a few fat tears.

"Yeah, I do. That's why I feel comfortable crying in your driveway."

"It's a good place to cry."

"Shiit." Evie laughed, more tears slipping down her face. "I knew this would be hard without them, but your mom just really brought it all to the surface. She's been asking me all of these questions, and I didn't realize how delicate Miss Leona has been. How you all have. You've just been letting me navigate this, but she really wants to remind me she's the only mother in this situation."

"Yeah. That's kind of her brand, unfortunately. It's how she shows she cares. Putting her stamp on things, even if those things are your face."

"That's it exactly." Evie laughed. "No, she's been great. And I love the idea of Senior walking me down the aisle. I just—yeah."

"Anything I can do?"

"Nah. Well, actually. You can tell me why you sent Lily-Grace and Jenny that bottle of wine."

"I have no idea what you're talking about. Goodnight, Evie." Jesse turned and headed back to his house.

"You're just gonna leave a bride-to-be out here all alone?" she called after him.

"I thought you wanted me time."

"Get back here, Jess." With a sigh he made his way back to where Evie was waiting with her hands on her hips.

"Spill it, Pleasant. I know there was drama at the ranch this morning. Delfi texted me."

"Remind me to fire her tomorrow."

"Yeah, try it. She'll just stop showing up but lock you out of the payroll system."

Jesse smiled to himself because he knew Evie was right. Delfi would give him a piece of her mind for even joking about letting her go. She was a big part of what made the ranch tick.

"What happened with Lily-Grace?"

"Just giving me a piece of her mind for almost murdering her father."

"Geez, you're getting it from all sides."

Jesse just sniffed and straightened his shoulders.

"So you gonna ask her out?"

"Why the hell would I do that?"

Evie stopped walking and shot him that classic *really bruh?* look.

"For real. Tell me."

"Tell me why you sent her a bottle of wine at dinner."

"There's nothing to tell."

"That right there. That's why you should ask her out."

"I don't follow."

"Jesse, the whole time I've known you you've never had secrets. Well, except the whole not telling Zach that you and I were still keeping in touch, but that was my secret too."

"It's getting late, Buck. Make your point."

"My point is, she said she just got back to town?"

"Yeah."

"And you two have already had a public blowup, what I think might be some kind of passive-aggressive making up, and now you're acting like nothing happened. You got a big ole juicy secret and it involves Lily-Grace."

"Not telling you my business isn't keeping secrets. Besides, isn't it against the law to draw focus away from the bride this close to the wedding? Wouldn't my sudden involvement with any woman shatter the bedrock of this entire community? No one would even be thinking about your dress or how hard Zach is gonna cry while he tries to get through his vows. Everyone will be focused on a simple bottle of wine."

"Hey, buddy, you should have thought of that before

you body slammed an old man in cold blood," she said with a cheap-shot giggle.

"Ha ha."

"Promise me something."

"What's that?"

"When we get back from the honeymoon you'll let us girls set you up. It's time, Jesse. I know you don't want to be alone like this. It doesn't have to be Lily-Grace, though that would be *amazing*. She seems over-the-top in the best possible way. But I see what you're doing. You're putting the ranch, all of this, before yourself, just like Zach used to. And you don't have to, it's just an excuse to push love away."

"Who are we including in the *girls*?" he asked, ignoring the pain that suddenly bloomed in his chest.

"Hmm, me, Lilah, and Blaire."

"I should have asked Blaire out when I had the chance." The pretty high school teacher and Evie's former roommate had always been kind to Jesse, kind to everyone. He could see himself with a woman like that.

"Excuse me?!?! Why didn't you?"

"Someone I know had a traumatic brain injury, and by the time she was feeling back to herself and speaking to my brother again, her best friend was dating a doctor, who she's now engaged to. Plus, she lives in New York."

"Damn it. I mean I love David. But you and Blaire would have been fun. Mostly for me."

"That's what I need most in a partner. Someone who is perfect for you," Jesse teased, his tone dry.

"At least let us try."

"No. Never." He trusted Evie with a lot of things, but not his love life.

"Okay, well, how about this. Enter yourself in the date auction."

"No." Every spring the Charming Chamber of Commerce helped sponsor a community date auction. Jesse and Lilah were on the planning committee. It brought in a shitton of money and in recent years a few happy couples and even a marriage had come out of it, but Jesse would rather stab himself in the eye than be put up center stage.

"Hear me out."

"No."

"Jesse!" She laughed. "I'm serious. Enter the date auction. You'll be raising money for your own project and you'll at least go out on a date. One date. Break the seal, man! Also you remember Lilah's terms. She said she'd join if you did. I think it would be good for you both. There is no reason for the two of you to be single because I *know* it's not what you want."

"Revenge is her reason, and it's a good one."

"God, you Pleasants are stubborn."

Jesse reached over and lightly punched her shoulder. "Welcome to the family."

"Oof. I've made a terrible mistake. It's late. And cold. Let's go back." They turned on the driveway and walked back toward Zach's house on the far end of the cul-de-sac. Evie stepped up on the porch. "Just think about it, okay. All jokes aside. I—I see how you can get lost in all of this. And I see how you hold yourself back and what happens when it all comes bubbling out. You deserve something of your own. A love of your own. No need to keep punishing yourself."

"Who says I'm punishing myself?"

Evie looked at him for a moment, before she stepped off the porch and wrapped her arms around his waist. He held her back, soaking in the way she seemed to squeeze him tighter. No one in his family hugged him the way Evie did, not even his grandmother. But for some reason, in the moment he thought of how much taller Lily-Grace was and how well she would fit against his body. How warm she might feel against his chest.

"Love you, Jess," Evie said, before she stepped back into the porch light.

"Yeah, yeah, grumble grumble. Love you too."

"Night."

Jesse waited until she was back inside and he heard the door lock before he made his way back to his house, Sugar Plum trailing behind him. He got the dogs settled and climbed back into bed. Before he did something stupid, like texting Jenny Yang to see if he could get Lily-Grace's number, he put up his phone and went to sleep.

The sun in the cloudless sky beat down on Jesse's shoulders as he and Lilah made their way to the stables. They could have taken a staff golf cart, but it was Jesse's bright idea to walk. He looked forward to returning to the AC in his office as soon as their meeting with Dr. Vasquez was over.

"Why is California so hot?" Lilah whined.

"Climate change. Proximity to the equator. You want my hat?" Jesse slathered sunscreen on his bald head every day. He could spare his Stetson for another five hundred yards.

"No. It doesn't go with my outfit. Also it'll look like I'm playing dress-up cowgirl. Your head's so big."

"Thanks."

"I mean that in a good way. Your brain is huge."

"That is true. You don't have to be here for this though. I was gonna catch you and Zach up next week." He'd given Lilah the week off so she could help Evie with wedding stuff, but she'd hopped in his truck with him that morning and come over to the ranch with him like it was a regular Tuesday.

"No, it's fine. I needed a wedding break. Your dad asked me like forty questions about my dad last night, and I almost asked him if he knew how to use a phone. Being here with you is safer than being around Senior and Aunt Regina right now. She keeps telling me how pretty I am and then just stares at my face."

"How come people think your temper is cute?" Jesse asked his cousin.

"'Cause I am cute. Also no one takes my temper seriously. Pick your struggle, Jess."

He couldn't argue with that. People were afraid of him, and that came with a certain level of respect. When Lilah tried to assert herself, with her dimples and her soft, sweet voice, people just patted her on the head and went about their business. "You think if I start crying, Dr. Vasquez will put off his retirement for like another ten, fifteen years?"

"Maybe if we both cry. It's worth a shot."

They continued walking in silence, the main reason he and his cousin got along so well. As they got closer, Dr. Vasquez stepped out into the sun. Jesse could see his bright smile at a distance. Jesse really didn't want to go through the process of finding a replacement. Dr. Vasquez's smile shifted as Jesse got closer, and he cocked his head a little to the side. Jesse knew that look. Dr. Vasquez was in full caregiver-grandpa mode.

"Who told you?"

"Delfi. We're gonna miss you, Doc."

"Not leaving town. Just freeing-up time to help with the grandkids. I don't want to miss any more moments with them. It's official at the end of the month, but this will be my last visit to the ranch."

Lilah stepped forward and let Dr. Vasquez take her hand. "But who is going to sing to the goats?"

"I'm sure you can carry a tune." He smiled back at her. "Before we head inside, I just want you to know I brought my replacement along. Chris is showing him around."

Jesse immediately felt his blood pressure spiking, his jaw tensing. This was not how he wanted to do things. "Doc, you know I can't just take him on—"

"I know, I know. He's a young guy, about Zach's age. His family is back in LA. I just wanted to introduce him to some good people before he's off on his own."

"This his first solo gig?" Jesse asked as he followed Dr. Vasquez back into the barn.

"Yes, but he was practicing up in Valencia. He knows his stuff." Jesse looked at the tall, broad-shouldered Brown man standing beside Chris. The two of them were having an animated conversation, and Zach's horse Steve had his head over the door of his stall, listening intently.

"Oh, here's the boss man," Chris said. He turned and led the young vet back in their direction.

"This is Fetu Kuaea. He'll be taking over my practice,"

Dr. Vasquez said. "Fetu, this is Jesse Pleasant, co-owner of Big Rock Ranch."

"Nice to meet you," Fetu said, taking Jesse's hand in a firm handshake.

"Likewise. This is our assistant operations manager, Lilah."

"Nice to meet you, Lilah."

"Uh, all-pro linebacker Fetuilelagi Kuaea?" Lilah said, the awe in her voice obvious. Jesse realized then why he looked familiar. Dr. Vasquez's replacement had had two amazing seasons with the Steelers.

"Yeah." Fetu laughed. "Good eye. You ball?" he asked Jesse.

"Yeah, three years in college, but my knees had other plans before I could make it to a combine."

"Looks like it worked out okay."

"So far, so good."

"I thought I'd introduce Dr. Kuaea to our toughest patient," Dr. Vasquez said.

"Oh, you mean Majesty." Jesse held back a cringe. Sam's horse was a complete asshole, but for some reason she let guests ride her on the trails, so they kept her in the rotation. "I'll hang back and let you do that."

"She that bad?" Dr. Kuaea asked.

"Oh, you'll see." Chris laughed. "Come on. Lil, you wanna show him?"

"I'll try," she said. "She doesn't love me either."

Jesse watched as his cousin led the new vet and their ranch hand down to the other end of the barn where Majesty was no doubt plotting a murder in her stall.

"He's a good egg, Jesse," Dr. Vasquez said quietly.

"I don't doubt that, but I gotta talk to Zach and my

cousin Walker. Lilah's brother. He's two years out of vet school and I gotta at least offer it to him."

"You think he'll take it?"

"No. He's out on the idea of family business, but I still have to go through the motions."

"How does an interim gentleman's handshake sound? You don't find anyone you like better and you give Fetu a chance? And maybe let him tag along to Claim Jumpers with you every once in a while?"

Jesse moved farther down the stalls, walking down the center of the space. He could feel the doctor smiling beside him. Dr. Vasquez knew how much Jesse didn't like the larger animals. Jesse ignored his laughing gaze though, and focused on Dr. Kuaea. He had to make sure he wasn't seeing things. Majesty poked her head out over the stall door and gave Dr. Kuaea's shoulder a playful bump with her muzzle. Dr. Kuaea leaned closer and gave the horse a gentle scratch under her chin. She didn't seem to hate it.

"See?" Dr. Vasquez said. "He's got the touch."

"Clearly." Jesse turned, and held out his hand for that gentleman's shake. "We're going to miss you."

Dr. Vasquez gripped Jesse's palm. Jesse could feel the calluses among the wrinkles in the man's hand. He'd done his work, done right by the ranch. He'd more than earned a break and time with his family.

Jesse hung around a little longer, sharing some small talk with the doctors and watching carefully as Lilah and Chris helped with more personal introductions to their exhibition steers and the new baby lambs who had just joined their petting zoo. Eventually he excused himself to get to his next meeting. Lilah and Chris would fill him in on their impressions of Dr. Kuaea.

He pulled out his phone as he walked and sent Jenny Yang a text he immediately regretted. While he waited for Jenny's response and the shitstorm that would definitely come after, he googled therapists, specifically Black men who focused on families and anger management.

Chapter 6

Lily-Grace felt herself cringing as she watched some man try to explain why it was perfectly reasonable to hold his neighbor's dog ransom in exchange for some knee pads that were taken off his porch. It had been a literal eternity since she'd watched daytime TV. She usually spent her free time with her nose in a book. Her life felt so noisy, reading always offered her a little quiet.

She'd gotten a lot of quiet though, since she'd been home. All the books on her Kindle were romances and biographies of strong women, and she wasn't right there at the moment, emotionally. So today she settled on *Hot Bench*, aka Judge Judy on crank. That morning she'd silenced the email notifications on her phone. Someone had finally told someone she'd left Ulway for good and her inbox was blowing up.

Requests for interviews from various websites and magazines; former colleagues checking in; former colleagues wanting the truth about what had really happened and why she'd seemingly just disappeared without notice.

She knew at some point she should release a statement. Her friend and sometimes publicist, Margy, was in the loop and completely understood why Lily-Grace was hesitant to speak up. She knew she had to say something. She obviously couldn't go back in time and protect other women, and Ulway had made it clear that they weren't going to get rid of Douche Face, but she wanted something to go down in the Google of Record. People should know.

For a few more days though, peace and quiet, and quality time with her father. And back-to-back episodes of *Hot Bench*.

Her phone chimed in her lap. A text notification. She glanced at the screen. A smile wiped away her grimace as she looked at the screen. A text from Jenny.

> Please come help me fold linens right now. I need to tell you about the text I just got, in person.

"Uh, Vinny come crawling back?" Lily-Grace mumbled to herself. She sat up and lowered the volume on the television like that would help her type better.

> I don't have a whip right now.
> Papa is in town.
> He went back to work.
> Took his car.
> Just tell me.

> Okay I'm calling.
> Another text won't do it justice.

Lily-Grace glanced up at the Life Alert ad playing on the TV, until her phone started singing in her hand. She hit accept. "House of Beauty. You're talking to a cutie."

"You're on speaker and I'm only mostly alone," Jenny replied.

"What does that mean?" Lily-Grace laughed.

"Mama Yang is around here somewhere. We have a few clear days until more guests arrive. She's giving the rooms a real hose-down while I do the beds."

"Who doesn't love a hose-down?"

"You know I do, just don't swear."

"Like hell I won't. JK. What's up?"

"Jesse Pleasant just texted me and asked me for your number."

"Ugh, so disappointing."

"Why?"

"He couldn't even draw this out. It's been like forty-eight hours and he's already in love with me."

"Who's in love with who?" Mrs. Yang yelled in the background.

"No one, Mommy! Hold on." Lily-Grace chuckled to herself as she heard shuffling and then the clarity of Jenny's voice. She'd been freed from the speaker function. "See. There are ears everywhere."

"Is the line secure now?" Lily-Grace teased.

"Yeah. So yeah. He sent such a formal text. Very polite."

"Yeah, I'm not falling for it."

"What should I tell him?"

"Ummm . . . could you send me the text? Oh, and can you send me his number."

"Yeah. Hold on."

A second later the screen shot made her phone vibrate, along with Jesse's contact information. Lily-Grace skimmed the text, ignoring the way her heart fluttered. Not a romantic flutter. Something else, but it was there.

Good Morning, Jenny.
If it's okay with your dear friend Ms. LeRoux,
I wondered if you could pass along her phone
number. I'd like to speak to her again without either
of us showing up unannounced.

She read it two more times before she let out a deep breath. "Jesus."

"He's so . . . tight." Jenny laughed. "Sweet, but tight."

"Hmmm, would we jump right to sweet?" Lily-Grace knew she was giving Jesse a hard time, but he had gone nuclear on her father. She couldn't ignore that. She couldn't let it slide. She didn't want to be an enabler to a next time. Did she remember him as a sweet person? Yes, actually she did. Very sweet, thoughtful, and kind. She still had the pink glittery cowboy hat he'd given her for her birthday. It was in a wicker trunk somewhere. But that was then and this was now, and people can change a lot over the course of decades.

"He's an interesting guy."

"I don't trust it."

"So tell him to fuck off. It won't hurt my feelings."

"Let me call you back."

"What are you going to do?"

"I'm gonna call him. Put an end to this madness."

"Listen, I know things are complicated. You want to stab him. He's clearly been in love with you since eighth grade at least. But, for the good of womankind. For science—"

"I have to sleep with him."

"Oh my God, please sleep with him."

"I'm gonna tell Vinny you said that."

"Tell him!"

Lily-Grace's burst of laughter melted into a sigh. "I'll call you back." She ended the call with Jenny, then slid her thumb over Jesse's contact. She knew she should ignore him, but she knew she couldn't. She swallowed as the line rang, secretly hoping he didn't pick up, senselessly praying he did.

"This is Jesse," he said as soon as he answered. Without looking at him, without being in the same room with him, it was just brutal how deep and smooth his voice was. *Don't trust it, girl,* she told herself. *All men are trash. Especially this one.*

"Heard a rumor you were trying to get in touch with me."

"Lily-Grace, hi." Did he sound nervous?!?! "Ah, yes, I uh, reached out to Jenny Yang to see if I could get in touch with you."

"Well, you have me. What can I do for you?"

"I was wondering if you'd let me cook dinner for you tonight."

"What?" Lily-Grace let out a shocked burst of laughter.

"I wanted to cook dinner for you tonight."

Lily-Grace muted the television and sat up on the couch, thinking how the hell to respond. She had plans to torture him a bit longer. None of those plans involved him making her dinner.

"Are you still there?"

He should bottle his voice, Lily-Grace thought. *Sell it at different tones and levels. It could heal the world. Or at least the horniest people in need.*

"I'm here." She folded the corner of her throw blanket over her leg, then folded it back. "I'm just wondering how you spoke with a therapist and completed a full anger management course since Monday. That's impressive."

"I haven't done all that, but I do have an appointment with a Dr. Kenneth Brooks next Tuesday. He specializes in anger issues."

"The first step is admitting you have a problem. Bravo."

"So, about dinner."

Lily-Grace let out another sigh and glanced at the TV. *Hot Bench* was over. Suddenly this game with Jesse Pleasant wasn't fun anymore. "Look, Jesse, I'll be honest. I just got out of a thing. An intense thing that hurt to end. I don't think dinner is a good idea. Not tonight. But, if one day I decide to change my mind about spending time with you on purpose. . . who—who would tell me the truth about you?" Not that it mattered because she wouldn't change her mind.

The version of this scenario in her mind didn't exist. There wouldn't be a heated argument over sound investments that would boil over into a passionate make-out session, ending with some of the best, long dick sex she'd ever experienced. The reality would be awkward and unsatisfying and then she'd be left cold and full of regret, wondering still what the fuck she was going to do next.

Still, she liked to believe there was someone besides her in Jesse's life who wouldn't sugarcoat things if she did become sad and lonely enough. If she decided to stay in Charming.

"Lilah, my cousin. She knows me better than anyone and she'd give you an honest and thorough report and throw in some embarrassing stuff for shits and giggles."

"Hmm, good to know. One more thing: You tell me something about you, something no one knows. I like a man to be vulnerable with me before he poisons me with his bad cooking."

"I'm an amazing cook," he said, very seriously. That shift in his voice did something else to her, sparked something between her legs she should absolutely ignore. It was the sadness and the disappointment talking. Not genuine attraction.

"Well, no one knows I'm going to therapy, but they'll know eventually. I don't keep many things from my family."

"Okay, fine—"

"I might run for office," he said, suddenly. "I've been approached to consider filling the district seat. Paul Cooger isn't going to run again."

"Good, I hate that demon. Wait. Is that why you asked me to dinner? Looking to grease up a first lady?"

"What? No."

"I get it. Even Booker managed to get a girlfriend for the primaries, but politics aren't for me, Pleasant. Though I am pretty tall. We'd photograph together well."

"No, I—Lily-Grace, I just wanted to have you over for dinner, as friends." Lily-Grace squeezed her eyes shut. The sounds of her ego deflating echoed like loud fart noises in her ears. "You've been away so long, and I obviously didn't help you feel that great about coming back to town. I just thought we could catch up. I'd love to hear about your time at Clutch and Ulway. If you're up for it."

"Dinner as friends."

"I grill a mean steak or if need be, Evie has been helping me perfect some vegetarian options."

"I'm fine with meat, but um—tonight is no good. I have plans tonight with my dad."

"Lily-Grace," he said slowly, his voice sliding over her skin like a kiss. "How are you going to give me all this shit about my temper and you can't even tell me the truth? Your dad has plans with my grandmother tonight. My cousin told me so I wouldn't be caught off guard again."

"Where are you right now?" she blurted out. For some reason dirty thoughts of Jesse in his office filled her mind. She really needed help.

"I'm in my office."

"Oh. Well, I'm just—tonight is not a good night. Maybe some other time. As friends, of course."

"I'm leaving on Thursday for Zach's wedding, but I'll be back on Monday afternoon. May I text you in the meantime, as friends?"

"Right. Family weddings. It is important to have a contact on the outside, though four days in Malibu doesn't sound too bad."

"I'm sure we'll have a great time, and of course the most important part is that Zach and Evie actually get married."

"I guess you can text me. No nudes though."

"What's the point in texting you then?"

"Fine, send nudes. Just be prepared for a full critique and I will definitely show them to Jenny."

"I don't think nudes will do much for my chances when it comes to running for Cogger's seat."

"Are you really thinking about running?"

"I am. I—"

"Need to 'take these broken wings and learn to fly again'?"

"Something like that. Excuse me . . . Yes?" Lily-Grace heard a muffled female voice in the background. "Thank you. I'll take it." To Lily-Grace, he said, "I have to go."

"Go do business things. And have fun at the wedding. Don't hurt anyone."

"I promise to keep my hands and my temper to myself." Jesse ended the call and Lily-Grace sat there on the edge of her couch wondering what the fuck had just happened. She was still angry with Jesse Pleasant, but for some reason she'd just agreed to be texting buddies with him. And the worst part was that she actually wanted to talk to him again. She wanted to hear about this bid for office. She wanted to know what his plans for the ranch were. She wanted to be a fly on the wall when he told his family. This was the perfect time for her to plan the next move. Like right that moment, as if Jesse Pleasant's life and family business were suddenly super interesting to her.

Did she google Dr. Kenneth Brooks just to see if there was a shred of truth to what Jesse was saying? Yes, Brooks was practicing out of LA and offered online therapy, so that checked out. And that should have been the end of it. Still, two hours and a rerun of *Judge Mathis* later, she was still thinking about Jesse Pleasant. She grabbed her phone and headed up to her room, getting out of her pajamas, and getting her mind off things was a smart move. She started her shower and sent Jenny another text.

Wanna go to a mid-week movie tonight?
Snacks on me.

Heck yeah!

Pick you up at 7.
And then you can tell me what happened with Jesse.

Chapter 7

Jesse waited patiently on the couch in Zach's grooms-men suite. The photographer was arriving in five min-utes. The last few days had been draining as hell. More Pleasant family members and his mom's parents, Grammy and Gramps Johnson, made their way to Malibu. The planner, Bailey, had put together a packed schedule, fac-toring in arrival times and meals and breaks to recharge.

Yesterday afternoon and evening the rest of the family had arrived, along with Evie's side of the wedding party. Jesse tried not to think of just how many people were actually showing up for this event. He had his role for the day: Support Zach as a groomsman and make sure to act as an emotional and possible physical barrier between Lilah and her father, Gerald, if they decided today was the day for them to finally have it out.

He hadn't found the time to text Lily-Grace, because even during their scheduled breaks the only time he was alone was in the restroom. He'd taken a twenty-minute power nap on the couch in Sam's suite, before Sam and Amanda bust into the room for a little afternoon delight.

It was nice to catch up with his cousins, it was amazing to come together to celebrate Zach and Evie, especially after everything they had been through, together and apart. Still, he was now in the fifth day of receiving the silent treatment from his grandmother and day three of his parents acting like he didn't matter for one glaringly obvious reason. He didn't have a girlfriend.

He wanted his parents to catch up with Evie and he was glad that Amanda had managed to charm them. His dad had even taken a shine to Vega, making sure she and Corie weren't left out of the family fun, even though they weren't technically Pleasants. Everyone was happy. Everyone was having a good time. There was no reason for the shitty ball of pain and frustration to be lodged at the height of his throat. It was dulled at the moment, overshadowed by his genuine excitement for his brother.

But this was always the way with his family. Always how he felt when they were all together.

Jesse smoothed his hands over his dress pants and let out a slow deep breath before he felt Senior lean in his direction.

"Before the reception, your mother wants a photo with just the family," his father said quietly.

"Immediate or extended."

"Extended."

Jesse nodded. "I can get with Bailey and make that happen."

Senior nodded in kind, and then leaned back into his corner of the couch. Nothing else to say between then.

Jesse stood as Zach walked out to the bedroom. Jesse immediately noticed that Zach's tie was a little off center, but before he reached him his father was up and at Zach's side.

"Your tie." Senior fixed it with his confident, capable hands, then gave Zach a fatherly pat on the shoulder. Jesse settled back on his heels, suddenly too anxious to sit down again. He let out a slow breath through his nose and then another and another. He knew that later Zach would be honest with him about this moment. He had his own issues with Senior and his own opinions about their father's choices, but that wasn't the focus today. Zach's gaze shot to him and then Sam, his smile brightening.

"I should have gone with the bolo," Zach joked.

"Trying to jack my style," Sam said, deadpan from his spot on the arm of the love seat.

"Shouldn't be anyone's style," their cousin Brandon laughed.

Senior let out his own chuckle before he straightened Zach's lapels. "No, the bolo is style, class, and function all the way. It takes a certain kind of man to pull that off."

"Like I said, the bolo is all mine," Sam insisted.

"You look great," Jesse said.

"Thanks, man," Zach said, before he crossed the room and clasped palms with Jesse. "You ready?"

"Are you?"

"You know I am," Zach replied, his eyes shining already. "I get to marry Evie Buchanan."

Heads turned toward the knock at the door before they could all do the manly posturing of dashing away tears of joy. Cole, one of Zach's roommates from college, opened the door. Miss Leona stepped into the room, plumes of dove-gray fabric trailing behind her.

"Look at you all. So handsome."

"Just trying to keep up with you, Miss Leona."

"Stop sucking up, Christopher."

"Yes, ma'am." He laughed.

"Jesse Junior," his grandmother said. There was still an edge of ice to her tone, but at least she was speaking to him.

"Yes, ma'am?" She beckoned him forward, the bangles on her wrist chiming together, and then nodded toward the door. He followed her out into the hallway, closing the door behind them. She turned back to face him, waiting a beat before she said anything, her stage training at work. Whatever she had to say, she wanted to make sure that he heard her loud and clear.

"You look very sharp." She adjusted his boutonniere. "And tall."

"You fed me too well."

"Not possible. I wanted to give you a chance to apologize."

"I am very sorry. I was caught off guard and being overprotective when it wasn't my place. It won't happen again. I think I managed to apologize to Mr. LeRoux and his daughter."

"He told me you came by. I accept your apology and I wanted to let you know that Mr. LeRoux and I plan to keep seeing each other. He is a wonderfully kind man and he makes me laugh. I haven't felt this way about anyone since your grandfather."

"So it's serious?"

"It is serious. We were just trying to enjoy ourselves for a while before we got the families involved. I haven't told your father yet. Or your uncles. We were going to wait until after the wedding."

"But?"

"But I just want to prepare you. August will be around more, and I need you to—"

"Keep it together. I will. And I'm happy for you."

"Thank you. Are you ready for your speech?"

"I am. Keeping it short and sweet like Evie requested."

"Good. Nothing good comes from a long-winded wedding toast."

"It'll be the quickest toast of all time. I swear."

"Good." Miss Leona reached up and gently stroked his cheek. "Deep breaths," she said. Jesse had to force himself not to flinch away. He'd made one mistake. He wasn't out of control. But apparently that didn't matter anymore.

"I should get back inside. We still have some male bonding to do before the photographer gets here."

"I'm here!"

Jesse looked up as the photographer, Stephy, and her assistant came power walking down the hall.

"It's go time," Jesse said. He managed to pull up a smile, as he pulled open the door to the suite.

"Mrs. Lovell, since you're here, I'd love to get some photos with you and your grandsons."

"Absolutely."

Jesse held the door open and ushered the ladies inside. He tried not to let what his grandmother had said get under his skin, even though it started making slow, silent progress as the morning went on. He decided as they made their way down to the site of the ceremony to focus on other things instead, like possibly texting Lily-Grace later, and in the long term, taking A New Way Forward up on their offer and leaving all of this, and Charming, behind.

Jesse made his way to the other side of the massive white tent and carefully sank down into the white-and-gold chair beside his mother. He sat back and finally gave in to the urge to loosen up his tie. He'd been on the dance floor the last hour straight, sharing the spotlight with Amanda, who had to have been some sort of dance-battle champion in a former life. She almost danced as well as Jesse. Almost.

It'd been a good day, a great day. The vows Evie and Zach exchanged were thoughtful and full of love as well as the biting humor that drew them to each other since they were kids. Jesse managed to hold back the tears, but it was a pretty close call.

By the time they said *I do*, Jesse's focus was right where it should be. On Zach and Evie, and how happy his whole family was together, celebrating this day. He and Sam had nailed their best man speeches. Jesse came with the heartfelt notes and Sam with the humor. Blaire somehow managed to combine the two, talking about her friendship with Evie, her accident, her recovery, and how Evie had somehow managed to hide the Pleasants and the magic of Charming from her.

Jesse ignored the twinge in the back of his neck, the work that he'd put into enhancing the illusion of Big Rock Ranch and the pretty picture his family painted when they were all together. The good with the bad. He knew he couldn't change it, or them, but as Blaire raised her glass, Jesse knew he had some decisions to make soon. Not now, but soon.

"You know what people have been telling me all night?" his mother said. She'd been running around all night, mixing and mingling, on and off the dance floor. Her baby was married to a beautiful, successful woman and the ceremony had gone off without a hitch. Regina Pleasant was on cloud nine and not a single strand of her hair was out of place.

"What's that, Mom?"

"Everyone has been telling me how lovely your speech was and just how handsome you are."

"I'm a man of many talents. And I appreciate the contributions your DNA made to my face."

"Of course. I am so happy to do my part—Umph, I need a drink."

"You want me to grab something for you from the bar?" Jesse asked, already halfway out of his seat.

"Oh no, honey. I need to do another lap anyway. Catch your breath and maybe stop moving long enough for some of these single ladies to shoot their shot."

"What are you talking about?"

"Nothing." His mom winked at him and headed off to the other side of the dance floor where his dad was talking to Evie's agent, Nicole. Jesse looked around the room and tried to see what single ladies his mother was talking about, but as far as he knew all the age appropriate women in attendance were currently standing with their dates, in most cases their actual husbands or wives. He shook off his mother's comments and grabbed the full pitcher of ice water from the center of the table and poured himself a glass. He took a deep sip, realizing just how thirsty he was, when Amanda came over and plopped down in the chair beside him with a dramatic huff.

She dabbed her face with a folded napkin she had clutched in her hand. "I have bad news or good news. No, bad news," Amanda said. She looked over at him, gauging his reaction.

Jesse couldn't stop his eyebrow from going up. "Which is it?"

"Not great news. There is a woman at your . . . eleven o'clock. Green dress." Jess looked over and saw the woman in question swaying to a Pointer Sisters song blaring through the DJ's sound system. She was nursing a glass of champagne.

"Yes, that's Fabien. She's one of the producers on Evie's documentary." They'd wrapped taping on her journey to open her restaurant, Thyme, months ago, but the editing process trudged on.

"Yeah. So she and pink dress over there and black dress standing beside her, they have a bet going to see who can get you back to their hotel room tonight. I heard them talking about it a few minutes ago."

Jesse felt strange heat shoot up the front of his neck and over the crown of his head. Suddenly his brain felt tight and a dull ringing started up in his ears. He swallowed and tried to ignore the way his vision was suddenly blurring.

"I figured I had to tell you because I have a feeling this is not your bag, but also I'm not all up in your business when it comes to the ladies."

Jesse felt his chest swelling up again. "Thank you, Amanda. Excuse me for a second."

"Are you okay? Should I have kept that to myself?"

"No. Thank you. Thank you for telling me." Jesse couldn't muster up a smile, but he did give her shoulder a light squeeze of reassurance as he stood up from the table. "Excuse me."

He needed to get the hell out of there, or least walk it off. This was why he didn't date. The real reason. Every woman he met saw him as a challenge. Not a person. He knew he had his own stuff to deal with, but how the hell was he supposed to start a romantic relationship with people who viewed him that way? What was the plan? What did they think would win him over? He wasn't a one-night-stand kind of guy, so even if one of those women had come up to him to claim that prize, they would have been disappointed. He wasn't going to hop in bed or duck behind a large bush for a quickie at his brother's wedding. His grandmother would love that.

Carefully, but quickly, he walked away from the main tent and headed for the bathroom inside the villa. He spotted his cousin Sage smoking near the path leading down to the parking lot and decided to ignore her.

"Jesse," Sage called out to him with a laugh as he stormed by.

"What?" He didn't mean to snap, but that didn't make his reaction any less shocking or unnecessary. He could just hear Lily-Grace's mocking voice, see the disappointment on his grandmother's face. He couldn't even make it through the night without losing his cool. But Sage didn't seem to take it personally. She was from the

Pleasant side of the family that didn't decide to go into some sort of family business. Her side of the family had gotten all the chill.

"You okay?" she asked.

"Yeah, what's going on?"

"Is it true you know all of Cardi's choreography?"

Jesse fought the urge to snap again, and this time he was able to keep it under control. "Yes, it's true. Lilah bet me fifty bucks I couldn't learn the moves to 'WAP' in fifteen minutes. And I enjoyed my winnings. It spiraled from there."

"That is amazing."

"We like to have fun," Jesse said, trying to keep his tone level because now he was pissed for a whole new reason. "Please tell Corie I know her business too. We can both keep to ourselves."

"I will tell Corie that. But just know there were like six other people at the table when she told us. You were cutting it up on the dance floor and I think she just wanted to give a little back story. You got moves, cuz."

"Thanks. Excuse me."

"Uh, I wouldn't go in there," Sage said suddenly, nodding toward the entrance.

"Why? What's going on?"

"Uncle Gerald kicked like five employees out so he could finally have it out with Lilah."

Jesse let his head fall back on his shoulders and let out a loud groan.

"Yeah. That's the sound I made when he stopped me from following them. Has he always been such a dick?"

"To Lilah? Yes." Jesse eyed the door, then looked

down at his watch. He'd promised he wouldn't let Lilah and his uncle make a scene. Technically they weren't, but he also didn't know how long he should stand by while Uncle Gerald hammered his daughter with his outdated views on her life. His uncle wanted to see Lilah, his only daughter, settled and taken care of, but trying to *arrange* a marriage for her, without giving her a say was not the way to go.

It had been almost six years since she fled their vineyard up North, trying to get away from Uncle Gerald's brutish views and something told Jesse this conversation wasn't going to convince her to return home. He glanced back at Sage, who took one final drag before she stomped the butt out with her heel. Smoke billowed out of her nose when she spoke again.

"Get in there, champ. Use some of that pent-up aggression for good."

"I'm not—" Before he could finish his sentence, his uncle Gerald came storming out of the building. He saw them, but didn't say anything as he walked by.

"Hmmm, looks like Lilah won that round." Sage shrugged.

"Let me go check on her."

"Tell her I said to keep fighting the good fight. Marriage is only worth it if you actually like the person you're married to."

Jesse grunted in agreement and headed inside the building. He found Lilah sitting on the edge of the indoor fountain.

"You okay?" he asked.

"No. He's so—seriously. What is wrong with him? He offered me money, Jess. He said he would literally pay if I just come home. And he doesn't even want me there, really. He just wants me home so my mom will stop nagging him to apologize."

"Did he apologize?"

"Of course not. He told me I'd made my point and was, like, asking me how I thought it looked, abandoning the vineyard to come run Senior's business when he knows damn good and well that's not why I left."

Jesse felt himself frown. "Well, it's not Senior's business to start—"

"That's what I said. Ugh. Whatever. I gave him a piece of my mind and I did what everyone asked. I didn't make a scene."

"Maybe you should have."

"Yeah. Right."

Jesse took a seat on the wooden bench on the far wall, and gave Lilah the time she needed to catch her breath. She was the baby of their whole generation of Pleasants, but she was a smart, capable adult. Uncle Gerald needed to let this shit go if he even wanted to have a real relationship with his daughter again or if he cared the slightest bit about her happiness.

"Hey. I have a wild idea," he said after a few minutes. "I'm going to enter the date auction." The idea just popped in his head. He knew he'd regret it, but he needed to do something, gain some sort of fucking control. Yeah, women bidding on him was kind of like hedging bets for his attention, but at least he'd be in on it this time. At least it would be his choice. He told Lilah about Fabien and her friends and how he'd arrived at this decision. "We could enter it together."

"Yeah, and then maybe I'll just marry whoever bids

on me and then maybe my dad will chill the hell out once and for all." Her expression brightened as she finally looked up at him. "Jess. You're a genius. We should definitely enter the auction."

"It's not too late?"

"No, of course not." Lilah had nailed down participants a few weeks ago and the auction was only a week away. Jumping in now was cutting it a little close. "Plus, Mrs. Donatelli will be over the freaking moon."

"Okay. Let's do it."

"Let's get back out there. That cake is amazing and I want another slice."

"Right behind you. Just going to use the restroom." Jesse headed off to the men's room as his cousin went back to join the party. He felt better now that he had a plan. The rest of the night went smoothly, mostly because he made an effort to avoid Fabien and her friends. By the time he got back to his hotel room, it was too late to send Lily-Grace a text. As friends.

Chapter 8

Lily-Grace stepped out of her father's Buick and thanked the valet. When her father had first mentioned going to the date auction, she brushed off the idea of attending. For one, she didn't know if she'd still be in town. She was closing in on a month of whatever near-midlife crisis she was going through and thought by now she'd have some sort of plan sorted out. All she'd managed to do was hide the alerts to Dane's texts, which were constant and annoying as fuck.

She needed a closure with him she knew she wasn't going to get, but she was waiting for her final Fuck Off to come with a plan, which she didn't have. So she'd decided to extend her vacation mode, embrace her growing wardrobe of adult onesies. She'd just taken her new hooded onesie from Savage X Fenty out of the dryer when her dad explained his plan for the date auction. Once he'd explained everything, she couldn't say no.

"You ready?" Lily-Grace asked as she took her dad's arm. He looked sharp in his fresh black suit, and he finally had his cast off. His wrist was good as new.

"You know I am. Let's go." She smiled back at him as he led her through the front door of Charming's fancy new Marriott. Tonight was a big night for Mr. LeRoux. He'd entered himself in the date auction. This year the money was going toward a technology program for seniors, providing the funds for space, equipment, and instructors. Lily-Grace was glad her aging father was perfectly tech savvy, and she loved the idea of other seniors in Charming getting the chance to catch up.

But that wasn't the main attraction for the evening. He and Mrs. Lovell had hatched an elaborate plan. She'd bid a ridiculous amount of money for him, a tax deductible contribution; then, a week from now, they'd leak through the grapevine that their first date had been a success and they'd decided to go steady, and most importantly they had the auction to thank for it.

Lily-Grace joked that they needed to do a full press release, but she wouldn't put it past Miss Leona at this point. It was genius really, and completely in line with Mrs. Lovell's over-the-top, theatrical energy. She was happy for them though, and there was no way she'd miss their adorable display. She was so happy for them it was enough to ignore the fact that Jesse Pleasant would be in attendance. It had been almost two weeks and he'd never called her, never texted, never followed up about this so-called "dinner as friends" he'd initially suggested. It was fine. It was proof that whatever she had imagined had been bubbling between them, even if it was only distraction sparked by sheer boredom, was just that. Nothing serious. Nothing worth mentioning again.

Had she considered texting him? Yes. Had she scoped

out any and all of the photos from Zach and Evie's wedding that featured Jesse in that perfectly tailored suit? Perhaps. Had she caught a photo of Jesse, suit jacket cast aside, dancing his ass off during the reception? Yes, okay. Fine, she'd seen the picture on Evie's Instagram and gone back to it maybe two or three or eight times.

She looked at the few gossip posts pointing out the fact that Academy Award–winning actor Sam Pleasant had not one but two extremely attractive brothers, and the tallest, sexiest of the bunch with thighs that could crush a field of watermelons, was in fact single. Very much so single, and just a short drive across town. But none of that mattered. Jesse Pleasant was a distraction. A messy distraction. She had things she needed to do, and none of it included Jesse Pleasant.

She did want to ask him how therapy was going, if he'd actually followed through with it. Some other time though. A crowded ballroom wouldn't be the place to ask heavy questions about his anger management issues.

Her father left her at the door of the ballroom with a kiss on the cheek and went around the stage to join the rest of the hot dates putting themselves up for auction. She spotted Jenny and Mrs. Yang, and quickly picked her way across the ballroom to take her seat with them.

"Look at these gorgeous ladies!" She leaned over and kissed Mrs. Yang on the cheek as the older woman lightly pinched her thigh. She motioned toward the ruffled edge of Lily-Grace's off-the-shoulder jumpsuit.

"This is cute. You look so cute."

"Thank you."

Jenny moved her chair a bit so Lily-Grace could take the seat beside her. "I just told her the plan," she said.

"And I am devastated. I was going to bid on your dad," Mrs. Yang replied.

"With what money?" Jenny laughed.

"I'm secretly rich. Don't worry about it," Mrs. Yang said.

"Mrs. Yang. Question for you. What about Mr. Yang?" Lily-Grace asked. To her knowledge, Jenny's parents had been happily married for decades.

"There is nothing wrong with a backup husband."

Lily-Grace gasped, placing her hand on her chest. "Papa LeRoux is no one's runner-up."

"Just as well. I can't compete with Leona. Look at those earrings." Lily-Grace followed her gaze toward the ballroom door, where Miss Leona had just glided in with her granddaughters. Lily-Grace considered going over to greet them, but she didn't want to drop any hints that they were already in cahoots once the bidding started.

"She is quite the fashionista." Lily-Grace picked up the program on the table, filled mostly with ads from local small businesses, including the Yangs' B and B. She flipped to the first page of contestants. Each entrant was given a half page with their headshot and a short bio. "We know anyone else in this?" she asked Jenny.

"My stupid sometimes boyfriend. And I heard Neddy Davis's mom entered him."

"Aww, Ned." The short white kid sat next to Lily-Grace in seventh grade social studies. He was quiet and sweet, and loved telling Lily-Grace about his favorite R & B songs of the day. It would have been annoying as hell with anyone else, but there's something about Neddy. He was the best.

"He goes by Ned now," Mrs. Yang said. "His wife left him, which I think was a bad move. He makes a lot of money. Best Realtor in town."

"Well, dang." Lily Grace kept flipping through the program. She smiled when she got to her father's profile. He was wearing his "fancy" glasses and his favorite tie in the photo. Scanning his bio, she tried not to dwell too much on the mention of his four grown children. She hadn't asked if he'd told Mrs. Lovell about his other kids. He still loved them, but he didn't bring them up to Lily-Grace very often, for obvious reasons. She flipped to the next page and her eye almost twitched at the color insert highlighting two last-minute entries. Jesse and Lilah Pleasant.

She gave Jenny a light jab. "Did you see this?"

"Surprise?"

"You knew?"

"Yeah. I told you he'd be here."

"Yeah, 'cause he helps with the auction or 'cause his family donated a million dollars to the cause. Not because he was in the mix."

"He's in the mix. Get your wallet ready."

"Yeah, no. If he can't send a text, I'm definitely not paying for him to hang out with me. Sorry." Lily-Grace had more snark on the situation, right on the tip of her tongue, but Mrs. Donatelli, the owner of Chip Chip Hooray, the best ice cream spot in town, stepped onto the stage.

"Hello, everyone. Thank you so much for joining us

tonight for our annual community date auction. Just a few announcements before we get started." She lied about "a few," instead launching into an abridged but painfully long history of Charming before she got to the rules for the auctions. "There will be a reception, poolside, following the auction, for all of our donors, winners, and their dates. Now let me bring out our emcee for the evening. You might all know him from local fire station No. 332, right here in the heart of Charming. Proof that this auction can lead to true love, Omar Harrison. The room broke out in applause as the house lights dimmed a bit.

"His wife bid on him a couple years back," Mrs. Yang explained as Omar went to the mic and got the evening started. First up, Will Barzelay, the new assistant basketball coach over at the high school. Everything about him was pretty average, but he came with dinner for two at the Charming Inn. A giggly woman and her friend in the front row joined forces to come up with the winning bid. Lily-Grace smiled, taking in the charm of her hometown and the people in it.

As each entrant graced the stage and went to the highest bidder, Lily-Grace anxiously awaited her father's turn and did her best not to think about which woman was going to take Jesse Pleasant on whatever Pleasant family-related date he had planned. It would probably be a free snack from the mini bar at the ranch, followed by a really uncomfortable conversation about homemade dog food. She pitied whichever woman decided to pay for that outing.

Finally her father came onto the stage. For some silly reason tears rose to her eyes when he spotted her in the dim room and waved. She waved back and blew him a kiss.

"Now, ladies," the MC went on. "We have a real gem tonight. Mr. LeRoux is a pillar of our community who has probably given financial advice to half the people in this room. A father to extremely successful grown children, he is looking for someone to discuss the expanded *Star Trek* television universe with. Our winner will join this fine gentleman for an evening of dinner and your choice of dancing or a trip to the Trappman observatory."

"He's mine," some woman yelled from the far side of the room as Lily-Grace's dad held up his hand in Vulcan greeting. Lily-Grace couldn't see who it was, but the whole ballroom burst out in laughter.

"I think we should get this bidding started then." The MC took the first bid, from that same shouty woman. Two more women bid, including Mrs. Donatelli. Her husband passed away when Lily-Grace was an undergrad. She hadn't remarried. Maybe Mrs. Donatelli had an eye on her father. Finally, Mrs. Lovell piped in with a ridiculously high bid. Gasps around the room mirrored Lily-Grace's own shock.

"Oh, that's too much money," Mrs. Yang said sarcastically. People close to their table laughed.

"Who can top that, folks?" the MC said, giving Mr. LeRoux a light pat on the shoulder.

Shouty Gal's hand flew up in the air, adding a significant amount to Mrs. Leona's current bid. That's when the murmurs started. Ice cream must be doing very well, because Mrs. Donatelli was not out of the game yet, either. She called out her bid. Lily-Grace loved her father, but this she did not expect. He'd already topped the bid for Mike Crowe, the sheriff's deputy with an eight-pack and a jaw that could cut glass. He was so fine, Lily-Grace and Jenny almost bid on him. But he was old news now.

Lily-Grace watched as Mrs. Lovell slowly rose from her seat, and a literal hush fell over the room. The fabric of the light blue tunic she was wearing seemed to swirl around her. Lily-Grace had always looked up to Mrs. Pleasant with her glamour-girl looks and beauty queen poise, but the dream was to be as confident, cool, and completely together.

Miss Leona would have a plan by now, the asshole part of her brain decided to say. Lily-Grace pushed away the shitty thought and ignored the lump lodged in the top of her throat as Miss Leona doubled her previous bid. She turned and looked at the woman at the other side of the room.

"I think we should end it there, sweetheart," she said, throwing the woman the iciest wink Lily-Grace had ever seen. In the near dark, Jenny reached over and gripped her hand, her gaze also locked on the epic standoff. The other woman stood and Lily-Grace finally saw who it was: Merry Sharpe, the first wife of Glen Sharpe, former governor of California.

"I know when I'm beat, Miss Lovell."

The MC swallowed, clearly terrified to be caught in the crossfire if high heels started flying across the room. "Well, unless someone else is brave enough to throw their hat in the ring, going once—going twice—sold to Mrs. Lovell for the price of a private island." Her dad tipped his imaginary hat in Mrs. Lovell's direction as she sent her granddaughter Corie to the stage to claim her winner's ticket. "That was exciting and terrifying. Up next we have one of our amazing volunteers. I feel personally indebted to this awesome woman for convincing me to enter the auction. Folks, put your hands together for Lilah Pleasant."

Lily-Grace wasn't the only one who gasped when Lilah stepped out onto the stage. They'd only met once, but at the time Lilah was dressed for a casual dinner with her family. Now she was dressed to break some hearts, the floor-length black dress she was wearing showing off her every curve.

"How will our winner be spending their time with you?"

"Since it's for a great cause, myself and the team at Big Rock Ranch have contributed four tickets to the Dodgers versus the Yankees, complete with car service to and from Los Angeles and an overnight stay at the Marriot Downtown. Separate rooms of course."

"So you heard the woman, no hanky panky."

"Unless we hit it off."

Lily-Grace couldn't help but laugh at the sickly sweet affect Lilah added to her voice. The men in the room and probably some others were eating it up. The bidding went quickly. Jenny explained that the three main bidders were one of the local firefighters and two guys from the ranch, which would make for an interesting day at work come Monday. When Lily-Grace spotted the winner, a large Brown guy—shorter, but just as wide as Jesse—making his way to the stage to claim his ticket, it was clear Lilah hadn't done too bad for herself.

"That's Dr. Kuaea. New veterinarian in town," Mrs. Yang said.

"Can't go wrong with an animal doctor," she replied.

"You ready?" Jenny asked as the MC reset for the next entrant.

"I have no idea what you're talking about."

"Mm-hmmm."

"Now folks," the MC said, "I have co-owner of Big Rock Ranch himself, Mr. Jesse Pleasant Jr."

There was plenty of applause, but when Jesse walked out on the stage wearing another impeccable, custom-made suit, all Lily-Grace could hear was the chorus to "Dream Weaver." Had he somehow gotten more attractive in the last two weeks? Who made his suits? Who took his measurements? How many quarters could you bounce off his thighs?

"Now, Jesse, is it true you've been single this whole time?"

"That is true. I've been very busy with the ranch."

"What's changed?" The MC laughed.

"Oh, I'll keep you company!" Merry Sharpe shouted. Another "Oow!" followed from another corner. It was all in good fun, but for some reason Lily-Grace felt the strong urge to tell both women to mind their damn manners. Especially when she noticed the way Jesse's cheek twitched. He was not enjoying this at all.

"And what can our winner expect from a date with you?"

"A picnic lunch, compliments of Blue Moon Tavern.

Followed by a taste testing at Chip Chip Hooray, thank
you to Mrs. Donatelli."

"I know what I'd like to taste!" another woman shouted
from the center of the room. That time Jesse flinched.
Actually flinched. He didn't laugh, he didn't smile. There
was no snappy comeback.

"Okay, okay, let's settle down." The MC chuckled
some more. "Let's get the bidding started." The woman
in the center of the room bid first, but what felt like seconds later six different women were tossing out numbers,
climbing higher and higher. The MC could barely keep
up. The whole time Jesse looked miserable, like he
wanted to so be anywhere but under this hot spotlight.
Whatever his reason, finally Lily-Grace felt for him, but
it would be over soon. He'd suffer through one awkward
date and go back to being a pain in someone's ass.

Merry Sharpe drove up the bidding.

Murmurs filled the room and Lily-Grace had to stop
herself from getting out of her seat. To do *what* she
wasn't sure, but something. She looked over at Mrs.
Lovell, who was clearly thinking the same.

"Back off, Merry," some woman shouted. "That V-card
is mine." The breath left Lily-Grace's lungs as she saw the
look of horror in Jesse's eyes. Closing in on forty and still
a virgin didn't matter. He was absolutely mortified.

Before she could stop herself, Lily-Grace shot out of
her seat and held her paddle high. The figure she threw
out was just absurd, double the highest bid of the night.
Her accountant and her father would have questions, but
it was too late.

With an impressed nod, the MC took her bid. "Can we

go higher, ladies?" There were some grumbles, but no one offered another bid. Lily-Grace's whole body flashed hot as she walked to the stage and claimed her winning ticket. She couldn't read the expression on Jesse's face, and she wasn't exactly sure she'd made the best choice. Once again, she had no plan.

Her face was still hot when she joined the other winners out on the hotel pool deck. Jenny and her mother had gone home because Mrs. Yang had "seen all she needed to see," but Lily-Grace promised she'd text Jenny as soon as she spoke to Jesse. The after-party was surprisingly packed. Every business owner in town, family members, winners and their dates. Except Jesse. He was the only person who hadn't made an appearance. Mrs. Lovell assured Lily-Grace he'd be out soon, but almost thirty minutes of appetizers and drinks later, she was still making small talk with Mrs. Lovell and her father.

"Maybe I should go find him," she finally said. "Make sure we're on the same page if I decide to shank Merry Sharpe with a wineglass."

"I think we're all fine with that, but that's not a bad idea. He'd probably like to talk to you without an audience," Mrs. Lovell replied.

"Check the employees' office right behind the ballroom. I saw him duck in there earlier," her father added. She kissed him on the cheek and then started the trek around the crowded pool deck. She stopped briefly to say hello to Ava and Wren, girls she knew from middle school who were now running their mom's bakery. Ava was just about to give birth and Lily-Grace did want to catch up with them. As soon as she found Jesse.

She carefully skirted around the edge of the pool, mindful of the new decorative tile that looked like it had been stepped on by many guests. She spotted Neddy and flashed him a smile. She'd have to catch up with him too. Some other time though, when he wasn't with his highest bidder. Fucking Merry Sharpe.

"My dad has your number?" Lily-Grace asked Ned as she scooted by. They should have kept this part of the affair in the ballroom where there was more space to move around.

"He sure does. You in town for a while longer?" Ned asked.

"I mean, I still have a romantic picnic to see about," she said with a laugh.

"What are you going to do with all that man?" Merry said like Neddy, her actual auction date, wasn't standing right beside her.

"Continue to mind my own business," she shot back. "Excuse me." She turned and tried to scoot around an elderly couple slow dancing to the ambient music that was coming through the speakers. She didn't quite make it though. She considered herself competent in heels, but she knew she'd made a mistake not watching exactly where her feet were going, even for a split second. Her heel caught that magical place where tile meets grout. Her ankle rolled and the world suddenly tilted.

Ned reached out for her, bless him. But he missed her hand by a good foot as she fell backwards. Her other hand shot out to break her fall as her hip slammed into the edge of the pool deck, but there was nothing solid under her upper body, just the shimmering blue water. Head and shoulders first, she went under. When she finally figured out what she wanted to do with her life, she'd fit swimming lessons into the schedule. If she didn't drown.

Chapter 9

Jesse knew he needed to get out to the reception. Lily-Grace could put down a deposit on a large home for what she paid for their picnic and ice cream date. But he wasn't ready yet. He did everything he could think of. The counting and breathing exercises. He even gave himself permission to cry, but none of that worked. He sat in the manager's office holding his head in his hands, searching his mind for ways to beat back the humiliation.

He knew virginity was a construct. And even if it was something real and true it wouldn't matter. He'd had sex before. But just twice, and both times had been an absolute disaster. The times he'd attempted in between— even worse. He had been young and clumsy and nervous and the young women he was with . . . well, they reminded him of the Merrys and Fabiens of the world. They just wanted a crack at him.

Obviously, no one in the audience knew that, but that it was said in a roomful of people, and Jesse had had no idea how to react, was bad enough.

This wasn't how he pictured his life. Every attempt to step up and be the type of man his grandfather would be proud of, that Jesse himself could be proud of, ended with some foolish blunder or cold underestimation that left Jesse wondering what the hell he was doing.

Maybe he shouldn't run for office. The public side of life would be infinitely more difficult, and when things got hard on the floor of Congress or in front of the press, he couldn't count to ten or go somewhere and hide. Or worse. Lose his temper. Maybe the ranch was the best place for him. At least there he was the boss.

After Jesse had been honest about what it felt like when he grew angry, Dr. Brooks had given him an emergency contact number. Jesse had pulled out his phone, but his vision had blurred before he could hit the call icon. This wasn't an emergency, he told himself. Being clowned in front of half the town was just a day in the life of Jesse Pleasant. He wasn't Zach, with his ease and confidence, and he wasn't Sam, with his charm and his open heart. And he couldn't call either of them to tell them what was happening. Zach was still on his honeymoon and Sam was away for the weekend with Amanda. His parents were on their next European adventure, and the rest of his family was currently enjoying the very poolside reception he was avoiding. He was just Jesse, and he was going to have to pull it the fuck together and deal with how lonely and depressing that sad fact was.

He closed his eyes one more time, slowly counting to ten.

"You're gonna go out there and ignore everyone but your family and Lily-Grace. That's your focus. Deal with the rest when you talk to Dr. Brooks." Two more quick breaths and he grabbed his Stetson off the desk and exited the manager's office. Vega was standing in the hallway waiting for him.

"Oh, hey," Jesse grumbled.

"Hey. Just wanted to be, you know, available. I know a little panic attack when I see one." Evie had had them a few times after her head injury and when Vega had been acting as her nurse, she was right beside her, holding her hand and walking her through some pretty difficult moments.

"I appreciate it. I'm okay now."

"What happened in there, Jesse—"

"I know. It wasn't my fault."

"It wasn't."

"Where's Corie?"

"She's in the bar. You and Miss Leona take your time. There's a game on."

"Okay, I should get out there."

"You know where to find us. And I'll be back at the house later if you want to talk."

"Thanks." Jesse turned and headed for the exit that led out to the hotel pool. He spotted Lily-Grace on the far side of the patio. She made the call-me gesture at Ned Davis before she said something to Merry Sharpe that made the woman's face curl up. Jesse focused on getting to her. He'd make small talk with everyone else after he apologized for leaving Lily-Grace waiting while he tried to pull it together.

Later, he'd have a conversation with Mrs. Donatelli and Lilah about next year's reception and not having it on a crowded pool deck. He winced at the way Lily-Grace rolled her ankle in those sinful strap heels, and then his heart dropped to his stomach when she fell into the pool, water splashing up all around her. Anyone would need a second to recover from a painful spill like that, but from the way her father rushed to the pool's edge, Jesse knew something was off.

"She can't swim!" Mr. LeRoux yelled. Jesse didn't think. He tossed his Stetson and dove into the water, lit from below with lights built into the simple tiling. He spotted Lily-Grace, struggling to get to the surface, no chance of it happening. He reached her as fast as he could and grabbed her with a firm arm around her waist. Dr. Kuaea was kneeling at the pool's edge when they came to the surface, reaching out for them.

Lily-Grace's sputtering cough was the best sound he had ever heard. She'd swallowed so much water, but she was breathing. She'd be okay. Jesse swam with all his strength in Fetu's direction and lifted Lily-Grace into his waiting grasp. When she was clear of the water, he swam back and grabbed her clutch purse that was floating in the middle of the pool. He tossed it to Lilah, then hoisted himself out of the water.

He rushed over to where Fetu and Dr. Ritch, one of Charming's local pediatricians, had settled Lily-Grace in a deck chair. She was still breathing heavily and her eyes were still wide from shock, but the coughing had stopped. Jesse stayed back, giving the doctor room to check her out. Someone appeared with a stack of towels and handed one to Jesse before wrapping one around Lily-Grace's shoulders.

"Quite the scare," the doctor said with a kind smile for them both. "I think you're going to be fine. How about you, Mr. Pleasant?"

"I'm fine. Just wet." He stared down at Lily-Grace.

Her hair was wrecked, curls plastered against her face, and some of her makeup was smudged. Despite the thick hotel towel wrapped around her body, she started to shiver as she stared back at him.

"I can't swim," she gasped.

"Yeah, your father mentioned that," Jesse replied. In that moment, for no damn reason, his tear ducts decided to fire up. Thank God his face was already wet. He lifted the towel and wiped his whole head, covering his face long enough for a few more tears to escape unimpeded. His heart was still pounding, but he knew it—and the tears—were just the shock. He'd be okay in a few minutes. Suddenly Jesse felt a hand on his back, and before he uncovered his face he knew who was at his side. He dropped the towel and looked over at Miss Leona.

"I think we should get you two home. And get you into some warm clothes," she said.

"I think that's an excellent idea," the doctor said. He had more instructions for Miss Leona and Mr. LeRoux, but Jesse wasn't listening. He was still focused on Lily-Grace. He had fifty different things he wanted to say when they weren't surrounded by people. Finally she stood, wincing as she gripped the hotel towel. Jesse reached forward and helped steady her.

"You okay?"

"Yeah, just bashed my hip on the ground. I'll be sore tomorrow, but I'm fine." She looked over at her father, eyes suddenly pleading. "Daddy, let's go."

Jesse knew that look, though he never thought he'd see it on her face. She was too proud and too strong, but Jesse suddenly knew the unique pain carried in her expression. She was embarrassed and she wanted to be anywhere but that pool deck. Hotel staff and auction volunteers were buzzing around, making sure everyone was okay. Apologizing, like the pool had suddenly appeared out of nowhere.

"I bet they planned this," Jesse heard someone say, and yeah, right then, it was definitely time to go.

"Okay, okay," Mr. LeRoux said. He accepted Lily-Grace's purse from Lilah's outstretched hand. Someone produced Jesse's Stetson and handed it over to Miss Leona, and they all began making their way back to the valet stand. He realized as he held the door open for their small entourage that Lilah was following right behind him.

"You can stay if you want, hang out with Dr. Kuaea."

Lilah glanced back to where the vet was dabbing off his pants with one of the extra towels. "No, it's okay. I told him we'd catch up tomorrow."

"Alright. Can you get Vega and Corie? They are in the bar."

"Sure."

For a few minutes that was the last thing Jesse remembered. The next thing he knew he was watching Lily-Grace climb into her father's Buick. He helped his grandmother into the back seat of her SUV before he climbed in the passenger's seat beside Corie. She kept her jokes to herself as they drove back to Pleasant Lane. Out of habit, Jesse reached into his pocket for his phone. The feeling of his still wet pants snapped him back to the present. He pulled out his phone. The screen wouldn't light up.

"Gotta put that thing on rice," Corie said.

"I will," Jesse muttered. It was just a phone. He'd get

a new one in the morning if he had to. All he could think about though—the whole way back to the house, as he pulled off his ruined suit and got into a hot shower, and later when he took Clementine for her stroll around the yard—was getting in touch with Lily-Grace and thanking her for saving him up there.

The sound of the front doorbell ringing made him cringe. New rule now that Miss Leona and Mr. LeRoux were dating: no more barging into each other's houses. He knew it was probably Corie or Lilah coming to see if he was ready for church, but for the first time in a long time, he didn't feel like going. He went to the door, still dressed in the sweats he'd put on to let Clem out that morning, to break the news to whoever was waiting. He knew the Lord would understand, especially after the night he'd had.

He could see from the silhouette in the fogged glass that Miss Leona was waiting on his front step.

"If it's okay with you, I'd rather skip church today," he said when he opened the door. It wasn't mandatory, but he'd spent most Sundays since Lilah moved in, in their usual row at St. Timothy's Episcopal church.

"Jesus walks with you everywhere, baby, it's fine." She held up her cell phone. "Lily-Grace wanted to speak with you."

"Oh, thank you." Jesse took the phone and tried not to make a big show of clearing his throat. "Hello."

"Hi, Jesse. Fun night last night, huh?"

"An absolute blast. How are you feeling?"

"I'm fine, thanks to you. Was a little jittery for a while when I got home, but sleep helped."

Jesse almost asked if she'd bundled herself up in that Baby Yoda onesie, but he kept that comment to himself. "Good."

"So, I put my phone on rice last night, but it's still dead, so I'm calling it. I wanted to go get a new one, but my dad is meeting your grandmother after church to rub their love in people's faces on the town square—"

"Damn straight," Jesse heard Mr. LeRoux say in the background.

"I'm very happy for you, Dad. Anyway, I don't have a car here and I figured you could take me to the closest cellular device retailer and we could talk."

"I think that's a good idea." Jesse checked his smart watch, which had survived the plunge. "Pick you up in two hours?"

"See ya then."

Jesse handed back the phone. "Thank you. I'll see you this afternoon."

"Maybe tonight," Miss Leona said, lifting her shoulder. "I might have plans."

"I'll make sure the kids are fed then," Jesse joked. Kinda.

"No. They are big girls and they can feed themselves. Go have fun with your date."

Jesse held up his hands in surrender as Miss Leona tilted up her cheek in his direction. He gave her a light kiss, then watched as she practically skipped across the cul-de-sac, talking to her new boyfriend on the phone.

* * *

Jesse arrived at LeRoux's house right on time. Before he could turn off the engine, Lily-Grace walked out the front door and turned to lock up behind her. Jesse didn't know how to be anything other than a gentleman, but his mouth ran dry when he got a good look at her. Her outfit was simple, just skintight jeans and a pair of white sneakers and a pink crop top, but Jesse had to wonder if she understood just how good she looked. He climbed out of his truck and walked around to open the passenger-side door for her. She walked right up to him, then lightly punched him in the shoulder. A love tap really. Was she nervous?

"What was that for?"

"No idea. Couldn't kiss you, so it seemed like a good idea at the time."

"Did you want to kiss me?" Jesse asked, shocked.

"No. I don't kiss friends."

"Oh."

"Hey. Let's go get new phones." She started to move around him, but stopped when he didn't budge. "Or not?"

Jesse cleared his throat. "There's something I want to tell you before we go."

"Okay, what is it?"

"I'm not a virgin."

"Oh that? Jesse, I don't care. That's your private business and whoever that hag was last night did not have the right to—to—I don't know. She wanted to get your attention and tried to be cute doing it, but it backfired. I get to go shopping with you today."

"Well, that had more to do with the pool, but yes. In working on my . . . temper, I'm trying to be more open and honest. Most of the women last night were pretty out of control, but I was upset because I don't have a lot of experience with women. I have my reasons, and while I know I shouldn't be, I am embarrassed."

"I appreciate you telling me, and you don't have to be embarrassed with me. In my opinion, sex is best when it's with someone you love or someone who is really fucking good at it. Both of those things are hard to find, so I don't think you're missing out."

"Yeah, well." Jesse let out another breath and told Lily-Grace what he'd never told anyone else out loud before. "I'm not very good at it. There are layers to this embarrassment."

"Let's get in the car and you can tell me on the way."

"Okay." Jesse waited for her to climb in the passenger seat before he closed the door and went around to the driver's seat.

"Target sound good? If we go to our carriers, we'll be in there for hours for no reason."

"Target sounds great. They put up a SuperTarget on the way out to Ontario, right?"

"Yeah. It's pretty super." He glanced over and caught Lily-Grace's smile.

"Yeah, Target's good. I was thinking of getting a new number, but nah."

Jesse looked at the road before he glanced at her again. Something was off about her tone. "Trying to avoid someone?"

"No, I'm just talking. So keep going. You think you're not very good at sex."

"I'm sorry. We don't have to talk about this. It's—I wanted to be honest, but talking to you about my sexual experiences is very inappropriate. We can talk about something else."

"I never thought I'd say this, but you're very sweet. Thank you for saying that. I'm fine talking about this if you are, and if we get into not-cool territory, I'll tell you."

"Okay. Well, I've only been with two women, success-fully."

"What do you mean *successfully*?"

"Sex was actually had. Those two times were a good ten years apart. I tried three different times along the way, but I—had issues. I couldn't maintain an erection."

"Hmm, do you know why?"

"I think deep down I didn't want to be having sex with those people, so my body just shut things down."

"Okay, so we have a kinda *40-Year-Old Virgin* scenario here, mixed with the chicken-or-the-egg situation."

"What?" Jesse chuckled. He glanced over and Lily-Grace was staring at him. "What?"

"I've never seen you laugh. Like ever, I just realized."

"I was a very serious kid."

"I know you were. And now you're a serious adult. Anyway, you feel like you waited too long to get in that teens-to-early-twenties practice, where a lot of people remain bad at sex. Please believe me when I say that, and now it feels like too big of a deal."

"Exactly."

"So you want to have sex?"

It took Jesse a moment to answer. He'd never been asked that, or asked himself that, so plainly before. There were always so many other factors, like not having a girlfriend or even being socially involved with women who he was attracted to and didn't treat him like a piece of meat or a challenge. Jesse wanted to have sex, yes. He also wanted to be in love. He wanted to have sex with someone who understood him and someone he understood.

"I do, I just don't see it happening."

"Oh no. That won't work. I'm not saying we're going to go on a quest to get you laid, 'cause that's just weird. But I don't think you should just give up on yourself like that. I think if you meet someone you like, just be honest with them, like you're being honest with me, and if they aren't a complete asshole they'll understand and want to experience these things with you—What are you thinking about?"

"Nothing."

"Come on. Out with it. We've opened the circle of trust here."

"You're right. So you can tell me how you've never learned to swim."

"Oh." Lily-Grace sucked her teeth. "I just never learned, and then I developed a nice aversion to water. We had to pass a swim test too, in high school, but I was sick that day and no one followed up. And here we are. I just never learned, and then I almost died last night." She was trying to keep her tone light, but her voice wobbled a little. Jesse thought he was the only one in the truck who was carrying around some baggage, but something was going on with Lily-Grace. Not something from her past, something in her present. He wanted to know what was happening, he wanted to know how he could help, but he didn't want to push her.

"My emergency lifeguard skills aren't too shabby, but

I'm also a good swimmer. It's one of my favorite things to do."

"Huh. I mean I can picture it now."

Jesse turned to her as they waited at a light. He could see the Target up in the distance. "I have a pool at my house. I could teach you."

"I don't know how much longer I'm going to be in town, but a few lessons won't hurt. But you have to let me—"

"Let you what?" The light turned green and Jesse eased his truck back into traffic.

"Nothing. I was going to say I would give you sex lessons, but that's a little more intimate, and like you mentioned, really inappropriate."

His throat was suddenly dry. All he could picture now was just how badly he needed Lily-Grace's help in that department. "I would appreciate the help, actually."

"Cool."

Chapter 10

Lily-Grace slowly turned her head toward the window and squeezed her eyes shut. Cool. *Cool?* She'd just blurted out her most recent erotic fantasy. Jesse Poured-Into-Those XXXL-Tall-Jeans Pleasant had agreed to it, and all she could say was *cool*.

"Under one condition?" he said suddenly. Lily-Grace suddenly appreciated his serious side. Of course he wouldn't let this get out of hand. He'd ask for a full curriculum first, with slides and tasteful stock photos. She'd have to use a doll for demonstrations, which was probably for the best, but—

This had to be some sort of post-traumatic response. She was downplaying how scary her trip to the bottom of the pool had been. She really couldn't swim and neither could her father; she'd been up half the night trembling from the residual adrenaline, wondering what would have happened if Jesse hadn't shown up in time.

Before, she just wanted to mess with him—payback for her father's wrist—but something had changed. She'd wanted to kiss him the second she stepped out her front door. She wanted to hug him and she wanted him to hold her. Through the haze of nearly certain death she hadn't forgotten how strong and sure his arms felt around her when he hauled her from the water. And she was not a small woman.

She wanted Jesse, bad, but she knew it wasn't real. Just a reaction to the fall, and the intensity of the auction, and the way things had ended with Dane, and how he was still texting her like things hadn't ended at all, and the fact that Jesse was so fine it made no sense, and the fact that she still had no fucking plan. None of what she was feeling for him in the air-conditioned cab of his fancy pickup truck was real. And Jesse Pleasant deserved real, so for the sake of their lessons, both swim and sex, she promised to be on her best behavior.

"Gimme your condition," she said, still playing it so cool.

"You have to promise not to fall in love with me."

Lily-Grace leaned back and glared at him. "How many times have you seen *A Walk To Remember*?"

"I don't know, like ten. Lilah and I watch a lot of movies."

"Ah, I see. You have any real conditions there, Romeo?"

"Only that you let me know if you're uncomfortable and want to stop. Learning to swim can be an intense experience. I want to help, but I'm not trying to push you. If you need me to back off or would rather take lessons from someone else, I'll understand."

"I definitely will. I'm not very good at hiding my discomfort *or* my displeasure."

They pulled into the Target parking lot and Jesse found a space way in the back where there were a lot of open spots. He cut off the engine then rushed around her side of the truck. She didn't wait for him to open the door, but she did appreciate the gesture and the way he seemed to hover, like he was ready to catch a bullet or tackle a bear at any moment.

"You're just like this, aren't you?"

"Like what?" he replied. Lily-Grace almost laughed out loud at the not-so-subtle way he put himself between her and a car that was slowing in the pedestrian walkway.

"So . . . protective."

Jesse glanced over at her before he stopped again and let her walk in front of him through the automatic doors. "Duty and habit. You want to hit electronics and see if they have the latest in smartphone technology, and then we can wander around?"

"Let's do it." They walked to the back of the store and the whole way, Lily-Grace had to stop herself from giving in to the urge to hold Jesse's hand.

"Should we talk about last night?" Jesse asked as they took a shortcut through menswear into the toy section.

"Which part?"

"The part where you paid a lot of money to save me from Merry Sharpe."

"I mean, you saved me back, so I think we're even."

"Nah, try again. You could have let me suffer. Especially since you think I'm an uncontrollable madman." Jesse walked right up to the young man at the electronics counter who looked like he'd mentally checked out of his shift. Quick conversation and they discovered that this particular Target didn't have the phones they both wanted.

"Sorry. I thought they would have them. They have everything."

"It's okay. We can still enjoy the rest of what the Target has to offer, and we'll hit up the carrier stores or hit the mall over in Ontario. I think they have have a Mac store. We can grow old together while they make us sit there to activate our phones and upsell us on shitty cases. But while we're here, I need a swimsuit, and you"—she looked up at him, trying to picture the whole package, naked—"you need condoms."

"Is that right?"

"Yes. Come on." She grabbed his hand and tugged him in the direction of the pharmacy.

"What do I need condoms for?—Forget I said that."

Lily-Grace managed to keep her snort of laughter to herself. They stopped in front of the shelves of contraceptive items, which unlike the phones were fully stocked. "Okay, yeah, we are definitely starting your sex lessons right now. Two big things you need for sexy good times: consent and protection. You, oddly enough for all initial impressions, seem to understand the consent side. But if you're a little out of practice, being comfortable putting on a condom will help ease your anxiety in the moment. Also, they are useful for quick cleanup when you're alone."

"Hmmm," was all Jesse said.

"So. The sizes do matter. Do you think you have more of a slim to average base?" She held her thumb and forefinger up in a little circle before she expanded it to make the circle bigger. "Or a larger base?"

"Uh, a larger base."

Do not think about his dick. Do not think about his dick. "Okay. So we'll grab some of these in latex and a box of latex-free condoms. I personally am allergic to latex. Lots of fun trial-and-error to figure that out, but once I did . . . It's a good idea to test drive a few to see how you like them." She handed him the boxes and waited patiently as he turned them both over and carefully read every single word written on the backs. She stepped back when he went back to the rack and selected a few more boxes and read those too. Finally he seemed to settle on the boxed she initially handed him.

"Okay. I'll get these. Should I get some lubricant too?"

"Uh, sure," Lily-Grace said, trying not to sound too shocked. He was really jumping right into this, taking it seriously. She half expected gross jokes and sly comments, but then she remembered who she was dealing with. Jesse Pleasant. Filled with a little bit of rage, but definitely serious. He picked two different brands of lube that seemed to do the trick, then looked back at her, ready for her next set of instructions. "All good?"

"Yeah. You need anything?"

"Oh no. I'm on a sex embargo right now, but let's go check out the bathing suits. Let's go." She looped her arm with his and guided him to the front of the store for a handbasket before they headed back to the clothing section.

"You never answered my question," he said when they reached the racks of brightly colored two-pieces. "Why did you jump into the auction last night?"

"I . . . I've been asking myself the same thing." She grabbed a lime-green ruffly affair with lemons on it and put it in the basket. "Why didn't you text me from the wedding?"

"I was busier than I expected I'd be, and I thought it would be rude to sit in a corner on my phone. When I got back, I figured—I had a feeling the fact that I wanted to talk to you was pretty one-sided, so it seemed better to leave you alone."

"Of course. You're the one man who actually gets that hint." When she got her phone back she really needed to block Dane. She dropped a simple black one-piece into the basket, then put her hands on her hips. Jesse had been brutally honest and she could be too. "Though I had vowed to ruin your life and steal your dog, I didn't like seeing you so uncomfortable up there. It was supposed to be this fun night, and then you got up there and shit got real unfun real fast. Your grandmother was this close to bailing you out, but I think in the back of my mind your Grammy bidding on you would have just made things worse. So I spent a year's tuition at Harvard to end it. Also you looked really good in that suit." She mumbled the last bit.

"Wait, say that again?"

"You looked really good in that suit, okay? You're handsome, Jesse." She lightly slapped his rock-solid chest with the back of her hand. "Just deal with it."

"That's the second time you've hit me. I thought I was the one with the anger issues."

"Sorry." She curled her fists at her side. She just really wanted to touch him. "I thought I should, like, hug you or something for saving me last night, but slapping you was the natural response. Maybe I should talk to someone about that." Lily-Grace watched Jesse as he carefully set their basket on the ground. He stood back to his full height, then opened his arms.

"Come on."

"You sure? I'm more emotionally fragile than I look

right now. I might just suction myself to you and never let go."

He dropped his arms, one eyebrow going up under the brim of his cowboy hat. "What's going on? You've been home for almost a month, but I thought you were just visiting. You made that comment about changing your number, and right now you look like you're trying not to cry and using really bad sarcasm to do it."

Lily-Grace scrunched her nose up, a pitiful effort to stop the tears from rushing to her eyes. "How about this? Some stuff is going on, but I really don't want to cry in the middle of a Target, so let's put a pin in it. For now. And later, in the cover of darkness, I'll tell you the whole story. And you"—she reached up and flicked the brim of his hat. Baby steps—"you can tell me why someone who is clearly not comfortable with the spotlight would run for office."

"Oh that?" Jesse grumbled.

"Yeah, that."

Jesse pointed to a purple number on the rack before he reached down and grabbed the basket. "You'd look amazing in that."

Lily-Grace grabbed her size and put it in the basket. "There. I think three suits should cover it."

"It's all on me. And your new phone too."

"Really?"

"Yeah. You wouldn't have been on that deck if it wasn't for me and my poor decision to join the date auction."

"Thank you."

"You're not gonna fight me on this?"

"On letting you pay? Hell no. Receiving gifts is one of my love languages. Some people call it gold digging, which I think is bullshit. If you want to buy me things and your intentions are on the level, I will accept those things."

"Well, in the context of friendship, I am more than happy to buy you things."

"Hmm, yes. Friendship. Come on, Pleasant." They walked around a little more, grabbing necessary and random things like waterproof sunscreen, an aloe and bergamot candle, and a cherry Coke energy drink that Lily-Grace wanted to try for science. Neither of them hated being off the grid for a little while longer, so they decided to stop and get lunch at this new sandwich place called Breakin' Bread. They kept things light, talking about Zach and Evie's wedding, how things are going at the ranch, and Jesse's love for the water. From there they went to get their phones.

Jesse was set up and ready to go in fifteen minutes, but for some reason the guy who helped Lily-Grace had never encountered a computer before and seemed to be extremely averse to any sort of assistance from his coworker or Lily-Grace. She just needed him to assign her info to a new SIM card and they'd be off to the races. Eventually they got it together and Jesse paid for their new phones. He'd spent the whole time waiting patiently by himself, not saying a word, but giving her small smiles of reassurance whenever she looked his way. It was oddly comforting and nice. And unexpected from someone she thought had such a bad temper.

She tried not to compare their trip to the cell phone store to all the times she'd attempted simple outings with Dane. And by *with* Dane, she meant all the times Dane had paced in proximity, talking on the phone until he eventually handed over his credit card and ditched her. That had happened at least a dozen times before Lily-Grace suggested they stop shopping together. Dane was more than happy with that decision. As she climbed back into Jesse's truck and he waited patiently for her to buckle her seat belt, she could only think about the reality of her relationship with Dane. He made her feel special, and the sex was amazing, but looking at how attentive Jesse could be, as a friend, opened her eyes to the possibilities of what future relationships could be like.

Not that this was Jesse's tryout to be her man, but as her new phone started to blow up with fresh notifications, she realized she had never felt this comfortable being around any man she wasn't related to.

"Do you want me to drop you off at your dad's place?"

"Actually, I was hoping we could start our swim lessons today. Unless you're busy. I'm sure you want to get some downtime before work tomorrow. This weekend has been a lot."

"It has, but no. I'm free. I'm off dinner duty tonight too."

"What do you mean?"

"We kinda rotate dinner duties. I cook, or my grandmother or my cousin. We have a lot of mouths to feed," he said, his mouth tipping up in this little smile. Lily-Grace could not comprehend how no woman had ever just slowed down and given Jesse a chance to show this sweet side of himself. *Hey, you were almost one of those women*, a loud voice in her head reminded her. "Miss Leona is making everyone fend for themselves tonight, so I don't have to make dinner for four to twelve people."

"I barely cook for myself. I can't imagine cooking for that many people."

"I love it. If I didn't, I wouldn't recommend it. Anyway. I don't have plans this afternoon or this evening. We can start swimming lessons today."

"Great. Let's do it."

Lily-Grace felt herself smiling as they pulled out of the parking lot. At least for this afternoon, they had a plan.

"Okay, so my dad told me you guys live on like a compound, but he wasn't joking." Lily-Grace looked out the window as Jesse drove them down the longest driveway on the face of God's green Earth. She could see three large houses up in the distance.

"Calling it a compound makes it sound cultish. It's just private property to grant my grandmother and my brother some privacy. Just turns out we all like privacy."

"Hey, I get it. This place is beautiful." They stopped at the first house in the cul-de-sac and Lily-Grace could hear barking in the distance. They walked over to Miss Leona's house in the center, first, and let out four dogs, including her favorite, Clementine. The dogs were very excited to see Jesse and curious enough about her that she was able to sneak in a few pats on their adorable heads. Maybe she should get a dog, whenever she came up with her plan.

"What are their names?"

"You know Clementine." He reached down and picked up the large black Lab like it was nothing. Clementine rested her head on Jesse's shoulder and let out the cutest doggy sigh.

"Ah, she missed you."

"She's my boo," he said, deadpan. "The little one is Poppy and that's Euca and Sugar Plum."

"I love it."

"They'll help with swim lessons too. Come on." They walked over to Jesse's house, where he gave her a tour while her new bathing suits were taking a quick tumble in his washing machine.

"You have this whole place to yourself?" she asked as they made their way back to his massive chef's kitchen that opened to the equally large living room with its football-field-sized TV. He showed her three guest rooms, his home office, and formal dining room. They'd skipped over his bedroom, but Lily-Grace was dying to see his closet. The man knew how to dress. It wasn't the best house she'd been in, but it was a lot of room for one person. And sometimes four dogs.

"Well, this was my parents' place. I was supposed to live in the other house with Zach and Sam, but my parents moved away. But it doesn't matter now. My cousins are here and they are always over, watching TV, or eating, or using my pool."

"That must be nice. I have half siblings, but my father and I don't speak to them. I always wondered what it would be like growing up with them."

"I saw that in the program last night."

"I'll tell you—" She shrugged. It wasn't a secret, but it was kind of awkward. "Their mom, my dad's first wife, is like evil-stepmother evil. She was really abusive to my dad, and then she did all this shady shit with the insurance business they ran together. He finally divorced her, but she told his kids all of these lies about him and she would, like, spend all the child support money, tell the kids my dad wasn't paying.

"My oldest brother, Ryan, reached out a few times, but his mom found out and lost it. It's not a healthy situation, but my father decided to just keep me away from it. Anyway, he met my mom and they were happy and they had me." Lily-Grace turned her face up with a bright smile. She didn't remember her mom, but she loved hearing stories about her, and her father assured her all the time that she would have been proud of her daughter every step of the way.

"I don't think family is truly a family without its fair bit of drama." The washing machine chose that exact moment to chime. He showed her to one of the guest rooms with a bathroom so she could change. She settled on the black one-piece, since this was a swim lesson and not a photoshoot, then neatly folded her clothes on the bed. When she stepped back out in the hallway, Jesse was waiting for her in a pair of neon yellow swim trunks. One look at his broad bare chest and her mouth literally started to water.

"I won't slap you this time, I promise," she said with an awkward laugh.

"I appreciate it."

"Uh, can you put sunscreen all over every inch of my back before we go outside? I burn easy."

"Oh sure."

She handed him the bottle and tried not to react as he

gently started doing exactly what she asked. He took his time, even getting the backs of her ankles where she had a few spots that lacked melanin. Lily-Grace loved her body, she loved herself. She always made sure she took care of her skin, especially as her vitiligo spread as she got older. She let out a short breath as she felt Jesse stand to his full height behind her. Her body had cooperated as his hands moved over every inch, but the way he lightly touched her shoulder, encouraging her to turn around, had goose bumps spreading all the way down to her wrist.

She looked up at him, his dark brown eyes hooded with something she never expected to see from Jesse Pleasant. Desire.

"I never took you up on that hug," she said quietly. Jesse didn't say a word. He just wrapped his arms around her, pulling her close. In the most natural, almost instinctual way, she wrapped her arms around his muscled torso, marveling at how soft his skin felt against her chest, under her fingertips. Jesse Pleasant understood the importance of full body exfoliation. He smelled nice too, like a warm spring breeze. She gave into the urge to nuzzle her face against his neck and he held her even tighter. Still, no real plan, but this was something she could get used to.

Chapter 11

It pained Jesse to put the slightest distance between his body and hers, but if he didn't end the hug soon, he'd want the hug to turn into a kiss. Maybe more. He moved his hands to her shoulders and took a half step back. The distance didn't help. He still wanted to kiss Lily-Grace.

"Ready to swim?"

"Absolutely not, but let's do this." She laughed. Jesse led her out to the pool. The dogs followed. "Are they joining us?" she asked.

"I thought it would be a good idea to have them demonstrate some simple techniques. Okay." Jesse stepped back and faced Lily-Grace. It was time to get serious. She snapped to attention, arms tight to her side. "At ease."

"Yes, sir."

"First thing you need to remember about being in and around water. You should never feel panicked. Swimming or even floating should be fun or relaxing or a form of exercise. If you are panicking something is wrong. Does that make sense?"

"Yes."

"You don't need to be an Olympic swimmer, but the

goal is get you comfortable treading water and to teach you a serviceable doggy paddle."

"Is that where the puppies come in?"

"Exactly. Now—" Jesse held out his hand. He ignored the tingle that spread out over his palm as her fingers slid over his. "All I want to do today is have you stand in the water. No deep-end diving."

He watched her carefully as she closed her eyes and pulled in a deep breath.

"I'm certified in first aid and CPR. I renewed my certificates two months ago."

Her eyes snapped open. "Oh, that's very good to know. Okay, let's *Baywatch* it up."

Jesse took the first step down into the shallow end of the pool. It was designed to look more like a natural lagoon, but there were stone steps and two underwater ledges where you could sit, one in the shallow end and one in the deep end. He walked down till the water was up to his thighs and waited patiently for Lily-Grace to follow him into the water.

"Ohh, it's warm. Fancy."

"Fancy's my middle name." They reached the bottom of the stairs, where the water came up to the top of Lily-Grace's thighs. Jesse turned and took both of her hands. "How's that?"

"Okay." She smiled. "Not bad. I don't hate it. Do not let go of my hands."

"I won't. I promise." Slowly, Jesse walked her deeper into the water until it came up right to her belly button. Then deeper, until the water was just below her breasts. Her large, perfectly round breasts that he definitely hadn't tried to steal a glance at. "How does that feel?"

"Strange, but I don't hate it. I can't believe I've never done this before. It's not as scary as I expected it to be."

"You want to try floating?"

"Yeah. Let's do that."

"Okay, so I'm going to support your back and you're gonna lean back. Like a slow motion trust fall. I won't let you go underwater."

"Okay." Lily-Grace was a little less confident this time, but that didn't stop her from gripping Jesse's arm as she slowly leaned back. Her feet left the bottom of the pool and of course she started panicking. "Don't drop me!" she screeched.

"I'm right here." He pressed his fingers more firmly against her back. "Just relax. I'm not going anywhere."

"Okay." She was tense as hell, but eventually Jesse got her flat on her back, floating on the surface of the water. One hand braced in the middle of her back and the other under her thighs, he watched her face carefully as she stared up at the wispy clouds in the sky above them. Her thick curls were still up in a bun, but Jesse took a mental picture of the way wet strands fanned around her face in a black halo, streaked in two spots with white. She closed her eyes and sighed. Jesse waited a few minutes more before he slowly started to move around the pool, carrying Lily-Grace in the water, in the palms of his hands.

He couldn't remember the last time he'd been close to a woman like this, touching in a way that didn't make *him* nervous. His eyes traveled over her face, down the smooth lines of her neck and the swells of her breasts. Never, he realized. He'd never touched a woman like this. He thought about how any level of intimacy he'd taken a shot at had left his hands literally shaking. How if it hadn't been for Miss Leona, who dealt in the currency of hugs, or Evie, who had always treated him with sisterly affection, he wouldn't know how to picture any kind of closeness.

But this was different. The whole day had been different. His hands weren't shaking.

"Okay," she said, her voice quivering, part nerves, part laughter. "I'm ready to come up now."

"Okay." Jesse lowered his left arm, letting her legs down into the water. They were near the shallow end and Jesse absolutely had her, but that didn't stop Lily-Grace from flailing as she struggled to find the bottom of the pool. Jesse stood her up and pulled her close to his chest.

"You're fine. I got you."

She gripped on to his shoulders, eyes wild as she peered down at the water. "This isn't as easy as I thought," she said.

"No. Learning to swim can be hard and scary, but I won't let anything happen to you. Here." Jesse reached up and placed her arms tighter around his neck, before he placed a firm hand on the small of her back. "Just hold on to me."

Her legs went around his waist and she gripped him even tighter, eyes still glued to the surface of the water.

"We can get out if you want to. Last night was—just last night. We didn't have to rush into this."

"No, I—I'm trying to figure out what I'm so afraid of. You're literally holding me and this water isn't even deep."

"Because you're programmed to be on land, but we started out in the water. You're battling against a lot of instinct and nurture."

She glanced up at him with a sarcastic smile before the look of terror returned to her face. "Don't get all philosophical on me, Pleasant."

"I meant the womb. We come out knowing how to swim and then we lose it if we don't keep it up."

"Oh, got it. I don't want to get out. The water feels nice. I just need to take it slow. Do not put me down."

"I won't. Hold on." He walked them into deeper water again, so the surface was up to his shoulders, but his feet were still touching the bottom. Jesse couldn't see Lily-Grace's face but he could feel the way she was breathing, feel her chest rising and falling against his. This wasn't the swim lesson he'd had in mind, but he was in no hurry to let her go. He moved back to the shallow end again, her body still clutched to his as he sat down on a lower step. The water was still up to their chests but he could rest there, still holding her weight.

"This is better," she practically moaned in his ear. At that moment they both realized their mistake. "Sorry, I didn't mean to sound so horny." She laughed as she pulled back and looked him in the eye. Jesse tried to think the unsexiest of thoughts to quiet his rising erection, but the way Lily-Grace shifted against him made it a lost cause. Her crotch was pressed firmly against his lap and her perfect plump ass rested against his thighs. He held still, knowing his natural instinct to toss Lily-Grace on the pool deck so he could run and hide wouldn't help the situation. He watched her face as she swallowed, her gaze dropping down to his lips and back up to his eyes again.

"Should I get up?"

"No," Jesse replied a little too quickly. He had no idea

what to do, but moving seemed like a bad idea. "I'm not sure what to do here."

"Well. You're hard. We both know it and it's no big deal."

"It's not?"

"No," Lily-Grace said with a firm nod. "There may be some fabric in the way, but you have my yoni basically pressed up against you. I'd be insulted if you weren't a little turned on. Am I making you uncomfortable?"

"No." Jesse didn't want to scare her off, saying something stupid like how he hadn't felt this good and terrified in a while. Lily-Grace leaned back a little so she could see his face more clearly. A simple motion he appreciated except for the fact that it pressed her lower body even tighter against his. He was fully erect now. "I've never been in this position before," he admitted.

"With a woman in your lap?"

"Yeah." His sex life had been filled with awkward missionary intercourse in beds too small for his body.

"Well, it's a day of firsts for us both. So there's something you should know about sex."

"What's that?"

"There's a lot more to it than penetration. There is building a connection, even if it's fleeting—and there's this." She glanced down to where their bodies were so close to being connected. Jesse's erection twitched, pressing hard against his swim trunks, hard against Lily-Grace.

"If it's okay, I'm going to kiss you now. Like for practice."

"I should practice."

"Let me show you then."

Jesse held still as Lily-Grace pressed her lips to his. He tried to soak in everything about that moment. The softness of her mouth, the way the sunscreen smelled on her skin. Slowly she tilted her head, just the slightest bit, and parted her lips. Just the tip of her tongue brushed the seam of his lips and Jesse had a sense then what heaven might be like. She did it again, coaxing his lips apart, and he did as she did, just parting them a little, letting his tongue gently brush against her. It was the most amazing thing he'd felt in his whole life.

Lily-Grace pulled back and Jesse was positive the dazed expression on his face matched hers. "Not too bad."

"You're a good teacher."

"We should keep working on it though. Just to be sure." Jesse leaned forward this time, gently capturing her lips. He took it as a good sign when Lily-Grace moaned against his mouth and an even better sign when her hips started to move under the surface of the water. Jesse let out a muffled groan of his own, his hands moving to her perfect ass, molding her vulva around his full erection. Dry humping like teenagers in his pool had not been a part of the plan, but Jesse was grateful for the lesson. He was so caught up in the moment he noticed a second too late they weren't alone.

"Jesse, fire up the—whoa!"

He broke away from their kiss to find Corie and Vega standing on the pool deck. The one time the dogs didn't bark. Didn't matter. Corie kept right on talking. "So this is what all that money bought last night. Damn, ya'll move fast. I didn't know you had it in you, Jess."

Jesse felt his neck tensing again, heat rushing over the crown of his head. This was Corie all the time. Usually he had his own comebacks or would simply tell her to shut up, but Lily-Grace wasn't usually in his lap.

"Can we help you?" Jesse said through gritted teeth.

"Man, calm down. We just want to know what time to fire up the grill."

He didn't know why exactly, but he felt his blood starting to boil. He didn't want to lose it in front of Lily-Grace. Not now. Like she could sense it though, she put a hand on his neck, trying to soothe him with her touch. He looked her in the eye as she offered him a subtle nod. Everything was okay. Bad timing, yeah, but not the end of the world. He closed his eyes for a brief second, then looked back at his cousin.

"For what?"

"What do you mean, for what? Miss Leona ain't cooking tonight. You know what that means. What time are we firing up the grill?"

"Um, never. And if you can't tell, we're kinda busy at the moment."

"Ya'll can keep doing what you're doing. I just wanna know what we're having for dinner. Burgers or steaks?"

Jesse and Corie hadn't gotten into it in any real way in a while, but now he was getting a little sick of her shit. Luckily Vega caught the look in his eye. She reached forward and lightly grabbed Corie's arm.

"Babe, stop. We're going, and we can definitely feed ourselves dinner. It was nice to see you again, Lily-Grace. You want us to take the dogs with us?"

"Yeah, sure," Jesse muttered. "Just leave Clementine."

"Okay. We'll see you guys."

Corie muttered some crap back, but let Vega tow her out of the backyard. Jesse let out a deep breath when they closed the door behind them, but the tension refused to leave his body. He wanted to go underwater and count to one hundred.

Lily- Grace lightly touched his chin, encouraging him to look at her. "What just happened? Tell me."

"I didn't want her—" Jesse had made some progress in a short time with Dr. Brooks but he wasn't ready to bare all his insecurities to Lily-Grace just yet. "We didn't need her running commentary."

"Well, she's gone now." Lily Grace frowned, then moved off his lap. She kept a death grip on his arm as she moved to the top step. "This might be out of line, but do you want me to say something to her? Like I get the ha-ha kiking that goes on between family, but she clearly knows how to push your buttons and doesn't seem to care that it actually bothers you."

"It doesn't bother me," Jesse lied. "Come on." Ignoring his still-present erection, Jesse stood and helped Lily-Grace out of the pool. They toweled off. Jesse would show her to the guest shower so she could rinse off, and then he'd take her home. Maybe he could recommend a good swim instructor down at the rec center. He started to lead the way inside, but Lily-Grace stopped him with a gentle touch to his side. He almost flinched away. Erection or not, he'd completely shut down.

"Hey. It's a big deal. Wait, that's not what I meant. I get that it's a big deal to you. Sometimes you get interrupted. Sometimes people say shitty things."

And that was Jesse's problem. Somewhere between nature and nurture everything felt like a big deal. And no one, not even him, seemed to understand why.

"So that was it? Mid boner, he just called it off?" Jenny took a forkful of chili cheese fries and shoved it in her mouth. Lily-Grace took a big bite of her own as she tried to figure out how to explain how this bizarre weekend had gotten even weirder. Jesse had dropped her off. Instead of moping around until her dad came back from his day-and-night date with Mrs. Lovell, she'd called Jenny. They'd gone to Claim Jumpers to drown their sorrows in cheap beer, bad food, and the best hip-hop and R & B from the nineties.

"I mean I get it. I think he was embarrassed. I just hate that I hate that I *care* so much. Ugh, I need to leave town."

"Why?" Jenny chuckled.

"Because! I've spent like five minutes with him and I hate how it's making me feel. We shopped. We went and got new phones. I somehow slip in the idea of giving him sex lessons. Which he agrees to!"

"What guy wouldn't? Hell, you wanna give me sex lessons? I could probably use them."

"'Cause he's Jesse Pleasant, and I would sex-lessons you any day of the week. Dude. I don't know. I don't know what I'm doing."

"You're due a life crisis. You've had your shit together since we were like nine. I'm glad, for once, you're the messy one."

"Have you talked to Vinny yet?"

"Yup. It's over."

"What? Why didn't you tell me?"

"You gave Jesse Pleasant sex lessons. My not-relationship is way less interesting."

"What happened?"

"Nothing. He called me this morning to basically gloat about the auction, and I had like this moment of clarity where I realized how unhappy I was, so I ended it."

"I'm sorry it went down like that, but you deserve to be with someone who is one hundred percent *with* you. Vinny seemed committed to some high school shit."

"And so was I. I'm old and tired now, though. I talked to Ned last night for a few minutes and I don't want to get with Ned, but he's so nice, and I had this moment where I realized I could have a conversation with a guy who didn't give me chest pains."

"Funny, that's how I felt with Jesse this morning."

Jenny raised her beer. "How about a little pact? We don't date again until we're *happy* happy. Not just mildly amused or distracted. The real thing or nothing, and if we don't find what we're looking for, we raise show ponies together and you give me sex lessons."

"Oh my God. Hell yeah." Lily-Grace clinked her beer to Jenny's and took a long swig. A perfect long-term plan.

A few hours later, as if sensing that she was even thinking about happiness, Dane texted her. She wouldn't even have noticed if she hadn't been lying in bed reading *Real Housewives* commentary on Twitter.

I spoke with Matt Rich today.

He's getting his feet wet with a new blockchain
developer. He might have something for you.
A fresh start when you come back.

An angry heat flashed all over Lily-Grace's body. She
didn't know whether to rage cry or throw her phone at
the wall. This had to stop: the texts and whatever the fuck
Dane was doing talking to other people about her future
careers.

Please don't do that.
I don't need your help finding a job.

I'm glad to see you haven't blocked me.
Come home so we can talk about this in person.

There's nothing to talk about.
I can worry about my professional life
and you should worry about treating
your partners better in the future.

I hear you.
The only person I want a future with is you.

Lily-Grace scoffed out loud, her body's way of blocking
the rising bile with humor.

We are done, Dane. Stop texting me, please.

There was nothing left to say. She didn't know what
she wanted for herself moving forward, but it didn't

have anything to do with Dane. Finally, she blocked his number.

It was definitely time to turn in. Fuck Dane. She set down her phone, then picked it up again. Bed. She should definitely go to bed before she made any angry decisions. Sleep was exactly what she needed, the proper reset button. Or maybe like a TikTok of a puppy doing something cute or a hot guy making a complicated dish, shirtless.

But why watch soothing videos on her phone when she could revisit her weird, *confusing* feelings about Jesse Pleasant. She didn't really have a choice but to text him.

> It's Lily-Grace. Texting you from my brand-new phone.

It's Jesse. Responding from my brand-new phone.

> I know it's so 80s, but can I call you?

Yes.

Lily-Grace hit send. It rang twice before Jesse answered.

"Hello." The bass in his voice made her toes curl.

"Hello. What are you doing?"

"Just preparing for my week."

"What does that involve?" Lily-Grace could just picture him doing exactly fifty sit-ups and fifty push-ups, before he ironed his socks and laid out his suit for the morning.

"I go over my calendar and then lay out my clothes. I try to get at least seven hours of sleep before I get up and workout and then go to the ranch. What are you doing?"

"Oh, you know, the usual. Looking at the ceiling of my childhood bedroom, wondering what I should do tomorrow while everyone I know in town is at work."

"I'd have to speak to my brother about creating a position for you. The good Lord has shown me what you've done for Ulway."

"Is that what this is all about? Teaching me how to swim so you can butter me up and use my enormous brain?"

"All a part of my evil plan."

"You know what I do need?"

"What's that?"

"A car. Jenny's probably sick of picking me up, and if I wanted to go see someone else I'd have to get a ride. I'm enjoying all the nostalgia of being back home, but waiting for my dad to come home from work so I can go to Walgreens is not the business."

"I'm free tomorrow at one."

"Free for what? To take me to Walgreens?"

"If you need to grab something from there, sure. But I was thinking we could hit the auto mile."

"You're just gonna cut out for lunch and go with me to pick out a car? That could take all afternoon."

"I own the ranch, Lily-Grace. I think I'm allowed to leave early."

"Okay, then. Well, I'll see you tomorrow around one. And we can talk about that friendly dinner you promised me."

"It can't be tomorrow night."

"Damn, Pleasant, I was just kidding."

"No, I mean tomorrow night is the season premiere of *The Bachelorette*. We watch it at my house."

"That sounds amazing."

"You and Jenny are welcome to come."

"Thank you. I'll ask her."

"I have to go," he said, and an inexplicable bundle of disappointment knotted itself in Lily-Grace's stomach. Of course he had to go. He'd made it clear this wouldn't be an all-night gab session the second he answered the phone. "I'll call you when I'm on my way tomorrow."

"Okay." Lily-Grace forced a light edge to her tone.

"I had fun with you today," Jesse replied.

"I had fun with you too."

"Good night, Lily-Grace."

"Good night."

Chapter 12

The doorbell rang and Lily-Grace told herself to relax. Jesse was just a friend, and he was doing her a favor coming with her to look at cars. She wanted to tell him the truth first, before their friendship went any further. He'd surprised her. He definitely had a lightning-quick temper, but she was starting to understand why, and she appreciated that he'd taken her advice to try and work on it. The way their afternoon had come to a screeching halt the day before was still bugging her a little, but she knew it was probably best to let it go.

She took a deep breath and opened the front door, and almost immediately started to drool on herself. He filled her door frame in another perfect suit, this time a dark forest green, and that black Stetson. She tried not to look up at his lips, think about the way they'd felt against hers the day before. It was a friendly kiss and a friendly underwater dry hump. Nothing to replay over and over in her mind.

"Hey! You wanna come in for a sec?"

"Sure. How are you doing?" Jesse took off his cowboy

hat before he ducked his head and stepped over the threshold, then followed Lily-Grace to the living room.

"I'm fine. Please have a seat. I didn't want to tell you in the car because, honestly, if you had a bad reaction I wouldn't be above jumping out of a moving vehicle."

"Is this about the article in the *Charming Newsletter*?" he asked as he sat carefully on the edge of the couch. Lily-Grace and her father were both tall, but none of their furniture was fit for his long legs.

"What article?"

"They wrote about the date auction and mentioned how your bid was the highest. And how I very romantically rescued you from the pool."

"Oh. Cute. No, I haven't seen it, but that is not what this is about."

"Okay."

Lily-Grace took a deep breath, then let the truth spill out. "You asked me why I was home for so long, even though I maintain a child shouldn't need a reason to visit a parent for an extended period of time."

"True. I see my parents about once a leap year, so I probably shouldn't speak on that subject."

Lily-Grace felt herself frown and filed that information away for another time. "We should talk about that, but I did come home for a reason, and I am, or was, kind of hiding from someone. I was sexually harassed by our head of marketing at Ulway. I reported it. The company did nothing, so I left. I'm pissed still, but I'm—okay. I probably would have stayed in San Francisco, but my partner at the time wasn't very supportive. We were in a very sexually intense relationship and I'd put a lot of trust in him in that respect, so I was *a lot* caught off guard when he told me it wasn't a big deal." Lily-Grace took a breath, then tried to gauge Jesse's reaction. His brow was crumpled in a frown and his jaw was very tense.

"Anyway, we ended things. I don't have a car now, because I didn't have a car up in the Bay Area. He's a very wealthy man and . . . as his submissive, he wanted me to use a driver. Which I did. I'm here, still trying to figure out what I want to do next. And I do want to go public with my harasser's name, if only to warn other women, but I'm scared." It felt good to admit that out loud. Jenny and her father had both been gentle and kind, not pushing her to talk more about the situation than she already had, but she realized she needed to say that last bit out loud.

"That's completely understandable," Jesse replied, his brow creasing down with concern. "I am very sorry this happened to you. I don't think my therapist would be on board, but say the word, I'll get some of the boys from the ranch and maybe we'll just go have a chat with these two gentlemen. And whoever at Ulway is lacking common sense."

"Well, for starters, none of them are gentlemen. They are complete scumbags. But. As much as I would love that, I'm gonna have to say no and keep you out of a NorCal county jail."

They were both quiet then. Lily-Grace watched the expression on Jesse's face closely. He wasn't Dane, she reminded herself and if the next thing out of his mouth was in any way shitty or generally unhelpful, she could just walk up to the dealership herself. Jesse sniffed then looked back into her eyes. "What sort of reaction were you expecting me to have?"

"I don't know—a bad one, a pointing-fingers-at-me

one. Or the *Whoa, I'm dealing with someone who has too much baggage* type reaction, where you pull away from me but act like it's just because you're busy," Lily-Grace replied, realizing then just how nervous she'd been about this conversation. Jesse had just entered the picture, but she wasn't ready for more emotional rejection or disappointment.

"I wouldn't do that to anyone, let alone my friend. But if you're not comfortable, we don't have to do the, uh, intimacy lessons anymore."

"No, no, that's actually consensual, unless you'd like to stop."

"No, your tips so far have been very helpful. It's given me a lot to think about. I did practice with putting on one condom last night, and you were right."

Lily-Grace managed not to bring up a mental picture of what that must have been like. "A little out of practice?"

"You could say that. But I'm glad you suggested it. I've never talked about this with anyone. It's easy with you," Jesse said.

"And I think that's why this whole thing makes me extra itchy. You can be a sexually confident person, you can talk constructively about sex and—"

"That doesn't give you the right to grope someone at work."

"Exactly, and not that I was talking about that stuff at work, I'm just—I'm just working out things in my head. There's a lot of shoulda-coulda that's not helpful."

"Well, I'm here if you want to talk about it."

"Thank you, Jesse."

"You're welcome. And I understand if you need time

to figure everything else out. Both of my brothers and Evie have had their periods of self-discovery."

"And what about you?" She grabbed her keys and her purse. Jesse continued talking as he followed her to the front door.

"Oh, I've always had my life figured out: next step, the Capitol."

She didn't say anything as she set the alarm and locked up. She had no idea if she'd be in Charming another month, but for some reason the idea of Jesse taking a job that would have him in Washington for chunks of the year didn't sit right with her.

"The head of the search committee saw the article, actually. She emailed me and said you seemed like First Lady material."

"What did you say?" She laughed.

"That we were just friends."

Right, Lily-Grace thought. *Friends are good.* "How are you feeling about the position? You think you're going to go for it?"

"I don't know. I have to let them know soon. The date-auction thing made them very happy." He opened the passenger-side door for her and waited for her to climb in.

"How did it make you feel?" she asked when he joined her behind the wheel.

"Not sure yet, but I'll definitely bring it up with my therapist in the morning."

"I might need one of those." It wasn't her intention, but she let out the most pathetic sigh as Jesse started backing out of the driveway. When they pulled back out onto the main road, he surprised her though, reaching over and taking her hand. She squeezed his fingers back and held on a little longer than a friend should.

The sun was shining over George Martin Chevrolet. Jesse mentioned going to middle school and high school with both of the Martin boys, but Lily-Grace didn't remember them. She led the way into the showroom, and a youngish white guy came from around his desk with a rather presumptuous greeting.

"What can we do for you and the missus today?"

He was behind her, but Lily-Grace had a feeling the look on Jesse's face matched the *what in the hell* expression written all over hers.

"Not the missus," Jesse said. "And she's buying for herself. I'm just here for the good times. Unless you want me to buy." He lightly touched her shoulder. She whipped her head around, eyes wide.

"You are not buying me a car."

"Bradley, do you know who you're talking to?" An older white man in a bright white cowboy hat, and the ugliest floral blazer she'd ever seen, came walking toward them. She recognized him from his commercials.

"Uh, no," Bradley said, looking between them like he was trying to decide who he was supposed to recognize.

Mr. Martin gripped Jesse's hand in a firm shake that would dislocate a normal person's arm.

"How are you doing, George?"

"Better now that you're here. Bradley, this is Jesse Pleasant. He's the brains and brawn behind Big Rock Ranch."

"Oh! My girl wants me to take her there."

"You should bring her by," Jesse replied. "We have great packages for couples."

"You'll just need to sell a few dozen trucks to afford it," Mr. George teased. "What can we do for you today? I'm sure the ranch has racked up a hefty discount at this point."

"Yeah, think a full fleet should garner a little extra. But nothing for me today. My friend is looking. I'm just tagging along." Lily-Grace flashed Mr. Martin a tight smile, waiting for them to wrap up their boys' chat. Jesse's hand sliding across the small of her back snuffed her mild annoyance right out. Especially when it lingered, brushing over her hip in a small circle. She glanced back at him and instantly he pulled his fingers away. It took everything in her not to tell him to put his hand back. She didn't mind soft touches from a friend like him.

"Lily-Grace LeRoux," she said. Mr. Martin gave her a more tempered but still enthusiastic handshake.

"August LeRoux's baby girl?"

"A grown woman now, but yeah, that's me."

"He's been helping my wife with the books down at her art studio for years. Any friend of August's is a friend of mine. What are we looking for today?"

"Something with a lot of legroom and headroom, because as you can see I am a tall drink of water. And something that I can hitch a horse trailer to if I decide to really spend my life in a completely different direction and get the filly I've always wanted."

"You sure you came here with the right Pleasant?" Mr. Martin said, eyebrows pitching up. She looked over at Jesse.

"What do you mean?"

"Oh, you haven't told her. Jesse Pleasant Junior here is the only rancher I know who doesn't care for horses. Doesn't ride them either."

"Excuse me, what?" Lily-Grace practically screeched.

"He's just told you," Jesse said. "Horses and I don't mix."

"How is that even possible? You are living my horse-girl dreams, surrounded by those beautiful animals, and you don't even take one for a spin around the valley every now and then?"

"Didn't we come here to get you a car? Don't worry about me and my life."

"Okay then. I'm paying cash today, Mr. Martin, so let's see what you can do for me," Lily-Grace said flatly.

"You two come right this way. Bradley, let's get our friends something to drink," Mr. Martin said. They spent their time looking at a few options, and Mr. Martin thoroughly answered all of her questions and the questions Jesse had too; things Lily-Grace hadn't considered, like towing uphill and through the mountains. They were in a desert valley, after all. Even if he didn't care for horses, Jesse knew a lot about transporting them.

After they looked at Martin Chevrolet's entire stock of trucks and full-sized SUVs, and taken three test drives, she climbed back behind the wheel of the first Tahoe she'd taken for a spin and asked him to give her a few minutes to make her final decision. He told her to take all the time she needed.

Once they were alone, Jesse leaned his head down and

looked through the open driver's-side window. "What do you think?"

"Get in here with me."

"Okay."

She realized, as she watched him walk around the front of the car, the butterflies in her stomach she'd been battling all day. Asking questions about trailer packages for extended-cab pickups and gas mileage, Lily-Grace soaked in the way it felt to have Jesse hovering around her. Patiently waiting, actually caring what she wanted, and doing his best to be helpful. Just the thought of it made it seem like the bar had indeed taken up residence in hell, but it was such a simple thing she now saw she'd been missing. She'd thought she demanded the world from men she'd been with before. Still, it took something as boring as looking at the form and function of trucks to open her eyes to what she was missing on her list of desirable traits in a man.

Jesse opened the door and moved the seat all the way back before he even bothered to climb in.

"How does that feel?" She chuckled.

"You should see me trying to fly coach. This is paradise in comparison."

"So you saying you'd ride shotgun with me, 'cause I have to be honest . . ." She hesitated for a second before she went on. She knew keeping what she was feeling to herself wouldn't work. When she wanted something, she went for it. "I think I'm starting to like you."

Jesse dropped his gaze to the center console and just one of his eyes twitched shut, like maybe she'd finally broken him and his nervous system needed time to reboot. Okay, maybe going for what she wanted worked for Lily-

Grace. She should have known the straightforward approach, when it came to something less practical, like romantic feelings, might catch him off guard a little. She had to remind herself Jesse was still dealing with a lot of firsts. "I'm sorry. I shouldn't—"

"I think the feeling is mutual."

"Really? 'Cause I know I all but threatened your life not too long ago, but in a shocking turn of events, I like being around you."

"That feeling is also mutual."

"Okay, then." Lily-Grace ran her fingers over the steering wheel, a small sense of hope blooming in her chest for the first time in months. Still, they needed more time together. She needed Jesse now, as he really was and not just her mind's image of the sensitive boy from middle school and the man who needed condoms with a wide base. She turned in her seat to face him. "Since we know there are mutual feelings of like, what do I have to do to get you on a horse?"

"Build a time machine and go back to the day my dad's horse bit the shit out of me."

"Oh my God! Jesse, no!" She grabbed him by the bicep, wincing at the thought. "I know that hurt."

"Yup. Demon steed had a taste for nine-year-old me, and I haven't even attempted getting on a horse since."

"What happens when you have to do fancy deals and shit and someone wants you to woo them, out on the old dusty trail?"

"That's what Zach is for."

"Amazing. I think if I have to learn how to swim, you should have to learn how to ride."

"Nah. Swimming is a survival skill. If I fall into a pit

of horses, I'm letting the light take me. It's a wrap. So you want me to ride shotgun in this particular Tahoe?" He reached up and ran his fingers over the edge of the sunroof like he was itching to touch her, but decided the fine leather interior would have to do. Lily-Grace knew then she was in big trouble. Over the years she'd had some amazing, climbing-the-rafters sex, but there was something about sitting close to Jesse Pleasant. She felt calm and safe and giddy all at the same time. She'd have to make out with him again, and soon, but she enjoyed just being around him.

She looked back at the steering wheel and thought about what would come next, where she saw herself. All the things she refused to go back to. Still no plan, beyond the plan to move on. "Yeah, I think I could see myself in this particular Tahoe. I like the color."

"What did he call it? Midnight blue. It's a nice color. Plenty of room for all of your Baby Yoda–related merchandise."

"Don't act like you didn't like my onesie. Okay. This is it. My new car."

"Sure you don't want me to buy it for you?" Jesse teased as he opened the passenger door.

"How would you explain that to the ranch accountant?"

"Oh, you think I don't have my own money. I have a money bin no one knows about, up the Central Coast."

"I bet you do." She hopped out and came around to his side of the car. Nerves suddenly jumping in her stomach, she took his hand and tugged him back toward

Mr. Martin's office. "Come on, money bags. I gotta sign some paperwork."

It took a bit longer than she appreciated because Mr. Martin thought she was joking when she said she was paying cash. But after she explained that she was Internet rich, Jesse corroborated her claims and Mr. Martin had a quick chat with his money guys, they finally got the ball properly rolling. She'd been enjoying being back in Charming, but she knew it would only be a matter of time before some man reminded her he belonged in a trash bin. She almost wished she'd taken her business elsewhere. When he finally handed over the keys, after they had her new baby scrubbed down and prepped, Lily-Grace knew she wouldn't be a two-peat customer of George Martin Chevrolet.

"I'm surprised he's letting me drive it. Maybe he'll feel more comfortable if you escort me," she said when they were finally alone.

"Bill Davis over at the Ford dealership across the way called me *boy* once. I figured George's old-school approach was the lesser of two evils."

"Yikes. Good call. Well, I guess I'll see you later? *Bachelorette* starts at eight sharp, I'm told."

"Yeah. If you want a good seat and some food."

"Are you cooking?"

"I'll be firing up the grill. Do you have any food allergies?"

"Nope. All good. Can I bring anything? An expensive wine, perhaps?"

"We have wine," he grumbled at her.

Lily-Grace leaned up and kissed him on the cheek. "Thanks for coming with me."

"It was my pleasure. You gonna go cruise downtown now? Show off your new ride?"

"You know it. Actually, I'm gonna text Jenny and see if she wants to drive over to the pond so we can blast some Spice Girls."

"You should check out Little Mix. You might enjoy them."

"Who?"

Jesse pulled out his phone and sent her a link to an album with four girls strutting in front of a purple sunset.

"Jesse Pleasant approved?"

"Absolutely."

She didn't want to leave him, which was definitely a sign it was time to go. Also staring into Jesse's eyes in the parking lot of a car dealership wasn't as romantic as it sounded. She said her final goodbye, then kissed him on the cheek one more time before she climbed behind the wheel of her Tahoe. She'd definitely go over the manual before bed. She had to get to know her new whip and of course she had to name it.

She waved at Jesse as he drove out of the lot, then triple-checked to make sure Bradley and Mr. Martin weren't watching her as she snapped a few selfies. She sent the one featuring her biggest smile to her dad.

Baby got her own wheels!

It would take him a smooth fifteen minutes to text back if he didn't just call her first. She sent the best of the bunch to Jenny.

I'm on my way over. I gotta show you my new
car!!!!!!! *breakdance gif.com*

She and Jenny would never outgrow their sixteen-year-old bullshit.

Yes bitch! Come pick me up.
I have to run out and get green onions.

Lily-Grace synced her phone to the car, then safely stowed it away before she headed toward her friend's house.

Chapter 13

Jesse stopped by the grocery store. He went back to Pleasant Lane to check on his grandmother—after he knocked, of course. He changed his clothes and took care of the dogs, and still he couldn't shake the warm feeling radiating from his chest.

He was still pacing up and down their road, with Clementine and Eucalyptus by his side, when Lilah pulled up in Zach's truck. She rolled down the window and frowned at him. "What are you doing?"

"Thinking. I might need to talk to you about something."

"Oh good. I need to talk to you too. Gimme one sec."

She continued on and parked Zach's truck in his garage, then came back over and met Jesse and the dogs in front of his house. She sat down on one of the large rocks by his front door and arched her back.

"Ugh, I need to stop wearing flats. My back is freaking killing me."

"You're getting old, kid."

She rolled her eyes as she reset her shoulders. "Okay,

what do you need to talk to me about? Did Lily-Grace get her car?"

"Yeah, nice Tahoe. She's very happy."

"Good. What's up?"

Jesse considered his words and then just spit it out. "How do you know when you like someone?"

Lilah grew very still, her eyes wide. "Jess," she said slowly. She turned toward him, then covered her mouth for a second before she dropped her hands to her lap.

"What?"

"I don't know."

"Great. Thanks. I'm gonna go start prepping dinner." Jesse felt his jaw clench. He guessed he'd have to discuss his complicated feelings about Lily-Grace and women in general with his therapist. It would be embarrassing as hell, but it looked like he had no choice, if he wanted answers.

"No wait! I'm serious. I really don't know."

This was news to Jesse. They didn't talk about his personal life a lot, but Zach and Sam had gone to Lilah for advice about their own love lives. "I figured you'd have some pearls of wisdom for me in that huge brain of yours."

"I mean, my brain is huge. But I haven't liked a guy—well, a boy—since freshman year in college, and he sucked so bad I just gave up. I've been so busy with work and avoiding my dad, it just hasn't come up again."

Jesse knew what she meant, but that didn't stop him from giving his best *You sure?* eyebrow.

"What?"

"Li, every single human at the ranch is into you."

"I have a few admirers. I can admit that, but *I* haven't

felt those feelings in a long time. Wow." She looked off into the distance for a moment before her gaze snapped back to his. A big smile spread across her lips.

"So you like Lily-Grace, huh?"

"I don't know."

"What do you mean, you don't know?"

"Lilah. Please keep up."

"Right. If you knew, we wouldn't be having this conversation. Okay, well what do you feel so far? There's gotta be something there, 'cause you left the office early on a Monday to go do something with her."

Jesse considered what parts he was comfortable sharing with his baby cousin. "Yeah, I guess that could have waited until the weekend, but I wanted to see her again. I, uh—I think about her all the time. We did kiss yesterday, though it was more in an educational context."

"Corie mentioned that, but not that educational part. What's going on there?"

"Nothing."

"Alright, so you kissed and you've been thinking about her a lot. Hmmm . . . do you have any idea how she feels? She did pay a lot of money for you at the auction, and then you literally saved her life."

"That's part of the problem. She said today that she's starting to like me, but—"

"But what?"

"Nothing." The last few weeks had been filled with heightened emotions, and after what Lily-Grace had told him about her ex and her harasser, he thought maybe her feelings for him were a pendulum swing away from her own stress. And now, he wondered if he was rushing to protect her and keep her close like he did with the women in his family, just now on a whole different level. He wasn't trying to deny her own agency, but his train of thought was heading dangerously in that direction, and that wasn't fair or right. "I was about to do a deep dive into some assuming."

"Don't do that. So she's starting to like you. You obviously feel something for her, otherwise we wouldn't be having this conversation. Best I can say is just be honest with her and take it slow maybe? You're a great guy, Jesse, and she's clearly forgiven you for the thing with her dad. If you two want it to become something, or you want to explore your feelings, tell her. That way she can make an informed decision and so can you." Lilah smiled and gave him a firm nod, like her intellectual mojo had just returned and she'd cracked the case.

She was right though. He had two options: Tell her how he felt, or keep it to himself. And he could see how well bottling shit up had worked out for him. "Thanks. I'll do that. What's your news?"

"Oh, this is great. You're gonna love it. Fetu is gonna pretend to be my boyfriend."

"Dr. Kuaea?"

"Yeah, we talked after church, just to figure out when we were gonna go on our auction date, and realized my dad will absolutely have to back off if he thinks I'm finally seeing someone. Also, he's like the perfect, absolutely believable stand-in. He's smart, great career, churchgoer, former athlete. We had a great conversation about Perry Saysmith's chances in the draft. He's super polite, and you know I hate rude people."

"So why don't you actually date him?"

"Oh, he's not my person, but I think we could be great

friends, and he looks so good on paper my mom will love him. Gerald will have no choice but to deal. Don't tell anyone though. I'm only telling you because of our circle of trust." She held up her pinky. Jesse stepped forward and linked his pinky with hers, a quick up, down, side-to-side motion before they snapped and bumped elbows. Yes, they still acted like they were twelve because that's what cousins do.

"Anyway, we're gonna do this for a few months and then I'll release Fetu to the wind so he may find his own true love among the singles of Charming. He's gonna swing by for *The Bachelorette* tonight, if that's cool. We gotta start sowing the seeds of our new love."

"Yeah, that's fine. There's plenty of food. Lily-Grace will be here too."

"Great!" Lilah jumped up and groaned, grabbing the small of her back. "Yeah, new shoes are definitely in order."

Jesse's plan wasn't going according to plan. He hoped he would have time to give Lily-Grace the gift he'd grabbed for her at the store and then maybe they could talk before *The Bachelorette* started, but he got a text that she was running a little late and by the time she arrived, Jesse's cousins were already buzzing around the kitchen, fixing up their burgers and bratwursts that he had grilled to perfection. Jesse hung back, directing traffic, making sure everyone had drinks and napkins. His leather furniture had been loved over the years, but he still liked to keep it nice and clean.

Lily-Grace and Fetu arrived within two minutes of each other, so Jesse felt the need to be the gracious host, as his home training dictated, instead of whisking Lily-Grace off to a quiet corner of the house before *The Bachelorette* started. He'd have to speak to her after the show or maybe another time. Which was probably a good idea. The minute she walked through his door, he felt like he wasn't thinking straight. His whole mind was on her and what it might be like if they were more than friends who might like each other and had kissed under educational circumstances. He needed to sleep on it and see if having feelings for someone was for him. If this feeling in the pit of his stomach was what his brothers experienced every moment they spent with Evie and Amanda, he wasn't sure he wanted to mess with it.

"Everyone good? Last call from the kitchen until the commercial break." He almost grabbed a fresh tub of cheese balls out of the pantry to go along with his burgers, but reconsidered presenting Lily-Grace the oh-so-sexy image of him licking cheese dust off his fingers.

"I'm good," Lilah said.

"All good, boss," Fetu said from his spot next to her on the sectional. Vega shot Jesse a thumbs-up. She was already shoving her burger into her mouth as she watched some woman win her way to the final round of *Wheel of Fortune*. Corie mumbled something that Jesse interpreted as *I'm all set*.

"Oh wait," Lily-Grace called out from her place on the couch where she was balancing her plate on her thighs. She carefully rushed into the kitchen and brushed by him to get to the cabinet where he'd pointed out the cups when she first arrived. "Lilah mentioned some punch."

"You gotta try it!" Lilah yelled.

He grabbed the pitcher of pomegranate punch Lilah had made and a beer for himself out of the fridge. Lily-Grace took the pitcher from him and poured herself a glass. "You really pull out all the stops. Four kinds of chips and lemon cupcakes?"

"Miss Leona sent over the cupcakes."

"Well, this is the fanciest *Bachelorette* watch party I've ever been to. It's the only, but still."

Jesse took the pitcher and put it back in the fridge. When he turned back around, Lily-Grace was still standing behind him. It wasn't the privacy he'd hoped for, but they were near each other, with the kitchen island and a couple pieces of furniture between them and everyone else. Jesse stepped closer so he could lower his voice. He didn't miss the way Lily-Grace's gaze dropped to his lips before he spoke. "I usually sit in my recliner, but I can sit on the couch with you. If you want."

"I mean, I don't want to mess with tradition, but I am your guest and sitting with me would be the polite thing to do."

"Then I'll join you on the couch. But first I got you a little something." Jesse set down his beer and grabbed the small plastic bag he'd stashed near the microwave. "Sorry I didn't wrap it."

"Wrapping just gets tossed anyway." She stuck her hand inside and pulled out a keychain that said I LEFT MY HEART IN CHARMING and a piña colada air freshener. Jesse felt like a fist was squeezing his heart when she looked up at him with the biggest, most genuine smile he'd ever seen. "I love it."

"Yeah?"

"Yes. I was feeling—I kinda crashed after we parted ways this afternoon. You know—big day, big purchase. All of that and this—" She turned the keychain over in her hand, rubbing it between her thumb and forefinger. "I don't know, this makes today a little more real. Like when you get a new place and you finally decorate it so it feels like yours. This'll make my car feel more like mine and not like an impulse purchase to use as a distraction."

"You needed a car. You could afford it. I don't think you've run anyone over since I saw you last. It's okay to enjoy it."

"Yeah, there's just this feeling. I'm not a big fan of self-doubt."

"What do you mean?"

"*Wheel*'s over!" Corie said.

"I'll explain later. Come on. I don't want to miss a minute of this train wreck." They grabbed their food and went back over to the empty end of the sectional.

As the opening voice over waxed dramatic about what to expect from Clarissal's journey to love, Vega looked over at Jesse and subtly nodded toward his empty recliner. Her mouth curved down in an impressed smirk he hoped Lily-Grace hadn't noticed.

The two hours that followed were fucking painful. Clarissal had to be Jesse's least favorite bachelorette in years, which was a shame considering they gave her age appropriate men who all appeared to have real jobs. Everyone had their opinions about Clarissal and her suitors, and shouted them at the TV at will. Everyone ate their fill, and only one cupcake made it to the nine o'clock hour.

Fetu seemed to be enjoying himself. The performance he and Lilah were putting on was convincing enough. They seemed happy on their end of the couch, cuddled up together, periodically whispering in each other's ear. It made Jesse regret not telling Lily-Grace how he felt before the show started. They could have missed the opening B roll of Clarissal skipping around her hometown of Ann Arbor if it meant they could talk and if it meant Jesse wouldn't be sitting on the end of the couch, pressed against the armrest, thinking about what it would be like to put his arm around Lily-Grace.

Embarrassing. That was the word that bounced around in his head. He was a grown fucking man and he couldn't just lean over and ask Lily-Grace if it was okay. Embarrassing as hell that he was almost forty and he'd never put his arm around a woman before in a situation that didn't involve a group photo. How had it gotten this bad? How had he gone this far in his life, with so many walls up, and some junior high school achievement had passed him by? He tried not to think about what she'd said about her relationship with her ex. What their relationship had been like before he'd dropped the ball and left her out in the cold. The sexual intensity of it, what she must be used to when it came to the bedroom. And he was thinking of how he could hold her hand.

Comparing himself to some dude he'd never met and who Lily-Grace had dumped was a real smart idea. He rolled his eyes at himself and let out a deep sigh, maybe a little too loud. Everyone turned and looked at him.

"Damn, man. She'll send him home soon," Corie joked.

"Not soon enough," Jesse said, playing along, like he actually cared that Clarissal was talking to a man who had been going on about his outfit for a good five minutes while Clarissal nodded and smiled. He'd earned the first night elimination that was coming his way, but Jesse didn't actually care. He was too busy overthinking his own problems. He practically flinched when Lily-Grace nudged his leg with hers.

"You okay?" she whispered.

"Yeah. I forgot how long this show is."

"I don't know if I'm gonna make it," she said, before she gently poked his side. "I might need to rest right here."

"Oh. Here." Jesse shifted his weight on the couch, then moved his arm so Lily-Grace could fit against his side. She wiggled around until she was tight against his chest, her head leaning back against his shoulder. Jesse moved his head to the side a bit so her hair wouldn't tickle his chin, and then focused on controlling his thudding heart. Heat flashed over his face and met the warmth blooming from his chest. He could do this. He could do this.

He made it to the next commercial break. An ad for the Vermont tourism board started up and Jesse leaned down and tried to whisper in her ear.

"Can we go talk for a sec?"

"Yeah," she said, her voice light. "Let's go."

Jesse stood up and led the way out the front door. Poppy tried to follow them, but he shooed her back inside after Lily-Grace stepped out. He didn't need an audience for this. Not even a canine one. Lily-Grace turned to face him, wrapping her arms around herself.

"Oh, my bad. Are you cold?"

"No, it feels nice. I'm just in swaddle mode. What's going on?"

"I thought I could wait until my favorite reality show was over, but I had to say this now. I like you."

"I know. You mentioned that this afternoon. I like hearing it."

"No. I think I need to explain. When I said before that I didn't have much sexual experience, I have even less relationship experience."

"Okay."

Her tone was light again, like she wasn't shocked, but she was trying to be nice about it. He did appreciate the effort, but he was still confused. "That doesn't bother you?"

"No. You've been working. Feeling as if you're responsible for what seems like at least ten people at a time, plus the ranch. I understand focusing on your career. Trust me. Why do you think I'm not married?"

"Some people don't want to get married," Jesse said with a shrug. He could see Lily-Grace living to an old age, enjoying her life without a single man holding her back. She seemed that confident and free in the best possible way. He thought of Lilah for a moment and how she was currently putting on the show of a lifetime to hold on to that freedom.

"Well, I'm one of the people who does, but I think for a while I was surrounded by such awful men that I convinced myself I didn't want to be a wife to any of them."

"Well, Lilah told me to be honest with you so—"

"You talked to your cousin about me?"

"I did. Lilah has her own grievance with men and she always gives it to me straight."

"I knew I liked her."

"We had a somewhat pathetic conversation that made it clear that it's been a long time since I've actually had feelings for someone."

"You know I'm not judging you, right? Like, I'll judge you for being an unrepentant asshole, but I won't judge you for not having a line of ex-girlfriends trailing behind you."

"It's funny 'cause the asshole thing doesn't seem to be a problem for other women. Anyway, I was trying to figure out why this feels different and I was a little shocked when I figured out just how long it's been since I had a hint of a crush."

"Yeah?" Lily-Grace sat down on the rock where Lilah had posted up that afternoon. "How long are we talking?"

"I think I had a crush on Evie when she first got here, but I think I was trying to force something I'd felt before. The summer after eighth grade." If his pathetic history didn't scare Lily-Grace off, the truth that had dawned on him in the middle of the limo introductions definitely would. He watched the emotions play over Lily-Grace's face as her lips gently parted, but nothing came out. It couldn't get worse, he thought. Putting the final nail in the coffin seemed like the right thing to do. Perfect conditions for a clean break before anything really started, and now he had a therapist. He had something to start their session with tomorrow.

Jesse went on "I think it started before that though. I think it was third grade. When you brought yourself for show and tell, told everyone how your vitiligo made you special. Going up to the church craft fair with my mom and picking out that pink cowboy hat for your birthday. I told my mom we were cool and you should have a cool cowboy hat."

"I still have it." Lily-Grace laughed, her eyes glinting.

"You do?"

"Yeah. My dad moved half of my shit to the crawl space, but I was looking for some pictures of me and Jenny a few weeks ago and I found it. Sadly, it doesn't fit anymore."

"I'll try and find you a new one."

"Jesse, are you saying you've been secretly pining for me this whole time?"

"Pining is a strong word."

"You ass." She chuckled again.

"I think I had a feeling about you, being around you, and it went away when you left and I never felt it again. I didn't realize what that feeling was or what I was feeling again, until today."

"Can I be honest with you?"

"Yes." Jesse swallowed and squared his shoulders, like puffing up his chest would save him from the blow of rejection. She'd try to soften it with pity, but he knew it was going to hurt.

"I'm a little overwhelmed."

And there it is, he thought. "I get it. It's kinda why I haven't really tried this before, with anyone. Had a feeling I would come on too strong. Well." He let out a deep breath and tried to switch his gears back to friend mode. He'd cry like a baby after he kicked everyone out of his house. "We can get back inside. Clarissal had a tough decision to make."

"Jesse, no. That's not what I meant. I'm overwhelmed because this feels a little too good to be true."

"I'm sorry?"

"When I said I was starting to like you today, that was me trying to cover my own ass. I've always trusted my gut in a professional sense, and friends come easily to me. Either we get along or we don't, but I'm finally seeing how complicated matters of the heart are. I don't mean to bring him up, but I didn't love Dane. We were together for five years and I didn't love him at all. I enjoyed what we had because it was easy. We had a deal and we got along well enough that I thought we were friends. But he wasn't even that. He was just some guy.

"I feel different with you, and I don't want to trust it because it feels easy. But it should be easy. And then I remember we have plenty to stress us out. I have no fucking idea what I'm doing with my life. Like being retired before forty sounds fun, but I'm not cut out for a life of leisure. I'm bored out of my mind, while at the same trying not to spend every moment thinking about my aging father. My only parent. And you?"

"And me."

"Maybe off to Washington in a few months or a year."

"Right."

"We have plenty of hurdles, plenty to sort out, but why can't this"—she motioned between them—"why can't this be easy?"

"I would have gotten you that car today," Jesse admitted, thinking of that ease. He could just picture the look on his brothers' faces if they could hear him now.

How they would clown the hell out of him, but ultimately understand. They wanted the world for Evie and Amanda, gave it to them when the ladies were cool with it. Lily-Grace stood and walked over to him. Jesse lifted his arms enough for her to wrap herself around his waist. She looked up at him with a small smile on her face.

"I still want a horse."

"We'll get you one this weekend."

Chapter 14

"Wait!" Lily-Grace put her hands on Jesse's rock-solid waist, and took a step back. She did her best to ignore the way his muscles felt through his shirt. "Jenny told me you had a big fat crush on her."

"I tried."

"What do you mean, you tried?"

"Junior year before homecoming. I decided it was time for me to at least try to get a girlfriend. Jenny has always been nice to me and she is pretty. Always has been."

"So you're saying you had the hots for my best friend?" she teased, kinda.

"I tried. But I only saw her as a friend. And she turned me down anyway. But the whole school found out, and my brothers found out, and Sam let it slip to my mom, and then she and Mrs. Yang had an *oh, aren't they so cute* laugh about it. It was embarrassing as hell and I took a vow of silence. Jenny let me down easy though. She wanted to go to the dance with Vinny."

"Hmmm."

"What?"

"Nothing. Fuck Vinny. Well, if you're sure you're not secretly still pining for Jenny too."

"I'm very sure."

"Okay. Then I think you and I can work something out." Lily-Grace stepped back into his arms, ignoring the voice in the back of her head warning her to maybe rethink this whole situation. Was it a possible disaster waiting to happen? Hell yes. Even if it ended in a week, she still wanted to see it through. Plus she figured she needed more than one swim lesson. "Should we go back inside? Clarissal is a fucking disaster."

"Yeah, we should, but I'd like to kiss you first."

"Well, you should definitely kiss me," Lily-Grace replied, closing the small gap between them. Jesse was hesitant at first, but like he'd done in the swimming pool, he caught on quickly. Lily-Grace tried not to moan when his lips parted and his tongue brushed against hers. She almost managed to keep how bad she wanted him at bay, until his hand slipped lower down her back and pulled her closer. She just could picture it, skipping the rest of this reality show so they could slip back to his bedroom and finish what this kiss was absolutely starting.

"Jesse," she breathed. He looked back at her with impossibly dark brown eyes. "You have to promise me we take this part slow."

She shivered as he reached up and drew his thumb lightly over her cheek. "Why?"

"Because I don't want to scare you away."

"You won't."

"You don't know what I'm thinking. What I want to do to you right now. What I want you to do to me." She could picture the kind of fun they could have with a riding crop and a pair of handcuffs.

"You're assuming that I'm not having those same thoughts. Lack of experience doesn't mean there's a lack of desire. I'm trying to be a gentleman."

Lily-Grace wanted to press him, see how far she could go with this hypothetical conversation, expressing those dirty thoughts out loud, but that would ruin things. She had no doubt Jesse had some vanilla fantasies of her stored in his special alone-time files. But even if he'd conjured up some thoughts of her that were more on the risqué side of things, he wasn't ready to go there yet, not in real life. What she had in mind? That was his deep end of the pool, and she needed time and his trust to get them to the same depth together. She leaned up and kissed him on the mouth one more time. "Let's go inside."

He hesitated, but before he could argue she took his hand and pulled him. She ignored the way her palm tingled against his massive palm, and stored away the thoughts of what he could do with those strong fingers, for another time.

They rejoined the gang and made it through the most drawn-out rose ceremony. Clarissal kept some real stinkers around, but that would only add to the drama to come, on this season of *The Bachelorette*. Lily-Grace knew it would be bad form to stay over, but she wasn't ready to leave quite yet. The whole experience was torture for Lily-Grace, because she ended up back in Jesse's arms on their end of the sectional. Pressed up against him while his fingers drew lazy circles over her hip. Instead of her brain doing the kind, charitable thing and luring her to sleep for the remaining thirty-five minutes of the watch party, her brain decided to delve into those fantasies she thought Jesse wasn't ready to hear.

Images of her sitting naked on those tree-trunk thighs, while he's still fully dressed in another of his perfectly tailored suits. Wearing his Stetson of course. Or maybe she's wearing it and only it. She thought about what it would be like to get a spanking from one of those large hands. There was more, much more that she wanted to do, some of it on her knees. By the time the show ended she was warm all over and hot and wet between her legs.

When Jesse stood up and headed into the kitchen, she followed. "Let me help with cleanup," she offered, her voice coming off a little too light and fluffy.

"We'd love to help, but we have some making out to do in the driveway," Lilah said. Apparently the date auction had worked out for her and Dr. Kuaea too.

"Thanks for having me. This was fun." Fetu shouted his goodbyes as Lilah dragged him toward the front door.

"Can't stop a woman on a mission," Jesse said as he opened the dishwasher. Lily-Grace started rinsing and handing him plates and cups, while Vega and Corie put the living room back in order.

"Okay, I have to get going too," Vega announced as she pulled on her jacket. "New patient in the morning."

"Vega's a private care nurse," Jesse explained.

"Oh cool."

"It's definitely an experience. I do love it though."

Corie zipped up her own hoodie, then took Vega's hand. "Uh. So I guess I owe you two an apology?"

"For what?"

"You guess?" Lily-Grace and Jesse said at once.

"For the other day out at the pool. I thought you two

were just playing hide the pickle or whatever. I didn't know you were feeling each other like that. Lily-Grace, I just met you, so I shouldn't be fucking with you like that."

"Can you fight?" Lily-Grace joked, kinda.

"Oh, it's like that?"

"Yeah, it's like that. I just wanna know."

"Can you—actually, I know you can. If you're fucking with this one." Corie nodded in Jesse's direction. "Anyway, I'll get to know you and then I can get back to clowning you both, on an appropriate level."

"You could learn how to cook too," Jesse suggested.

"Man, nah. I drive, run errands, and make sure your grandmother isn't on the Internet doing wild shit. The least this family can do is feed me."

"Corie, we pay you."

"Yeah, whatever. When are your brothers and wives coming back?"

"Sam and Amanda are back this weekend. Amanda wants to take Bam Bam out. I think Zach will be back on Thursday and Evie will be back on Sunday."

"Okay. Well, leave a sock on the front door."

"Or you could just text me before you come over. Or knock. I thought we went over this. Half the family stopped talking to me because I didn't knock first."

"We'll knock," Vega said. "Lily-Grace, always a pleasure. Night, Jess." Corie rolled her eyes but let Vega pull her toward the front door. Lily-Grace and Jesse both waited until they heard it close.

"I'm trying to picture you in a fight," Jesse suddenly said.

"I've only fought dudes. Some guy called me the

N-word in college and I milly-rocked his ass to the Stone Age. And then I had to fight a guy at my friend's bachelorette party. It wasn't cute but I definitely won," she said with a shrug. She didn't like violence, but she wasn't no punk either. "Anyway. That was nice of Corie to apologize."

"Always feel free to tell her to shut up."

"Thanks for the tip." Lily-Grace laughed and then a heavy silence fell between them, the low hum of the dishwasher the only sound filling the room. She looked around the kitchen, which was now spotless. "I should probably go before I do something horny I can't take back."

Just one of Jesse's eyebrows shot up. "Again, I think you're taking my lack of experience for something else. I'm not scared."

Suddenly, Lily-Grace's face grew warm and her eyes started to sting. She realized what she was doing and she wasn't proud of herself. This was a game she'd played with former lovers. A game she'd played with Dane, and she didn't want that anymore. The seduction through not-so-subtle manipulation. It worked for the erotic power exchange, but Jesse hadn't agreed to that. He'd agreed to honesty, earnest expressions of desire, and open communication. It was what she liked about him. She wasn't going to scare him away, but if she kept on she was definitely going to fuck this up. She let out a shaky breath and tried to smile.

Jesse stepped forward and placed a heavy hand on her shoulder as he frowned down at her. "Hey, are you alright?"

Another shaky breath and this time the smile was real.

"Yes, I'm fine. I'd like to stay over. We don't have to have sex, but I'd be lying if I said I didn't want to touch you with your clothes off. I also fully understand if you want to be gentlemanly and send me home with a chaste kiss on the forehead. Or hell, even a handshake."

His other hand went to her other shoulder, like he was gently trying to bring her back down to earth. She was the sexual goddess. He was the novice, and for some reason *she* was losing it.

"Why don't you call or text your dad and tell him you're spending the night out?"

"Are you sure? It is a Monday and a school night. I know how important a good night's sleep is. Blowing it on Monday can throw off your whole week," she said, like a moron who didn't want to stay over when she absolutely did.

"I won't let you throw off my routine."

That she believed. They'd made a lot of progress in the last forty-eight hours, but that wasn't enough time to *undo* Jesse Pleasant. "Okay. I'll call my dad."

Jesse leaned against the counter, another rare smile spreading across his lips. "Don't act so excited about it."

"I gotta play it cool for August." She dug her phone out of her bag and brought up her father's contact information. He answered after a few rings.

"Daughter of mine."

"Hi, Papa. I'm going to spend the night out."

"And where will you be spending the night?" No judgment. He was just being a dad and she wouldn't want it any other way.

"At Jesse's. I'll be back in the morning."

"Okay. I know Jesse has his own place, but Leona is

a little particular still about sex before marriage when it comes to her grandkids. Commitment, unwanted pregnancies, all that. I know you're responsible, but that's the way she feels. Just be respectful if you cross paths."

Lily-Grace didn't like the sound of that, but she knew better than to say anything about it to her father. "Will do. I'll see you tomorrow."

"Until then."

She ended the call and shoved her phone in the back pocket of her jeans before she turned back to Jesse. "Am I going to have to sneak out of here at five a.m. to keep your grandmother off my scent?"

"No," he said, serious again. "You can leave when I leave for work. I'll talk to her."

"Okay. I'm fine being a hussy, but I want to be a hussy she likes."

"I'll take care of it."

"Okay. So walk me through your nightly routine." A different kind of thrill ran through her as she said the words. They didn't need a riding crop or any handcuffs. She wanted to spend the night with Jesse. She just wanted to be with him.

"I've successfully removed all family members, guests, and remaining dogs from my house. First, I ask Clementine if she has to use the bathroom."

Lily-Grace looked back into the living room where the dog had been snoring on her dog bed since Clarissal's first limo introduction.

Jesse walked back into the living room, and whispered in the softest voice, "Hey, Clementine." The dog's eyes snapped open and her head popped up. "Let's go outside."

"What if she doesn't have to go?" Lily-Grace asked

quietly. Jesse didn't answer right away. Just waited as Clementine slowly rolled to her feet. She made a few steps of progress, then stopped to stretch and let out the most adorable doggy groan. She walked by them and headed right for the front door.

Jesse took Lily-Grace's hand and they followed. "If she's too lazy, she stays on her dog bed out here, but usually she knows it's bedtime and she better relieve herself before I call it a night." Lily-Grace watched as Jesse opened the front door and let Clementine out. They stood in the doorway and watched as she doggy-jogged over to the grassy acreage that made up the center of the cul-de-sac. She did her business then jogged back inside, walking right past them, in the direction of Jesse's bedroom.

"She's independent."

"She's the best dog on Earth," he said, his expression deadly serious. He talked baby talk to that dog, she just knew it. "Next, I get ready for bed. If you'll follow me. Please." He led her down to his bedroom and into his massive closet. Her closet up north was impressive. Room for her ridiculous amount of clothes. Her handbag collection, all of her shoes, but she had a hard time keeping it organized and tidy. Jesse's closet was immaculate. His suits all hung with care. Shoes placed lovingly on organized shelves. There were drawers she assumed were for his accessories and an assortment of Stetsons in different colors hanging artfully on the far wall. The black one he usually rocked was on the coatrack near the front door.

"I don't think I've seen you wear any of these," she said, touching the brim of a cream-colored cowboy hat.

She turned and did a double take at the huge mirror just inside the closet door. Jesse walked toward her and she watched both of their reflections in the large reflective glass. Jesse stepped up behind her, pressing against her back. She leaned against him, soaking in the warmth of his body.

"I got my black Stetson from my dad. His 'you're a man now' gifts to me and my brothers. We each have one from him. I'm just used to wearing it."

"Well, it suits you. So which drawer do you keep your man jammies in?"

"When I'm home alone, I sleep naked. I came in here to grab something for you." He opened one of the drawers and pulled out a Lakers T-shirt.

"Do you have one that comes in Golden State?" Lily-Grace said, then immediately burst into laughter at the deeply horrified look on Jesse's face.

"Get out of my house."

She snatched the T-shirt from him. "I'm kidding. I remember how much of a Lakers fan you are. You wore that Starter jacket nonstop. It would be like a hundred degrees and you'd be on the swings just sweating in that thing."

"I miss that jacket. This way." They headed out of the closet and out of Jesse's bedroom. He showed her into one of the guest rooms and turned on the light.

"Oh. Am I sleeping in here?"

"Hell no." He walked into the bathroom and turned on the light. "You can get changed here. There are extra toothbrushes, lotion, washcloths, in the restroom."

"Do you get many overnight guests?"

"I do. Not the fun kind. Just a revolving door of baby

brothers and cousins and family friends. When everyone is here we play musical houses a lot, depending on Miss Leona's mood. I got tired of people complaining about how they got locked out of Zach's or my grandmother's and forgot their toothbrush."

"Ah, makes sense. Well, let me freshen up then and we'll regroup in your bed?"

"See you soon."

She watched him as he walked out the door, then closed it behind him. She wasn't trying to rush, but she rushed. She quickly used the restroom, then checked out this stocked cabinet he spoke of. Sure enough, extra everything, including some very expensive face washes and lotions. Jesse Pleasant had taste. She changed out of her clothes and into her borrowed shirt that fell just above her knees. She took off her makeup and brushed her teeth, then twisted up her hair. Jesse didn't have extra bonnets, but she'd survive for one night. She checked herself one more time in the mirror, then grabbed her phone and went to find Jesse.

She tried not to swallow her tongue at the sight of him standing beside his bed in nothing but a pair of thigh-*and* crotch-hugging boxer briefs. His eyes were glued to his phone, which worked for Lily-Grace. She needed a few seconds to take him all in.

"Sorry." He dimmed his phone and set it on his night-stand. She didn't say anything about the handful of con-doms he'd placed there as well. Ready and within reach was always a good idea. Just in case. "I always go over my calendar before bed."

"No, of course. What else do you need to do?"

"Nothing." He walked to the edge of his neatly made

bed and pulled back the sheets, revealing a respectable number of pillows. Two of which were draped with satin pillow cases. She didn't need a bonnet after all. "Please," he went on, his voice deep and raw. "Ladies first."

"Why, thank you." She climbed into the bed and waited for him to shut off most of the lights so he could join her. A blue ambient glow coming from the TV mounted above his fireplace gave off just enough light for Lily-Grace to see his handsome face as she snuggled close and rested her chin on his chest. His hand slowly rubbed over the small of her back. She wanted him to move his hand a little lower and lift the hem of her T-shirt. He'd discover pretty quickly that she didn't have any underwear on. A little more exploration and he'd see just how wet she was for him. But she wasn't sure if he was ready for that, and she didn't want to push or force him to rise to the occasion if he wasn't ready. She was happy to wait, for now.

"So what's next in your bedtime routine?"

"Usually, I'll lie here for a little and then remember I have a pretty busy schedule. And then I usually fall asleep."

"Well, let's go to sleep then."

"Can *you* sleep right now?"

"I mean, not right this second, but this is nice." She snuggled closer and kissed his stubbled chin. Her heart started to pound when he shifted a little so he could kiss her on her mouth. When they broke apart she looked up at him as his eyes ran over her face. She knew what he saw, the way the portion of vitiligo had spread over her right eye and the smaller portion that stretched from the left side of her chin and up over the corner of her mouth.

She'd stopped covering it up with makeup years ago. His hand continued its smooth circles up and down her back.

"I want to know what you think will scare me away."

"Nope. We're still on level one of your sex lessons. I'm like level forty-five. I want us both to feel comfortable talking about that stuff, and I don't think we're there yet. Why don't you tell me what you're holding on to in that gentlemanly imagination of yours."

"Through my research I've learned that I need to get to know your body and what you like."

"Is that right? You want to get to know my body?"

"Yes. I want to please you."

"And what about your body? What about what you like?"

He was quiet for a second, looking down where their fingers were intertwined. "It'll be easier for me if we start with you."

"Okay. But just know that I do want you, and I want all of this to be good for you too. So much of sex seems to focus on men just getting off, but there's more than that. If you're open to it."

"I am," he said hesitantly. There was something else. Maybe something to do with his past experiences or his own self–body image. Lily-Grace understood all of it. She just wanted them both to have a good time.

"I like being fingered," she admitted. She liked being fingered and paddled or fingered and spanked, a lot, but that wasn't necessary at the moment. Jesse swallowed, his gaze dipping to her lips again.

"What else?"

Lily-Grace sat up on her elbow and gently placed her

hand on his stomach. His whole body clenched under her touch. "Is this okay?"

"Yeah. Your hands are cold."

"Oh shit. My bad." She laughed.

"It's okay. Keep going."

She slid her hand lower, over his cloth-clad penis, which was starting to fill with arousal. "Let's see. I like being fingered. I like dirty talk, hearing it, saying it."

"So if I told you I've been thinking about eating your pussy all day long, in every room of my house, out by the pool, on the kitchen counter. Would you like that?"

"Yes," Lily-Grace breathed, her hand stilling over his hardening erection. "I'd like that a lot."

Her breath hitched again as he rolled her onto her back. His hand slid down between her legs and even in the dim light she could see the intense look spread across his brow when the side of his finger brushed against her bare slit. "Show me what else you like."

Lily-Grace took hold of his wrist and spread her legs apart a little farther.

Chapter 15

"This can be lesson number two," Lily-Grace said as she slowly guided Jesse's fingers over the part in her soaking lips.

"Have you been this wet all night?"

"Yes. Right there." She led his fingertips over her swollen clit. He gently stroked over it, once and then twice as she arched against his hand. "Sometimes that's enough and sometimes . . . sometimes I like it harder, but right now, that's perfect."

He learned very quickly, exploring with a tentative touch. Lily-Grace knew she would come if he kept going that way. One of those soft orgasms that put you to sleep with a smile on your lips, but she didn't want that at the moment. She wanted something a little rougher. She swallowed the thick lust building in her throat and guided his hand lower, pushing the tip of his middle finger into her aching entrance. She let out a pitiful gasp at the fresh sensation. Jesse froze above her, his eyes going wide in the dim blue light.

"Did that hurt?"

Lily-Grace snorted. "No, babe. It feels nice. Like

this." She pushed his finger in deeper, past his second knuckle, squirming against the welcome intrusion. She flexed her hips slowly, up and down for a few moments before he caught on to the rhythm. Another sigh slipped out of her mouth as he pushed in and out of her without her assistance. "Try one and then work up to three."

Jesse stilled again. "Three? Are you sure? My fingers aren't small."

"I'm sure." She licked her lips and spread her legs even wider. Her eyes sprang open though, as Jesse suddenly pulled his hand away, then tossed the covers back.

"Hey!" She giggled. "It was warm under there."

"I know, I'm sorry. I just like to see what I'm doing. I want to see you." He moved back close to her, his hips bumping against her side. Her mouth started to water at the sight of his erection pressing against the pocket of his boxers. Four fingers wouldn't warm her up for his girth, but she was willing to take on that challenge when the moment was right. The expression on his face was all sorts of clinical, but his touch was warm. Jesse closed his eyes for just a second, but in a purposeful way that Lily-Grace couldn't ignore, like he was trying to hit a reset button. He opened them again and a calm seemed to come over him. "So let me try this again."

Jesse's fingers returned to the perfect spot at the height of her slit again, gently gliding over her clit. She exhaled, trying to keep her eyes open so she could watch. He followed the same path they'd just traveled, touching her in all the right ways. He pushed one finger inside her, only halfway, in and out in the softest rhythm. It felt good, so good, but it wasn't enough. Before she could ask though, before she started to beg, he added another finger.

"Tell me if this hurts."

"It doesn't. Don't stop, please," she moaned. "I can handle more." Jesse didn't hold back. He gave her exactly what she asked for, pressing three fingers now deep inside her aching, wet pussy. Lily-Grace closed her eyes then, pressing down against the thick invasion of his hand. Deep and slow. The way his fingers moved was perfect, everything was almost perfect, but as she worked her hips against the pressure of his palm, all she could think of was how badly she wanted his lips on her lips. His lips anywhere, really. She wanted him to kiss her. All over her body. Her eyes opened again and a desperate whimper slipped from her mouth when she saw the way Jesse was looking down at his own fingers and what they were doing to her. He was so dedicated, so focused.

She slid her hand up his shoulder and almost laughed at the way his gaze shot up to her face, like he was on high alert for her next bit of feedback. "Kiss me, Jess. Kiss me on my lips and then move down to my neck, but"—she quickly moved her hand over his—"keep this right where it is."

"I can do that," he replied, his voice rougher than she'd heard it before. He moved up her body just a bit and softly kissed her on the mouth. She leaned up, pressing closer, wanting this kiss to be more, and he seemed happy to oblige. He kissed her deeper, worked her deeper, until she was gripping his side, writhing against the motion of his hand. After a few blissful moments, he did like she asked, he broke from her lips and made his way down to the sensitive spot in the crook of her neck. Shamelessly, she arched closer, moaning his name as his tongue swirled over her skin.

She felt his erection, hotter and heavier, pressed against her side, and as an orgasm crashed over her, all she could think about was how badly she didn't want to wait. Jesse eased up on the movement of his fingers, but didn't completely withdraw as she started to come down. She wasn't entirely sure it was his first time making a woman come that way. She settled back into the sheets, a ragged sob escaping from her chest. She needed more.

"Tell me what you want," Jesse said against her ear. Like a complete dumbass, Lily-Grace shook her head no. "Why won't you tell me?"

"Because," she gasped. "I'm trying to be a lady."

"Uh-uh, none of that. I don't want you to be a lady right now. I want you to tell me."

Lily-Grace licked her lips and raised her hand to cover her eyes. "I want you to fuck me, Jess. I want you to fuck me."

She wanted to hold off. They were still getting to know each other. There was no rush, but in the moment her body screamed to be filled by him. His hand was good, his fingers were perfect, but the greedy side of her libido had been activated. More. More was all she wanted. Jesse started moving his hand again then, and Lily-Grace let out another shuddering breath. She opened her eyes and saw the softened expression on his face.

"What's wrong?" he asked sweetly.

"Nothing. I don't know."

"We don't have to go slow for my sake," he said again.

"I know, I just—" A strange laugh slipped out of her. She'd been so concerned about Jesse she hadn't paused to think of how a first time after Dane would feel. She refused to say that out loud. She'd had enough sex lessons of her own to know you don't bring up what you used to do with your ex while a new man's fingers are gently stroking your vulva. "I think I underestimated how badly I wanted you. I think I was trying to play it cool."

"Don't do that," Jesse said, his voice firm, his expression grave. "I want to try new things with you, but I don't want you to pretend or fake anything or play anything up. If you want me to fuck you right now, I'm going to fuck you."

Lily-Grace chewed the inside of her lip and turned her options over in her mind. "Okay," she replied. "I want you to fuck me."

Jesse climbed off the bed. Lily-Grace couldn't take her eyes off of him as he stripped out of his boxer briefs, revealing the largest erection she'd ever seen in real life. She shifted her gaze up to his face while he grabbed the protection so they could keep this party going. She watched impatiently as he deftly slid the condom into place. He'd clearly been practicing.

"Do you have a favorite position?" he asked.

"Yes, but kiss me first." She rose up on her knees and moved to the edge of the bed. He stepped closer, pulling her in with his arms around her waist. She shivered as their lips met again and his hands slid under the hem of the T-shirt, lightly gripping her ass with both hands.

"I can't kiss you during," she said.

"Okay. Show me what you like."

Lily-Grace pulled the T-shirt over her head and tossed it at the foot of the bed, then moved to the middle of the mattress so she could situate herself on her stomach. She spread her knees and arched her hips off the bed to make room for him.

"Come here, babe. Come up behind me." She tried to breathe as the mattress dipped under his weight. She ignored the goose bumps that spread out all over her body when his large hand smoothed its way over her hip. She closed her eyes, more than ready to take what he was about to give her, but Jesse stilled behind her, his hand seemingly frozen against her skin.

She turned her head, but only his shoulders and the silhouette of his bald head were backlit by the ambient light. "You okay?" she asked softly.

"Yeah, I just—yes. I'll go slow."

"Probably a good idea. I'll tell you if I can't take all of you." But she knew she could, she wanted him that bad. As if to agree, her pussy clenched on itself, begging politely to be filled. She faced forward again, and pressed her hips back as she heard him let out a deep breath. Another breath and he gently nudged at her entrance with the head of his penis. She shifted back farther, letting him know it was okay for him to keep going. And he did, finally pushing his way inside. She wanted to give him more time, but the impatience and the ache became too much. Shameless, she dropped her hips back until she'd taken almost every inch of him and then again and again until she'd taken him to the root, spurred on in every single thrust by the sexy groans Jesse couldn't seem to hold back.

"How does that feel?" she asked, her forehead pressed into the sheets.

"Good," Jesse ground out. "Really good."

Lily-Grace smiled to herself and swung her hips back and forth once again. It took a few moments, but Jesse caught on, matching the pace she set perfectly. Pressing in hard and deep, just the way she liked it. She felt another orgasm creeping up on her.

"Here," she managed to say before she reached back and grabbed Jesse's hip. Carefully he followed her forward as she lay flat on her stomach. Tears sprung to her eyes at the feeling of his perfect, heavy weight on top of her. She knew this position could be a little tricky. She could feel Jesse fumbling a bit to get situated, balancing the full brunt of his body onto her, but he quickly sorted it out and started moving inside of her again.

Lily-Grace bore back down, working her clit against the sheets as his erection massaged the tight embrace of her slick cunt. She fucked Jesse back with the same slow intensity he was giving her. She was coming, her orgasm deep and consuming. She cried out Jesse's name as her orgasms seemed to roll on and on. She hadn't come this hard in a while, and all she wanted now was a repeat performance as soon as she could breathe again. Above her, Jesse stilled and a pinch of terror ran through her, her eyes snapping open. He was going to pull out. She reached up and gripped his fingers in the sheets.

"Come, babe," she said. "This isn't just about me. Don't stop until you come."

He didn't respond, but after a beat, he slid his hand free from hers and sat back up. He cupped both her hips again and started fucking her with a little more speed, but still the same perfect pressure. He was being so careful, she couldn't help but love him a little for it. She clenched down around him again, coming as he pleasured them both with his amazing body. Soon she felt

the telltale tension in his hips and a harsh "Oh shit," as
he filled the condom. Relief rushed over her. She hated
the idea of him not finishing because he was afraid to
be that free with her. She sighed and reached back, giving
his thigh a gentle pat.

"Condom in the trash," she said, shocked that her brain
could still focus on the practical bits and not just the wild
emotions running through her mind.

"Got it." Jesse slid off the bed and into the bathroom.
He was back a few moments later and Lily-Grace was
still lying limp in the same position. He climbed back
into the bed and she let him pull her back into his mus-
cular arms. She snuggled close, taking in the amazing
way he smelled, like sun-kissed man and a job well done.

"I'm sorry," he said.

"For what? You are getting absolutely no complaints
from me." Her body was still humming.

"I forgot the dirty talk."

"I'm willing to let it slide."

"Did you enjoy the fucking?"

Lily-Grace laughed. "I did. Very much. We still have
a lot more to cover so we should probably do this again."

"I'll clear my calendar. We should get as much practice in as possible."

Lily-Grace loved that idea and also dreaded what the
next day would bring. She knew this bubble, or at least
the shape of it and the illusion it presented. Also she was
definitely still dick drunk. Tomorrow she'd be able to
think more realistically about what had just happened and
what might happen next. She still needed to make a plan,
figure out what was next for *her*, but she settled into an
idea of *them*. She could play it by ear, but that wasn't the

way her brain worked. There was a good chance Jesse was headed to Washington, and a small chance he'd ask her to join him.

Several long, quiet minutes had passed when she realized how much overthinking she was doing. Definitely play this by ear, she reminded herself. This was easy, being with Jesse, and trying to plan it to death would definitely ruin it. She closed her eyes and decided communicating was for the best.

"Are you awake?" Lily-Grace's whisper melted into a giggle as Jesse squeezed her shoulder.

"Yes, I'm awake."

"What are you thinking about?" she asked.

"How soft your skin is." She shivered as his thumb stroked down her shoulder in the most loving caress. Again, not to compare, but no man had ever touched her like that.

"Why, thank you. I like to take care of myself. It's amazing how you, and, well, other people can give you like five hundred different complexes about yourself. I have to say thank God for the Internet though. I found this super specific group online, Black women with vitiligo who also read romance novels. And it was nice to have people to talk to about things with and share tips with. I've made some good friends in that group." Which reminded her to check in. Her friend Bonnie was expecting, any day now. "Anyway, it's nice to feel empowered and supported. It makes it easier to take care of myself the way I want to."

"Hmmm," was all Jesse said in reply.

"What? Are you not a big romance reader or not wild about self-care?"

"I love a good skin-care routine," he said. "And I've never read a romance novel, but considering how many reality dating shows I watch with Lilah, I should probably start."

"Oh, I have plenty of recommendations for you."

"I'll take a list—Ah, no, I was thinking about the group chat part. It sounds nice."

"Oh, it is. You're not a part of a hot-guys-who-own-ranches group chat?"

Jesse's chest jostled her as he laughed. "No. I have a group chat with my family and one that's just me and my brothers, but that's it. I don't have many friends."

A pang of guilt touched Lily-Grace's throat. Jesse was capable of being a complete butthead, but he wasn't a bad person. She wanted him to have friends. She didn't have tons, but she couldn't imagine her life without Jenny or Bon and the girls. Jesse and his cousin seemed close, but she knew it wasn't the same thing.

"What about Fetu? He's new here. He seems pretty cool. You should hang out with him."

"Hmmm."

"What's wrong with Fetu?" She laughed.

"Uh, nothing. Just thinking."

"So what's the next thing in the bedtime routine?" she went on, sensing he was done with the friendship portion of the conversation.

"This." Jesse rolled over on his side and pulled her into the curve of his body. The perfect big spoon–little spoon situation. He leaned over and dropped kisses on her neck and her shoulder over and over.

"Good night," he whispered.

"Good night," she whispered back. She had to fight the urge to hatch a plan just to keep Jesse Pleasant.

Jesse's alarm went off early as hell, but Lily-Grace happily accepted his offer for her to stay in bed. She dozed off again to the sound of the shower turning on. The scent of nutmeg woke her up an hour later. She climbed out of his bed and went to change back into her clothes. She rinsed her face and put on some fresh lotion before she went to find him. She'd take a nice long shower when she got home.

Jesse was in the kitchen, dressed for work, whipping up one of those eight-course breakfasts that make absolutely no sense on TV. He was back in his apron, covering his pristine dress shirt and tailored slacks.

"Hey, you look busy," she teased.

He glanced over to her as he turned off the stove and added two more pieces of French toast to one of the plates. The other had a stack fit for a lumberjack. Or a six-foot-seven rancher. "Morning. I was going to bring this to you in bed."

"Before you go to work? Damn, Pleasant. Are you looking for a girlfriend or a wife?" she joked. Yup, definitely joking.

"Nothing starts the day like a proper breakfast. Come sit."

She climbed up on the stool at the island and took the plate of French toast and eggs and bacon he'd masterfully arranged. The man had an eye for detail and presentation. He handed her a glass of the punch Lilah had made.

"Thank you, this looks amazing."

He came around the island and joined her with his own meal. "You're welcome."

They didn't rush, but they were both mindful of the clock as they ate. She asked Jesse about his plans for the day and then told him all about the disaster that was *Hot Bench*, a show he hadn't seen. Which was probably for the best. She helped him with a quick cleanup and then they grabbed their stuff and he walked her out to her Tahoe, Knight Rider. It was still cool out, but the temperature was clearly rising as the bright sun climbed higher in the cloudless sky. It would be seventy-five or more by lunchtime. She put her purse on the driver's seat, then turned to kiss Jesse goodbye.

"I know you might be leaving town sometime soon, but I'd like your permission to court you properly," he said when she was back in his arms.

"Is that right? You're not going to show up in a carriage and ask my father for permission to take me into town, are you, 'cause he doesn't play that caveman shit with me."

"Not unless you want me to."

"So what does being courted by Jesse Pleasant involve, I wonder." She hoped it meant more deep dicking-like she'd experienced the night before.

"Well, we still have our auction date to attend to, but that was a matter of business, so I'm not sure that counts. I think some proper dates, some lavish gifts, some very deep discussions about our hopes and dreams. Maybe a moonlit walk or two. Homemade baked goods."

"You bake too?"

"I do. It helps relax me. I've perfected a lemon bar recipe that is to die for."

Lily-Grace smiled up at him and accidentally let the most deranged thought cross through her mind. She was going to marry Jesse Pleasant. She swallowed, stopping herself from declaring how easy it would be for her to fall in love with him, and focused on the present.

"Oooh, this all sounds amazing. Oh! Can I come by the ranch sometime?"

"Of course. I'd be happy to show you around."

"I know there is a bit of genuine terror there, but I'd love to check out the horses. I haven't been riding in ages."

"Sure. I'm not getting on a horse with you, but we can arrange a ride—Don't pout on me. It's cute as hell, but it won't work this time."

Lily-Grace jutted her lip out even further. "Fine, you're drawing a boundary and I respect it. Well, you can watch me ride a horse. I'm sure it'll be equal parts awkward and sexy."

"I look forward to it. How does Saturday sound?"

"Perfect. I'll let you get to work."

"I'll text you later."

"It better be dirty."

"I'll do my best."

"Goodbye, Mr. Pleasant."

"Bye, Lily-Grace." She squealed as he helped her up into the cab with a firm hand on her butt. Settled behind the wheel, her heart fluttered when he winked at her. Boy, was she in trouble.

Chapter 16

As soon as Zach got back Jesse was going to ask him how he got anything done now that Evie was in his life. How did he concentrate? How did he remember to show up for anything on time? He'd have to ask Sam how he didn't spend all day literally pestering Amanda, asking when he could see her again. Heat had been fluttering in his chest—yes, fluttering— since he watched Lily-Grace drive away a few hours ago. He had to fix his face before he walked into the office. He didn't want to scare Erin with the smile that was still fighting its way to the surface. It took all of his willpower to dive into his emails instead of spending the morning replaying what it felt like to touch Lily-Grace, what it felt like to be inside of her, to feel her come on his fingers and again on his lap.

He finished his call with their feed vendor, then glanced down at his cell phone. He had a full day, including therapy, after a quick lunch, but he could take a break to text Lily-Grace. Right when he picked up his phone, the screen lit up with a text alert from the woman in question.

Let me know when it's safe to send you sexy
pictures.

Jesse looked up at his door, like Erin would bust in at
any moment and snatch his phone out of his hand.

I am free to accept such texts right now.

He swallowed as he hit send, prepared to enjoy whatever images Lily-Grace sent over, for no more than ten
minutes before he deleted them. Not that he'd ever received any, but he knew enough about the dangers of
having nudes hanging out on your phone. The photo she
sent was not what he expected: Lily-Grace in her pajamas with her hair wrapped up in a silk scarf. She'd pulled
the fabric of her pink pajama top just off her shoulder,
showing off the soft skin he'd pressed his lips against the
night before.

Since we're courting I thought this was the
appropriate level of racy.

It's working for me.

And it was. Their whole time together came rushing
back to him in full detail. How easy it was to be with her,
how natural it felt to wake up beside her. Jesse couldn't
wait to see her again. He wanted to send something
back, but he never, never took selfies. If it wasn't for his
cousins and brothers forcing him to be in pictures, there'd
be very little photographic evidence of his adult life.

Selfies for a new lover were definitely outside of his realm of expertise.

He thought for a moment before he pushed back from his desk and hiked up the leg of his pants and pulled off his boot. He was wearing a pair of cactus socks Miss Leona had given him for Christmas. He snapped a picture of his socked ankle and sent it to Lily-Grace. She replied immediately with a laughing emoji.

So hot. Omg.

Anything for you, baby.

Jesse glanced at his clock. He had a little time before he had to meet Delfi for a quick lunch, and then he had his therapy appointment. He wished he had more time to just bullshit with his . . . He wasn't sure what to call her. They hadn't talked about titles yet. He went over to Google and quickly searched what to call someone when you were courting them. He cringed, almost dropping his phone when his eyes scanned over the actual definition of courting. Maybe he should have looked it up before he put it out there that morning. He was clearly developing serious feelings for Lily-Grace, but it might be a little too soon to talk about marriage. Not that it was off the table, but he really needed to stop thinking like that and focus on a real first date.

Switching back over to his conversation with Lily-Grace, he figured *baby* or other endearments would have to do for now. He looked at his computer for a split second, his fight response pinging, as his inbox auto-updated. He did a double take to make sure he wasn't seeing things. There was a fresh email from Senior. Jesse sighed, skidding closer to his desk before he clicked on the message:

FWD: NEWS FROM GOLDEN GULCH RANCH

Talk to your brother, but I think you should move on this. —Dad.

Jesse's blood pressure cranked up another notch when he read the email again. Zach was cc'd on it, but whenever his dad emailed them both like that it was clear what he meant: *I'm talking to Jesse and acting like Zach's input is just a formality.* They both played their roles, but they were in this fifty-fifty.

He continued to scroll down and read the email Graham Major had sent to his father a few hours ago. Graham's luxury dude ranch sat on a massive spread of land just over the Nevada line. It was nice, but leaned a few inches too far into theme-park territory with its focus on the gold rush. Jesse skimmed over the part his dad had included for Zach's benefit, Graham's well wishes for his recent marriage and compliments on the photos his wife had shown him of the special day, on their mom's Instagram account.

When he finally got to the point, Jesse had to reread Graham's message twice before he started to process it.

Patty and I have given it a lot of thought and we'd like to sell the place to you and the boys.

Graham Major was planning to sell Golden Gulch and he wanted to sell it to them. This was big news. Huge news. He was glad Zach would be back that night so they could talk about it; something about this annoyed the fuck out of Jesse. The way his dad cc'd Zach but only addressed Jesse was a part of it. That their dad was still emailing them about ranch business at all pissed him off.

He knew it shouldn't bother him. Don't kill the messenger and all, but his father had walked away. He'd left the business in their clearly capable hands. How the fuck, after over ten years, was he anyone's idea of first contact when it came to the ranch, especially when he and Zach had a professional relationship with Graham Major? Zach and Sam had been up to the Gulch more than once to ride with Graham's sons when they were kids. None of this had anything to do with Senior, and Jesse already resented the fact that he was going to have to carefully remind his father of that, again.

Another text from Lily-Grace lit up his phone, but he was too angry to answer it. Then a text from Delfi. He blew out a harsh breath through his nose. And picked up his phone.

Delfi: Grabbed our table and put in our order.
Ready when you are.

Lily-Grace: Internet friends
are the wave of the future.

Lily-Grace had been kind enough to send over a couple of links, a podcast hosted by two guys who watched *The Bachelor* religiously called The Rosecast and a Reddit thread called *Bros and the Bachelor*.

Jesse closed his eyes and counted to ten, slowly, then

replied to his dad's email with a short *Thanks for the heads-up, will discuss with Zach*. He closed his eyes again before he went back to his phone. He didn't want the way he was feeling about his father to stain the way he was feeling about Lily-Grace or the way he spoke to her. Even if it was over text.

> Thank you.
> I am always on the lookout for fellow Bach bros.
> I have back-to-back meetings,
> But I'll call you this afternoon.

She replied as he locked his computer.

> Can't wait. ♥♥
> Don't show anyone else that ankle.
> *It's all mine.*

He was still hot, but her texts made him smile.

Jesse found Delfi at their usual table next to the terrace window. They had brief conversations every day, but once a week they sat down to a meal, for a random sampling of that week's menu. It helped keep things fresh for the guests and gave Jesse time to process his thoughts before he and Zach met with their executive chef, Brit.

"Sorry I'm late. I got an email from Senior." He took a seat and looked at the eight glasses filled with various beverages on the table.

Delfi flipped open the cover of her tablet and leaned forward. "Major is thinking about selling Gulch."

Jesse smiled and grabbed the glass closest to him. He smelled the golden beer before he took a sip.

"Not bad."

"Soul Sisters Brewery out of Oakland. I like what I've seen and tasted so far. You're not gonna say anything about the Gulch?"

"How did you find out?"

"You know I have my whisper network."

"Graham emailed Senior." Delfi frowned at that too. She got it. "He's thinking about selling to us. Or to Senior, and he'll just give it to Zach and me to play with."

"I'll keep my two cents to myself until you speak to Zach."

"No, please. Go ahead."

"I mean, I don't see a downside here. You get to expand and take on a well-established relationship with a ranch that's more kid *and* bachelor-party friendly. It's far enough away that it won't feel like it's encroaching on Big Rock, but you and Zach can get there in four hours by car. Three if Corie drives. And aside from what Senior thinks, I imagine positive expansion is what your grandfather would have wanted for you. Screw what Senior thinks. Talk to Miss Leona."

Delfi was right. Big Rock had been his grandparents' dream from the beginning. Senior wanted nothing to do with it. Jesse needed to remember that and save what he felt about that email for Dr. Brooks and his next brother-to-brother-to-brother talk with Sam and Zach.

"Now, you could also promote me again, give me a nice little raise and a new title and I'll happily oversee both places for you." She flashed him a toothy grin as one of those longtime servers, Hillary, brought out a plate of truffle Brussels sprouts and the chicken-and-chili frittata Britnay had just added to the Breakfast by the Pond menu. Jesse thanked her and took a forkful of the frittata.

"Damn," he said as he reached for another bite. "Britnay doesn't miss."

"It's why I married her," Delfi replied.

They continued on with their meeting, discussing ranch business while sharing eight different dishes as Hillary brought them out. Jesse finished half of them and he knew he'd be hungry again by six. They needed to hire two more housekeepers and one of their valets; Will had given his notice. He was moving with his girl-friend to Texas. A stupid guest had jumped off a horse, trying to show off for his teenage son, but he'd walked away injury-free and accepted the thorough scolding he'd earned from Felix, who'd happened to catch the whole spectacle. No earth-shattering news, which made Jesse happy. Basic personnel changes Lilah could handle on her own.

"That's all from me. You have anything else before you go back to the kitchen and tell Brit yourself how much you loved that frittata?"

Jesse chuckled and put his napkin back on the table. Brit did enjoy some positive reinforcement and she deserved it for that dish.

"What's too extravagant of a gift?" he asked.

Delfi's eyebrow rose. "Business or pleasure?"

"Pleasure."

"Just so we're clear, I'm gonna go ahead and believe the rumors. You and Lily-Grace LeRoux are a thing now?"

"There is something there, yes. No labels yet."

"Well since it's pretty fresh I think you can hold off

with the labels for a little while. I barely remember her from middle school, but you gotta admire a woman who can bust up a meeting, threaten your life, and then have you half in love with her inside thirty days."

"Back to the gifts."

"Oh, that depends on the person, and if you care what other people think."

Jesse considered that for a moment and thought of Lily-Grace. All he cared about was how he made her feel.

"That's not a problem."

"Well, I say go big or go home. Brit and I both love a quality extravagant gift. I think people just go wrong with the presentation. Like find out if Lily-Grace is the kind of person who wants to receive a big gift in front of an audience or if she's more of a private gal. And give her the emotional space to turn it down if it's a bit too much."

"I think I can handle that. One last stupid question, and then I'll go shower your wife with praise. You consider me a friend?"

"What? Of course I do. Brit and I love you. What makes you say that?"

"Some people enjoy Zach's company and include me as an add-on."

"No. Zach is great. He's my friend too, but in a 'baby brother you wanna fight' sort of way. You're . . . you," she said, her tone kind, which was odd for Delfi. She was the queen of tough love. "I definitely don't think of you as some sort of add-on. You shouldn't think of yourself that way either."

"Thank you. I appreciate that. I'm thinking of asking Dr. Kuaea if he wants to grab a beer at Claim Jumpers.

See if he wants to be a 'friend outside of the ranch' kind of friend."

"That's a great idea. He seems like a good guy. New in town. It would be downright neighborly of you. Two more of my cents?"

"Sure."

"Don't invite Zach," she said with a cool shrug.

"What do you mean?"

"I mean you guys do everything together, and maybe if you want to start fresh with a new friendship, go solo for once. Don't invite Lilah either, even though she told me they are dating. What the fuck is in the water over at Pleasant Lane?"

"Hell if I know, but I'm just gonna go with it."

Dr. Brooks was patient while Jesse gathered his thoughts. He had this hour to himself. His phone was on Do Not Disturb, and Erin had explicit instructions to hold all calls and visitors unless the ranch was on fire. This time was his, he'd finally come to accept, but he was having a hard time finding the words.

"Sorry. I have a lot to share, I'm just debating where to start."

"Why don't you start with the thing that's got you blocked up?"

Dr. Brooks didn't know Jesse's family. Well, he did from their respective films and television shows. *Rory's War* had just been renewed for two more seasons, so that would keep Miss Leona busy—but his therapist didn't *know* them. Not like Jesse did. He spit the words out before he buried them deep again. "I think I hate my father."

He thought saying it out loud would make him feel bad. Or guilty, but it didn't. "I love him. He's my father. He gave me a great life, set a good example of how to be a good husband, but I hate him."

"Jesse Senior."

"Yes. I'm named after him." It should have been a point of pride, but sometimes it just made him want to grind his teeth.

"You haven't mentioned your parents much since we've started talking. What's your relationship like with them?"

"Odd," Jesse said truthfully. He always had a sense his dad had wanted more sons, not to fill his house with kids, but because he felt like Jesse had been a test run that hadn't gone quite right. Jesse shared that with Dr. Brooks, ignoring the pain it opened up in his chest.

"Both of my parents and my grandparents are, were, really outgoing people, and I'm just not. My grandparents understood that, but my parents, they just . . . handed me off to my grandparents and tried again. Zachariah and Samuel, the true heir and the spare. And they made it clear they were extra disappointed in me for not getting married first. And then Sam started seeing someone they like." Jesse needed to stop talking about this. It wasn't important, not in the grand scheme of things, but he'd opened a release valve he didn't know how to shut off. "But now . . ."

"What's changed?"

"I'm seeing someone." Jesse glanced at the clock

and did his best to give Dr. Brooks a PG version of everything that had happened since they'd last spoken.

"It sounds like a busy weekend, but how are you feeling about that relationship?"

"Good. Really good. We started off on the wrong foot. I mean, I'm talking to you because of what happened with her father. We both have stuff going on in our professional lives, big stuff, but I think we've turned a good corner, on a personal level."

"And your parents?"

"I don't want to tell them."

"Why is that?"

"Because I know they'll treat me differently, or they won't and they'll just embrace her the way they do with Evie, and continue to ignore me."

"Do you want attention from your parents?"

He'd made it this many sessions. Jesse was not going to fucking cry. "I don't know. I don't think they are capable of what I want."

"And what do you think that is?"

"A certain level of warmth. I feel like they outsource that to my grandmother."

"What is their relationship with her?"

"Odd." Jesse chuckled. "My mom's an actual pageant queen, so their diva energy doesn't really jive together, and my dad is my grandmother's clear favorite and has his own shit with his own brothers."

"You all sound pretty human to me."

"Hmmm."

"Do you think you could tell your dad how you feel?"

"Maybe. Do I want to? No."

"Why is that?"

"'Cause I don't think that'll change anything."

"And if it does?"

Jesse wasn't ready to think about that yet either.

Jesse didn't know how a single email could ruin his whole day. But that email from Senior really pulled it off. Zach had landed and was back at Pleasant Lane, probably trying to acclimate to life back on Earth, away from his new bride. Jesse almost cut out early to go talk to him, but he didn't want his mood to ruin Zach's. He had already blown off his planned call to Lily-Grace, but she took the news over text just fine.

He tried to smooth things over by asking if she had a favorite jeweler. She'd replied with a whole Pinterest board she'd named Diamonds Are A Girl's Best Friend, filled with items that caught her eye but she'd never purchased for herself. The most recent pin was a brown-and-gray Percheron that reminded him of their horse Peanut. He'd start making inquiries about similar horses in the morning. In the meantime, he ordered some flowers and a tennis bracelet she'd recently pinned.

He said goodnight to Erin, and as he waited for Clementine to climb in the truck, he sent Fetu a text, asking if he wanted to get a drink sometime in the next week or so.

He listened to the podcast Lily-Grace had recommended, and it was pretty good. Two guys who'd been friends since they were kids, now grown, bonding over the madness that was *The Bachelor* franchise. It took his mind off things until he pulled up to his place and saw Zach walking across the cul-de-sac in the setting sun. He grabbed his laptop bag and opened the rear cabin door so Clementine could go greet him. He followed the dog and instantly caught the dark cloud hanging around his brother.

"Hey, man. Welcome back." They executed their elaborate handshake that Sam insisted upon. "How was the honeymoon? You don't look so happy."

"No, the honeymoon was great, better than great. I had a lot on my mind and I read that email Senior sent this morning. Why the fuck does he do that?"

"I don't know. I talked to my therapist about it."

Zach let out a surprised chuckle. "You did?"

"Yeah."

"What did the doctor have to say about it?"

"He asked if I was comfortable talking to Senior about my feelings."

"Yikes."

"Yeah, FaceTiming him an ocean away, between stage productions and television roles. Mom's in the background asking him about the next gala they are going to."

Zach shook his head. They still hadn't debriefed about the wedding itself.

"I know you just got home, so we can talk about it back at the office, but I have thoughts about Golden Gulch."

"Yeah, let's talk about it for sure. Some new developments popped up during our trip. Come on, Miss Leona's cooking." Zach turned toward their grandmother's house. Jesse knew his brother. He knew something was wrong.

"Hey, man, what's up? What's going on?"

Zach turned back and took off his tan Stetson. The one Senior gave him. He scrubbed his hand over his face, tugging on his beard like it would relieve the pressure. "Evie might want to give up the restaurant or maybe hire a new executive chef. One day on our honeymoon she just burst into tears because she realized how she was feeling months ago, and we invested all this money and time, and she thinks you and Sam and Miss Leona will be mad at her—"

"I mean, her walking this soon is not ideal, but shit happens." Like maybe running for office and leaving your brother to run two ranches. "But I'm not angry, and Sam and Miss Leona won't be either."

"Yeah, well, I found out yesterday that the tears may have been a hormonal reaction to something else. Evie's pregnant."

Chapter 17

Somehow Jesse channeled Dr. Brooks. Zach looked like he was about to fall over and cry.

"How do you feel about that?" Jesse asked. He was more than excited to welcome Zach and Evie's child into the world, but how he felt about it didn't matter. His brother was about to be a father.

"I'm happy? Terrified? Happy again? A little hungry?" They both laughed, which was a good sign. If Zach lost his sense of humor, they'd really be in trouble.

"Kids were in the plan. They are in the plan. We didn't want to wait too long because Miss Leona isn't immortal, but we weren't *trying*. When they say some birth control is only ninety percent effective, they aren't kidding."

"Well, congratulations. I had some news, but this is bigger. Let's eat and we'll talk about everything else tomorrow. Gulch, Dad, how much Mom is somehow going to make this baby about her."

"Now you wait. What's your news?"

"I'm seeing Lily-Grace LeRoux."

Zach blinked and took a dramatic step back. "Hold on. I—hold on." Zach walked back over to his house and sat down on the edge of the large planter sitting on his front porch. Jesse rolled his eyes and followed. Clementine tagged along.

"Hey!" Jesse turned and saw Corie's head poking out of Miss Leona's front door. "Soup's on."

"We're coming," Jesse yelled back.

Zach shook his head. "It's crazy. It's like she doesn't have our phone numbers or know how to text."

"Lily-Grace got an apology out of her last night," Jesse said, the pride swelling in his chest overriding all the conflicting emotions of the day.

"No shit."

"Vega had a word with her too. Corie walked in on us in the pool and thought it was all fun and jokes. She did apologize though, and Lily-Grace asked her if she could fight. It was a highlight of the evening."

Zach looked up at him, a strange expression taking over his face.

"What?" Jesse asked. "What's that look for?"

"I'm just wondering if it's the therapy or Lily-Grace. You never talk this much at once. You look happy."

"I think I am."

"Good. Let's go eat. Don't say anything about the baby yet, and definitely not in front of Corie."

"I'm never saying anything in front of Corie again."

Zach laughed as they walked across the driveway.

Dinner was good, but something about the mood was different. Maybe because Zach was married, and now there was a sense that in a few days, the next time he'd join Miss Leona's table, it would be with his wife. Zach told them about their trip to Barbados, and they caught him up on everything he'd missed, most importantly the wild night that had unfolded at the date auction. Zach shot Jesse a look when Jesse mentioned he was teaching Lily-Grace to swim. Corie, in a wise move, kept her comments to herself.

Jesse sat by quietly as Lilah went on and on about how well things were going with Fetu. Jesse made a mental note to ask her later if she planned to tell Zach the truth about her elaborate scheme to pass the veterinarian off as her boyfriend. Miss Leona announced her officially *taken* status, which was actually true, and her plans to have Mr. LeRoux join them more often around Pleasant Lane.

Seemed like love was in the air for all of the Charming Pleasants. It was good, but Jesse knew things would never be the same. Maybe this was what his mother was waiting for, for her boys to pair off so she could see this clear shift and adjust accordingly. Or maybe she just liked lavish weddings and the idea of grandchildren.

After they finished and helped Miss Leona clean up, she asked Zach and Jesse to join her in the den so they could talk about Golden Gulch. Senior had emailed her too, asking her to give the boys a nudge in what he viewed as the right direction.

Jesse walked down the hall toward the guest wing of the house, absently noting that she'd added the *Vanity Fair* cover celebrating Sam's Oscar win and the *People* magazine cover featuring Zach and Evie's wedding photos.

He glanced at the *Essence* cover he and Zach had graced four years ago where'd they'd been interviewed for their take on being successful young Black men in the world of luxury hotels, and suddenly the walk toward that wing of the house made that feeling he'd been carrying since the start of dinner even heavier. So much had changed. So much was changing, and it was definitely time for him to catch up.

When they reached the den, Miss Leona took a seat in the large armchair she'd recently replaced his grandfather's old recliner with. Clementine and Poppy made themselves comfortable by her feet. Zach and Jesse carefully sat down on either end of the new matching sofa. The old furniture had been old, but broken in. He didn't think anyone had been in this room, filled with their old sports and rodeo trophies, since the delivery guys had dropped off the new stuff.

"So let's talk business."

"You wanna start?" Zach asked.

"Sure." Jesse had a feeling Zach was gonna drop the pregnancy news at some point during this conversation. But he wasn't ready yet.

Jesse slid forward to the edge of the couch, which wasn't designed for his long legs. He couldn't talk to his parents, but even if they didn't understand him all the time, he knew he could talk to Zach and Miss Leona. "Before we talk about Graham's offer, I think we should have a conversation about everything that's going on right now. Zach's a husband now, and I've been considering some changes of my own."

"Okay," Miss Leona said, her tone carrying a positive lilt to it.

"Right before the wedding, A New Way Forward approached me and asked me to consider filling Paul Cogger's seat. I have until the end of this month to decide."

He glanced between his grandmother and his brother, trying to read the wide-eyed shock on both their faces. Zach spoke first. "Wow, Jess. That's huge."

"I don't think I can do it. You weren't here for the date auction, and Miss Leona, you missed the aftermath backstage. I had a panic attack, a bad one. That's why I was MIA for so long. The auction was bad, but the attack started before I got on stage. I want to help people and I want to do great things for Charming, but public speaking for a living sounds like my own personal hell."

"That's fine, baby. Do you feel bad for wanting to turn it down?"

"I feel—I was trying to understand why I wanted to run in the first place, when it's clearly not for me. This is difficult to say, but I wanted my chance to get away from Charming."

Zach let out a pained sigh as he turned to face him. "Evie and I talked about this."

"You did?"

"Yeah. You do everything around here. Everything. Make adjustments for all of us, including Mom and Dad, all the time. And no offense to you," he said to Miss Leona, "but Evie pointed out that Jesse somehow became the family rock, and maybe that wasn't exactly fair to him. We've spent the last three years just coming and going; and your trip with Sam, Jesse, was the last time you even left town for yourself."

"And that trip was cut short because of that mess with Amanda's boss," Miss Leona said, nodding slowly. Sam had been nice enough to plan a brothers' trip to Bali for just him and Jesse, but his girlfriend's then boss thought that would be the perfect time to try and ruin Amanda's life. Jesse had been glad to come back to support her, and them as a couple, but afterward things had gone back to normal, with Jesse left behind.

"You've been holding everything down at the ranch and here at Pleasant Lane. You've even taken Lilah under your wing in a way I haven't," Zach went on.

"During dinner I realized how everyone seems to be moving on and I need to decide what I want for me next," Jesse said.

"Do you want to walk away from Big Rock?" Miss Leona asked.

"No. I wanna buy Golden Gulch."

They spent the next two hours talking about pretty much everything. Miss Leona was admittedly glad they were almost done filming the current season of *Rory's War*. She was feeling stretched a little thin and wanted to spend more time with them and August, as she wanted them to call him now. Jesse still couldn't believe his grandmother had a boyfriend.

Zach didn't drop the news about Evie's pregnancy, but he laid the groundwork, explaining that they'd wanted to start trying, and soon. That made Miss Leona very happy. They decided to wait for Evie and Sam to get back before they discussed what to do with Evie's restaurant, Thyme. They said their good-nights to their grandmother even though it was still early, and headed back to their respective houses.

"I'm glad you spoke up. And I'm glad you're sticking with therapy. Anytime you want to talk to me, I'm here," Zach said when he and Jesse went back outside. Poppy had stayed behind, but Euca seemed intent on following Zach back to his place.

"Thank you."

"Bring it in, man." Zach threw his arms around Jesse's shoulder with a playfully dramatic sob. Jesse patted his head, his eyes rolling until his goofy-ass brother stepped back.

"I have to go call Lily-Grace."

"It's weird she might be your step-cousin or some shit if Mr. LeRoux ever pops the question."

"Jesus, I might have to beat him to it."

"Oh, it's like that."

"No comment. You coming to the office tomorrow?"

"Yeah I'll be there. I'm gonna take Steve out in the morning."

"I'm sure he misses you."

"You could have gone to visit him, ya know."

"Don't worry. Lilah looked in on your horse-son. Which reminds me, I'm gonna bring Lily-Grace by the stables on Saturday."

"Are you going to come inside the stables with her?"

"Haven't decided. Night." Jesse turned back to his house at the sound of Zach's laughter and receding steps. He pulled out his phone as Clementine fell into step beside him. He was feeling raw as hell, and all he wanted at the moment was to hear Lily-Grace's voice. A text wouldn't do. She answered right away.

"Oooh hey, sexy daddy," she giggled into the phone.

"Hey. Sorry I took so long to get back to you. It's been a long day."

"Maybe you cosmically balanced out the fact that I

did absolutely nothing. I'm afraid I'm starting to soul bond with my dad's couch."

"I don't think I can swing another late night, but can I see you?" Jesse asked as he stopped on his front steps.

"Do you want to come over for a little bit? We can talk and make out in my driveway."

"I think that'll do the trick. I'll be right over."

"I'll put on real pants."

Jesse tried not to trip himself up with thoughts of what she was actually wearing at the moment, and went inside to change.

Twenty minutes later he pulled up to the LeRouxs' house on Wildwood Canyon Road. A smile bloomed across his face when he spotted Lily-Grace waiting by her SUV. Her mass of curls was piled on her head and she was wrapped in a large sweater. She had, in fact, put on real pants—skintight jeans that made his fingers all the more eager to explore her body again. He parked his truck behind her dad's Buick and adjusted his half-engorged erection.

Hopping out, he let Clementine out of the back of the cab.

"Oh, you brought my favorite girl." Lily-Grace ruffled Clem's fur before she stepped close to Jesse and greeted him with a warm kiss on the lips. Jesse pulled her closer with a firm grasp on her ass. The way she moaned into his mouth did nothing to calm his arousal.

Lily-Grace pulled back just enough for him to look into her dark brown eyes. "So you're saying you missed me?" She pressed her hips tighter against his, and her breath hitched when his erection twitched against the crotch of his jeans.

"You could say so."

"Well, why don't you step into my office and tell me all about it," Lily-Grace proposed. She pulled her keys from her pocket and pressed the button to open the rear door of her shiny new car. It lifted up, revealing quite the setup in the rear bed of the SUV. Jesse stepped closer to inspect the blanket she'd laid down and the little hurricane lantern she'd used to light the space. There was a large bowl with two bottles of sparkling water on ice.

"This is pretty damn romantic."

"Come on, girl, up!" Clementine jumped right into the rear of the SUV and made herself comfortable in the far corner. Then Lily-Grace took Jesse's hand and pulled him down to sit beside her. She grabbed her phone and a second later Sade came floating through the speakers.

"What's on your mind, hot stuff?" she said as she gave his shoulder a nudge.

Jesse couldn't help but laugh. "Sexy daddy. Hot stuff. You're really trying to give me a big head."

"Nope, not gonna say it. That's too easy."

Jesse sighed as he picked up Lily-Grace's hand and held it between both of his. She moved closer and put her head on his shoulder. This was nice. He looked forward to being back in bed together, but he wanted this too. He needed it.

"How do you feel about kids?" he asked her.

"My, Mr. Pleasant. You sure do move fast!" She laughed.

"I'm serious."

"I love the idea of kids. I hope to have a few someday via surrogate. I will not be opening *this* baby factory for occupants," she said, patting her stomach.

"Hmmm." He wanted kids too, he just realized he didn't care how they arrived. "Good to know."

"What's got you thinking about babies?"

"I'm just thinking about my life. Thinking about what I want. I'm not going to run for office. I'm turning it down." He told her about the situation with Golden Gulch and how that gave him the light-bulb moment he needed. "I have a good feeling about it. I think Zach and I are ready for this."

"That's amazing. It sounds like a busy day, but a good day. What's got you so down?"

"I got to the *daddy doesn't love me* portion of therapy today."

"Oh! It goes well with *why can't I have a mom like the other girls at camp* moment. What did your therapist say?"

"He asked if I could tell Senior how I feel."

"Can you?"

"Baby steps. I'm just learning to channel my rage. Productive conversations with your parents about how they fucked you up is more a level-two move."

"What's the best-case scenario? If you did talk to him."

Jesse had pictured it, anytime his brothers had a problem or Lilah raged about her own dad. What would be different if Senior was someone Jesse felt he could rely on? Every time, the picture dissolved into a memory of his grandfather's smile, and then reality swooped back in and took its place. Senior had made his decision and his decision was to leave.

"Honestly. I don't know."

"Well, look, you've made epic strides in the department of man tackles emotions, so I think you can cut yourself a little slack here. You are definitely not the first person to have complicated relationships with their parents."

"True. Enough about us Pleasants. How was your day?"

"Oh, you know, using the fact that I had the best sex of my life last night to distract from the fact that I need to make some big decisions pretty soon."

Now that he knew a career in Washington was off the table, he hoped Lily-Grace would stick around, but he understood if she couldn't. Charming was growing, but it was still small in comparison to San Francisco. She clearly needed a break, but he could see her getting bored here by the middle of the summer. He wouldn't dwell on that though. They were together now.

"People keep reaching out to me to see if I'm available for this and that. Consulting gigs, investment opportunities, I'm just—"

Jesse looked over at her as she let out a watery laugh. He put his arm around her and held her tight. "What's wrong?"

"I'm afraid. Part of me feels like I need to go back and kick in the doors at Ulway, but part of me just wants to give up and hide. I mean, being harassed was super fun and all, but I keep thinking about how much I've never actually enjoyed any of my jobs, any of my projects. I enjoyed the thrill of being ahead of the curve in terms of where tech was heading. I really enjoyed the money I made, but I don't want to go back to that world, and that scares me. I feel like I failed, like I thought I was tough enough to power through the heartless aspects of it.

"And I'm ashamed too. I know I worked with some

shitty people and I should have walked away sooner or done something."

"I'm trying to picture you as some sort of Silicon Valley Batman. Righting the wrongs of the tech world."

"I would look good in the outfit."

"My therapist would say this is a time for you to be kind to yourself."

"Oh yeah? What would Jesse Pleasant say?"

"That I've never been in your shoes and I can't imagine how you feel, but I just want to be there for you."

"You're sweet, you know that? I can't believe I was ready to fight you."

"I'm a new man. You should expect some deliveries tomorrow," Jesse said, just as Sade was cut off by Lily-Grace's ringtone. She reached for her phone, then immediately silenced it. Jesse may have been imagining things, but he could have sworn she tensed at whatever number she saw there on the screen. "More spam callers?"

"Yes," she said, with a humorous scoff. "I just got this car, but the warranty is already in danger of expiring. My next gig should be putting an end to the spam calls. Wait, did you say something about a delivery?"

"Yeah. You had some good stuff on your Pinterest board."

"Will it be delivered in a horse trailer?"

"You really want a horse, don't you?" Jesse said, keeping the other thought that rolled through his head to himself. *Because I'll buy you a horse. I'll buy you anything.*

"I do, but I need to figure out where I'm going to be before I become a horse mom. One step at a time—Hey, you came over here so we could make out." Before Jesse could respond, Lily-Grace made herself comfortable in his lap. She draped her arms around his shoulders, looking into his eyes, the sweetest smile tipping up the corner of her beautifully full lips. He couldn't help but laugh when she met his wide-eyed look of awe with a wink. His fingers spread out over her back, feeling the dip of her waist, the curve of her hips.

Jesse wondered how long this feeling would last. This perfect thing between them that didn't magically fix everything, but that made Jesse feel he was capable of so much more. That he was finally capable of letting someone in. He wanted to share everything with Lily-Grace. He cared for her. He trusted her, and when he thought about what he planned to do next with Golden Gulch, he wanted to end every day talking to her about it. He realized as she closed the distance between them and took his lips in a soft kiss, he cherished Lily-Grace as a new lover and as a friend.

"Stay," Jesse said. It slipped out, but he couldn't take it back. "Stay in Charming."

"And raise horse children with you?" she whispered against his lips before she kissed him again.

"Girl, you're gonna be a single horse mom. But we can go half on some other things together."

She pulled back so she could see his face again. "I want to," she said, her voice soft. "I want to stay. I've missed my dad and—there's you. I need to think about it though. Okay?"

He knew what she wasn't saying, and it was the smart thing to do. She wanted to do what was the best for her, long term. He wanted that for her too. He wanted her to be as sure as he was. He wanted her to have that same moment of clarity that made her feel, without a doubt, she was taking the right next step. He'd survive if she walked away and returned to the Bay Area, or flew off to some other city or even country to start something fresh, but that piece of his heart she'd carried in her hand since they were nine years old would always be hers, forever.

Lily-Grace smoothed her hand over his chest, soothing the emotions warring inside of him.

"But," she said. "Your opinions have been added to the record and they will be taken into consideration by the board."

"I appreciate that consideration." Jesse pulled her close again, kissing her until they were both breathless.

Chapter 18

Lily-Grace sat on the edge of her bed, still wrapped in her towel. She looked at the jewelry gift box still sitting on top of her covers. She knew Jesse was serious when he said to expect a delivery, but she hadn't expected her morning to end with two dozen roses and a Vienza tennis bracelet she'd been meaning to buy herself for her birthday. She appreciated that he took her love language seriously and she hoped she was reciprocating in the ways he needed. Their night together hadn't been as pornographic as she would have liked, but she was happy he'd come over. She was still basking in the fuzzy glow of the time they'd spent together. She couldn't wait to see him again.

Her phone screen lit up from its spot on the bed, and even though it was a text from Jenny, her mood immediately shifted. He'd only left one message, but Dane had called her three times the night before from an unknown number. She didn't listen to the voicemail until she was in bed. Same shit over and over. *Come back. She'd made her point. No reason to throw things between them away.* And the worst part. He loved her. She knew he was getting desperate then, but in the most foolish way.

She'd felt strongly for Dane, but they'd never used the L-word out loud. Something in her gut wouldn't let her do it. She pinned that on the nature of the Dominant/ submissive relationship, the terms and conditions of that, and how the sex and the power exchange they shared behind closed doors came first. But now she could see the knot in her gut was trying to tell her something more. That relationship with him lacked a whole lot, including the ease, the silliness, and the warmth she was getting from Jesse. A warmth she realized she didn't want to live without ever again, even if Jesse wasn't her one true love.

Knowing that Jesse wanted her to stay, and the soft, gentle way he'd accepted her need to think about it, put Dane's behavior on stark display. Yes, the bar was in hell. But now she had no doubt in her mind that leaving Dane had been the right thing to do, and while she'd been de-tangling her hair in the shower, she'd finally come up with a plan. Wherever she ended up, she was going to tell Dane that if he contacted her again, she was going to the cops. They were done, and no amount of texts and calls was going to change that.

She looked at her phone again and knew she had to do it now. Waiting would just give him more time to think his persistent hounding was okay. Her finger hovered over his still-blocked contact page, and she realized the last thing she wanted to hear was his voice. She needed to email him. It would save her the stress of all the argu-ing and sweet-talking he would try to pull if he had her on the line. All the reminiscing. That motherfucker loved to reminisce. It used to be a part of their foreplay, but she wasn't his anymore, and she didn't care how hot and heavy things had been between them once upon a time. It was most certainly over, and she had moved on.

Emailing him would also create a paper trail in the event she needed to reach out to the authorities. She didn't think it would get to that point. Dane liked power and control. He didn't like to be inconvenienced, and even a friendly conversation with a cop would feel beneath him and a waste of time. He would know she was serious and finally move on himself.

She switched over to her email app and drafted something short and to the point. Their relationship was over. They had no outstanding business between them. She had none of his things, he had nothing of hers. His continued reaching out, especially from different numbers, was beginning to border on harassment and it needed to stop immediately. He had no reason to reach out to her in the future, and should refrain from doing so.

She thought of how to end the email seven or eight different ways, including a middle-finger emoji or a dramatic GOODBYE FOREVER, but she thought *This will be our final correspondence* was good enough. She read it twice and then hit send before she could talk herself out of it. She closed out her email and stared at her phone, foolishly afraid of how Dane would react. She didn't give a shit how Dane would feel when he read it. What his lingering feelings were and whatever emotions the email brought up were his and his alone to deal with, away from her phone and her in-box.

Lily-Grace jumped, her heart lodging tight in her throat as her phone started ringing in her hand. It was her father. She answered, adrenaline making her hand shake.

"Daddio, what can I do for you?" Hopefully he didn't

notice the tremor in her voice. She didn't want to worry him.

"My Lilybug. Could you please check my room and see if you can find my wallet? I've left without it, and I'm taking Miss Leona to lunch. I think I left it in my pants last night."

"One moment, please." Lily-Grace slipped on a T-shirt and hurried down to her father's bedroom. His pants were hanging over the end of his armchair, and sure enough, she could see his wallet weighing it down. She pulled it and smiled at how it was packed with neatly folded receipts. His personal bookkeeping system would horrify his clients.

"Got it."

"Do you mind bringing it over to the office?"

"Any excuse to take Knight Rider out for a spin. I'm on it."

"I would think you'd come up with a more appropriate name for that tank," he joked.

"Knight Tank it is. I just got out of the shower. I'll be there in . . . twenty-six minutes."

"Much appreciated."

She ended the call, then went to finish getting dressed. She didn't see a need to wait for a special occasion, so she slipped on her new bracelet from Jesse. It went perfectly with her T-shirt and jeans. She triple-checked to make sure she had all her things, including her own wallet, before she locked up the house and jumped in the car.

There was a new email alert on her phone when she

set it in its holder. She knew she shouldn't check it but she did. It was an email from Dane.

I assume you've moved on. Wishing you and Jesse all the best.

She scowled as she clicked on the link he'd included below the message. It was the link to the article about the date auction. Her eyes rolled on their own as she closed the article just as quickly and put her phone on Do Not Disturb. Dane probably had a Google alert on her name, which fine, whatever, if that was how he wanted to spend his pathetic time, have at it. She quickly snapped an adorable selfie with her fingers delicately placed under her chin, showing off the tennis bracelet, then sent it to Jesse. Maybe after she'd dropped off her father's wallet she'd see if he was free for lunch.

Jesse was gonna do it. He was gonna take a selfie. He'd just gotten off the phone with Cynthia, thanking her and the team at A New Way Forward for their interest and faith in him, but he was going to have to decline. She understood his reasoning, even though he didn't go into to detail, but she had siblings of her own and could see how hard it would be to walk away from his brother and the family business. She wished him well, which Jesse appreciated, but if he was keeping it all the way real, he'd already moved on from the conversation before the screen on his phone dimmed. He needed to text a certain someone back.

Jesse liked the idea of him and Lily-Grace sending pictures to each other throughout the day, but while she showed off the gift he'd bought her, she'd also sent over a beautiful picture of herself. He wanted to send something back, something more than a text that said *Damn, girl, you look good*, just to let her know he was thinking about her. He looked around his office, trying to find the best spot for this momentous occasion. Lilah and Vega were always taking selfies, and Evie had mastered the art of it, but he wasn't a beautiful woman. Sam took the occasional selfie for his fans on Instagram, but that was different. He had actual fans.

Jesse went over to the window that looked out over the front of the property all the way down to the road. He'd heard Lilah go on and on about how Black people looked best in natural sunlight. He sized himself up on screen and snapped five or six terrible pictures. He tried again and almost dropped his phone as Zach knocked and opened the door at the same time.

"Hey—what are you doing?"

"Uh, nothing." Jesse moved back over to his desk like he wasn't completely busted. "What's going on?"

"Nothing my ass. What the fuck are you doing?" Zach chuckled.

"I was . . . taking a picture to send to Lily-Grace."

"You are really into her." Zach smiled as he flopped down into one of the chairs on the other side of Jesse's desk.

"I may have been looking for stables closer to her house this morning."

"Stables for what—are you gonna buy her a horse?" Zach's eyebrows shot up to his hairline.

"She expressed an interest in acquiring a horse. There were some conversations about love languages, and I'm about twenty years behind, buying any romantic partner any kind of gifts. I figure what I could have spent over the years might add up to the price of a horse and a year of boarding."

"I mean, you could board it here."

"Yeah, but I would like it to be Lily-Grace's thing completely. Separate from the ranch. And if I find the right horse, say something as handsome as Bam Bam, the guests will want to ride him. I don't want that."

"First of all, you aren't going to find a horse as pretty as Bam Bam," Zach said, defending his youngest horsey son. Jesse was serious, though, he realized. He wanted to give Lily-Grace something special, something she wanted. When he didn't respond, Zach knew Jesse was serious too. "Call Peggy Garcia. The Whittiers are moving at the end of the month, and they are taking both of their mares with them. She'd happily take your stable fees."

Jesse knew Peggy well. He'd call her soon. "Thanks."

"So this is what it's like?" Zach said. He settled back in the leather chair, shaking his head as a knowing smile turned up the edges of his mustache.

"What do you mean?"

"This is Jesse in love."

"I'm not in love."

"The hell you aren't. I mean, I've never seen you with a girlfriend before—"

"She's not my girlfriend," Jesse amended. Yes, his feelings were strong, but Lily-Grace needed time to figure things out and he wanted to respect that, and he wanted his family to respect that too, even if they were just clowning him a bit. If Lily-Grace was going to be his anything, she was going to be the one to make that call.

Zach bit his lips, which was new. Usually he'd come back with some Corie-like quip, giving him a hard time for being sensitive or having a temper like Senior.

"Sorry," Zach said. "I've never seen you care about anyone like this, but it makes sense. Hell, you spoil Vega and she's your grandmother's assistant's girlfriend. It makes sense that you would go all out for a woman you have real feelings for."

"You don't think I'm making an ass out of myself?"

"Nah. I basically bought Evie a restaurant. You and Sam chipped in. And I'm not even mad that she doesn't want to run it anymore. That's what intense feelings do to you, man. I'd give Evie anything she wanted, on the right side of the law or whatever."

"Yeah." Jesse sighed. He wasn't in love, but Zach was right about one thing. The feelings were intense. "She said she wanted a horse, and my brain just said, well, buy her a horse then."

"You know who couldn't say shit about this?"

"Who?"

"Senior."

That made Jesse laugh a little. His brother was absolutely right. Their dad gave their mom everything and anything she wanted, and had their whole marriage. Any bit of prize money he won, part of it went right into a Whatever Regina Wants Fund. And now the woman was living large, shopping her way across Europe. Most of the money they'd spent on Zach and Evie's wedding, down to the elaborate centerpieces, had been to make their mom happy.

Zach leaned forward. "Majesty."

"Oh fuck!"

Zach put his hands up, the universal gesture for *See what I mean.* Sam's prized black Friesian, the bane of all of their existence, a walking asshole in horse form, had been a gift for their mother. A gift she waved off. She was sweet about it, but she waved the stunning filly off all the same. Worked out great for Sam. He loved that damn horse.

"You go ahead and buy your lady friend a horse. Worse case scenario, things don't work out—and they will, 'cause I know that look in your eye and that is the look of a man definitely headed to the altar. But if things don't work out"—Zach rapped his knuckles on the surface of Jesse's mahogany desk—"we give whatever horse you pick out a home right here. And the ranch will pay you back."

"Hmm, you really found that silver lining."

"It's what I do, baby. Anyway, I'll let you get back to your selfies."

"Bah, I bet they all came out like shit."

"Here, let me see."

Jesse pulled up his camera roll and reluctantly handed over his phone. Zach looked at the pictures like he was examining an X-ray. "Okay, you're trying to be too serious. You gotta loosen up a little bit. Or go full completely serious, but we gotta do a whole-ass photo shoot."

"Didn't you come in here to ask me something?"

"I did, but this is more important. Okay, stand up and push your chair back. Put your left foot on the seat of the chair." Jesse followed Zach's directions, feeling like a complete jackass as he hiked up his pant leg. "Okay, hand under your chin and make that face you make when I say some of the funniest shit you've ever heard."

Jesse blanked out his expression completely. His brother wasn't nearly as funny as he thought he was.

"That's it. Okay, send that to her." Zach handed over the phone.

"I look stupid as hell."

"Exactly. She'll appreciate that you can laugh at yourself. A little."

"Fine." Jesse quickly dropped the picture in their text thread and hit send.

Art Directed by Zach Pleasant.

He tossed his phone on the desk as the heat of first-hand embarrassment spread over his face. "What did you want to talk to me about?"

"Oh! I'm not supposed to say anything, but did you know this whole thing with Lilah and the vet is a sham?"

"Yes, and that's supposed to be a secret. She's trying to get Uncle Gerald off her back."

"That's genius. How can he be mad about an animal doctor who used to play for the Steelers?"

"Exactly. I'm just hoping none of this blows up in her face. Miss Leona thinks it's real. I'm having drinks with him tonight actually. I'll see if I can get his side of the story while I'm at it. I'm working on making friends."

"That's a great idea." The loud ping of Jesse's text alert filled the air. "That her?" Zach asked, waggling his eyebrows.

"Yeah." Jesse unlocked the phone and tried not to react to the message she'd sent back.

This is literally the best thing that has ever
happened to me. Tell Zach to order me a few
wallet-sized and one in a gilded frame to hang over
my mantel. *Hubba hubba*
Also your junk looks amazing.

Jesse's cheeks set full ablaze as he went back to the
picture and realized the way he'd lifted up his leg there
left a very clear outline of his bulge on display. He didn't
know how to respond to that other than to say thank you.

"What did she say?"

"She approves."

"See." Zach stood up and adjusted his suit jacket.
"Time to start looking for a horse."

Jesse had no idea why he was nervous. He'd met
plenty of people for drinks and meals before. When Fetu
agreed to meet him, Jesse had been pushing the reality
of their appointment around his head, pushing it off like
that Thursday was somehow months away and not that
night. Lily-Grace had done her best to psyche him up
when they met up for lunch, but Jesse was still having
mixed feelings about the whole thing. What were friends,
anyway?

He pulled into the parking lot of Claim Jumpers and
headed inside the bar. His brothers and cousins loved
the place, but he hadn't been in a while. Still, the food
was surprisingly good and it was the only cowboy bar in
the whole desert valley that played country and hip-hop.
The DJ had a gift.

He said what's up to the doorman, Judd, who he'd

played football with in high school, then spotted Fetu at the bar. He already had two beers in his hands.

Jesse made his way across the room as Beyoncé's "Daddy Lessons" blared through the speakers. He greeted a few members of the ranch staff that seemed shocked and terrified to see him outdoors after hours, not wearing a suit. He'd changed his clothes four times before he realized jeans and a long-sleeve T-shirt would be perfectly fine. He had his security blanket, aka his black Stetson to round out the look.

"Hey!" Fetu said, with a cheery smile Jesse couldn't reciprocate 'cause the muscles in his face just didn't react that way under pressure.

"Hey, how's it going?"

"Good, man. Good. I got the first round and ordered like two pounds of wings. Lilah said they were good."

"She's right."

"Good. Let's get a table."

Jesse took the Tecate from Fetu's hand and followed him over to an empty four-top in the corner. "Thanks for doing this," Fetu said.

"What do you mean?"

"Well, Doc Vasquez told me he told you to take me out, help me get my bearings around here. Even if it was a pity ask, I appreciate it."

"Well, if it makes you feel any better, it was a bit of a mutual pity ask. My therapist and my"—he almost said *my girl* but he caught himself—"my family think I could stand to make a few friends on my own."

"Yeah, Lilah mentioned you were more on the shy, reserved side. Listen, I get it. I'm loud and always down for a good time, but after I left the league I realized how hard it is to make real friends as an adult. Especially if you don't lead with your championship ring. Didn't make that easier on myself by moving all the way the fuck out here where I don't know anyone. Here"—Fetu held up his bottle in salute—"here's to being old as fuck and just figuring out how to schedule your own playdates."

"Jesus," Jesse said with a painful groan. "Amen to that." They both drank, and then Jesse remembered they'd have to follow up that toast with an actual conversation. "So how are things going so far?"

"Okay, I guess. I'm over on Rosewood, and so far my neighbors have been pretty welcoming. I got an honest-to-goodness fresh apple pie from the lady who runs Mom's Country Orchard."

"Ah. Miss Alison. She's great."

"I didn't realize there was such a thriving apple industry out here."

"If California is gonna do anything it's grow some produce," Jesse said. He decided to spare Fetu a whole explanation about how the desert part of Charming confused some people and how where they were in relationship to the southern tip of the Sierra Nevada range, the ground water was plentiful and made for perfect conditions for farming on the east side of town. "So I have to ask. This thing with you and Lilah? Everything's cool there?"

Fetu laughed and took another long swig from his beer. "Absolutely not."

"Why? What's going on?"

"Well, she told me all about her dad. And I get it. My family can be intense too. So when she came up with this plan I thought sure. What's the best thing to have when you move to a new town? A fake girlfriend."

Jesse did laugh a little at that. "But?"

"Well, now I have a crush on her, and I know as soon as I tell her she's gonna break it off. Which she should, because she doesn't feel the same way about me."

Jesse winced. He wished he could give Fetu some good news, the inside track to how Lilah has secretly confessed to developing feelings for him since they hatched this plan, but that wasn't the case. The only time she mentioned Fetu was to say how well their plan was going. "Do you want me to talk to her?"

"Nah. It's okay. I'm going to eventually. Besides, nothing builds character like a little heartache. I just need to mentally prepare to be fake-dumped and for real friend-zoned, all in one conversation. Not that I don't want to be friends with her. She's funny. She's smart. She's sweet as hell. She knows more about football—fuck, all sports—than I do. She was dropping stats from the cricket league on me yesterday. But sometimes it's hard to re-member all that fake kissing and cuddling we did for show wasn't real."

Jesse couldn't help but think of Lily-Grace, and the real possibility of her leaving town felt like a punch to the chest. Fetu was on to something though. He needed to prepare for it, just in case. Good thing he already had a therapist.

Chapter 19

Lily-Grace hadn't been up so early in a long time. When Jesse suggested she go for a trail ride with his family, she figured they'd set out sometime around noon. Have a glamping lunch out in the foothills and make their way back.

Nope. Zach Pleasant liked to be on his way out of the barn when the first wisp of a promise of daylight crested over the mountains. Which meant Lily-Grace had to be up and caffeinated before the sun came up. Even her father, who was an early riser, was still asleep when she left the house and headed toward Big Rock Ranch. Jesse wasn't going to ride with them. His horse-phobia was still a thing, but he wanted to escort her to the barn himself and see them off. After, they were all going to have brunch at Miss Leona's. And that was only phase one.

She had asked Jesse for another swim lesson, which she hoped would turn into a boning lesson, and then they were going to go down to the senior center that night to play bingo. Afterward, they were gonna meet Jenny and Ned at the Marriott for drinks. Lily-Grace was going to have to fit in a nap in there somewhere. Hopefully a naked nap with Jesse.

She pulled up to the gates of Big Rock, an even bigger smile touching her lips when Jesse and another man came into view out on the wide dirt road. Jesse was holding some sort of box in his hand, probably another gift. A rare edition of a title by her favorite author, and another dozen roses, had shown up at her house the morning before. She turned into the entrance and rolled down her window.

"Howdy, stranger. You looking for a lift?"

"I believe I am. Lily-Grace, this is Ted Melvin. He's a member of ranch security."

Ted smiled and tipped his cowboy hat in her direction. "I've heard a lot about you from the guest services staff. First person to slip into a conference room."

"Oh my God." She didn't know whether to be embarrassed or proud. She nodded in Jesse's direction. "Look, that was all his fault."

"He took the blame, but my crew still had a meeting about it. You revealed a weakness in the system."

"Great." She laughed. Jesse shook Ted's hand and climbed in the SUV. When he was buckled in they waved goodbye to Ted and she had Jesse direct her through the property toward the stables. There was another man dressed nearly exactly like Ted pacing near the stables, navy blue canvas coat and tan cowboy hat. He nodded at Jesse and kept up his pacing. Probably the night security guard just about to finish his shift. Jesse showed her where to park, then turned toward her as soon as the car was still.

"Good morning," he said, his voice rough and deep.

Lily-Grace knew it would take some convincing, but Jesse would be amazing at phone sex. Yes, it was barely six a.m., and that's where her mind decided to go. From the way Jesse was looking at her lips he may have been right there with her.

"Good morning. Do you want to kiss me?"

"I do."

"Alright then."

Jesse shifted the box in his lap and leaned over the center console, planting a sound kiss right on her mouth. Lily-Grace responded in kind, letting her tongue slip past the soft part in his lips. She didn't know if she could give this up, give him up. When she pulled back she could feel the goofy smile on her face. This was the perfect way to start an early day.

"What you got in that box there?" she teased.

"I'll show you in a minute," he replied before he hummed a few notes to the all-time classic "Dick in a Box."

"I mean, if that's what it is, I can happily go riding another time." It hadn't been a whole week, but Jesse had reawakened the full potential of her sex drive. Jonesing didn't begin to describe what she was struggling with.

"I'm joking. It's something a bit more wholesome than my genitals. Go ahead and open it." He held the box secure while Lily-Grace pulled off the lid. Inside was an adult sized, near replica of the pink cowboy hat he'd given her in elementary school. She turned on the overhead light before she pulled it out of the box so she could get a clear view of every piece of glitter, every fake rhinestone and, of course, the white and pink faux feathers tucked into the satin ribbon band.

"Jesse." She looked up at his handsome face, the truth

she knew she could share with him, right on the tip of her tongue.

"Yes."

She took him lightly by the chin, the soft hair of his goatee tickling her fingers as she kissed him again. "This is the ugliest cowboy hat I've ever seen." It was cute. So cute, an adorable nod to their past and the promise of a future, but there was no way she could be seen out in that thing in daylight. She'd be shamed in the papers.

"I had a feeling you'd say that. Lift that up right there."

There was a bit of tissue over what Lily-Grace thought was a cardboard hat form underneath. It was not. She let out a long breath of awe as she moved the paper all the way back and revealed a beautiful light gray cowboy hat. She pulled it out of the box and turned it around in her hand. This wasn't an item on her gift board, but it was perfect.

"Jesse," she said, her breath still tight her throat. "I love it." She slipped it on and it fit perfectly over the two braids currently hanging over her shoulders. "How do I look?"

"Beautiful. You can use that one for every day, and I was hoping you'd wear pinky-sparkles later with your birthday suit."

"Oh, so you have been thinking some ungentlemanly thoughts."

"All week long. I have one more thing to show you."

"Is it in your pants?"

"There's that, but I wanted to show you something else." Jesse pulled out his phone and showed her a listing for a spotted saddle horse named Monty. She looked at the specs, a six-year-old gray-and-white trail gelding for sale up north. "You'll see when you go inside. One of Zach's horses, Bam Bam, is the ranch's most popular horse. Evie will probably ride him. Monty looks different, but he reminds me of Bam Bam. What do you think?"

"He's gorgeous. I'm sure the guests will love him too. I can appreciate the spotted motif," she joked.

"He's not for the ranch," Jesse said. "He'd be for you. There's a spot to board him over at Sunrise Stables, so you wouldn't have to deal with ranch guests here. I also found a stable up in the Bay Area right outside of the city if you decide you're not going to stay."

"Are you serious?"

"Yes." He took his phone back and then showed her a beautiful brown thoroughbred with a black mane. "This little girl is available too, but Monty seemed more your style."

"She's beautiful, but Monty seems like he has a little more spunk. Are you sure? I was kidding. I mean I do want to get a horse. And a dog actually, but you don't have to do this."

"I want to. I'll pay for the stable fees for a year and if, you know—" He shrugged, like he couldn't say the words *if we break up*. Still, she knew what he was trying to say. "We can meet him next weekend if you like."

"I—I would like that. Thank you." Lily-Grace glanced up as another set of headlights appeared in the distance and then another behind that. She was a little relieved they were about to be interrupted. She was also in shock a little. She knew she was getting the real thing with Jesse, but she was feeling a little overwhelmed at the moment. She knew why. Still, now was definitely not the time to consider the ins and outs of it. "Looks like

your family is here. Are you sure you don't want to come
with us?"

"If I get on a horse for the first time in three decades,
it's not going to be in front of you. Let me hold on to a
slice of my dignity."

"Okay, okay." Lily-Grace laughed. It was like him
asking her if she wanted to go deep-sea diving. She was
a little disappointed they wouldn't be spending time out
on the trail together, but she understood. She'd have to
come up with her own fantasies about how good Jesse
looked on horseback. The two pickup trucks parked beside
them and she recognized one as Fetu's newly branded
truck from his practice. A moment later, Jesse's brothers
and cousin piled out along with two of their dogs.

"Oh, where's Clementine?"

"She's still sleeping. You'll see her later. Come on, let's
go," Jesse said, giving her thigh a squeeze. He took her
hand once she met him around the back of her SUV and
together they went to catch up with the group. He did a
quick round of re-introductions. Zach and Evie offered
their warm hellos, along with Jesse's baby brother, Sam,
who she knew for obvious actual famous-person reasons.
And his girlfriend, Amanda. She remembered everyone
from the night at the Charming Inn when things between
her and Jesse were a little more strained. And of course
Lilah and Fetu, who were real close to claiming the real
title of Charming's new hot couple.

"Thanks for having me along," she said to Zach as
they walked toward the barn.

"Of course. More the merrier. You can pick out a
horse you want to ride and we'll get you all set up." The

security guard opened the door for them, but she noticed Jesse was hanging back.

"Hey, what's up?" she asked.

"Nothing. Just wanted to give you a proper goodbye. You're in good hands with Zach. And Sam. I'll see you in a bit." Jesse leaned down to kiss her, but Lily-Grace backed up as she realized what he meant.

"Wait—you're not even coming inside?"

"No, I usually don't. You'll have fun with them. I know you will. I'll go make brunch with Miss Leona and you can finish your ride with a huge meal."

"Oh." He had a legit fear, but she'd hoped he would at least see her off. She shook off the thought and tried to muster a smile. "O-okay. That sounds good."

"But," he replied, his tone suddenly lighter, "I can come in with you while you pick out your trail companion for the day. Just keep Majesty the hell away from me." He called out the last bit to his brother Sam.

"Like she'd want anything to do with a peasant like you," Sam yelled back.

"Are you sure?" Lily-Grace laughed.

"Yeah, I'm sure. After you."

Lily-Grace walked into the barn and took in how spacious and modern it was. It was clear the space was massive from the exterior, and obviously they needed enough horses to accommodate all of their guests, but she wasn't expecting so many stalls. She looked back at Jesse, who looked like he'd just been told it was his turn for execution. Lily-Grace took his large hand in hers and pulled it behind her back so he was forced to walk close, right behind her.

"Okay, which one's Majesty? Over there with Sam?"

Sam and Amanda were greeting a beautiful dark chestnut horse about midway down the barn.

"No, that's Fickle. Amanda usually rides her. Majesty is down at the end." Like she'd been summoned, a gorgeous black mare stuck her muzzle out over the stall. "That's her. Little asshole."

"Sam, what's the deal with your horse?" Lily-Grace chuckled.

"Okay, so she is kind of an—"

"Babe." Amanda shook her head.

"I mean—" Sam tried again. "She's just spirited. She's a great horse. She hasn't maimed anyone in at least three months," Sam joked, his tone dry.

"Okay, Zach, who is the sweetest of the bunch?" she asked.

"Well, the sweetest is Françoise, but she's not a trail mount. Come on." Zach stepped away from Evie and the black-and-white painted horse she was chatting with, and led Lily-Grace deeper into the barn. He stopped a few stalls down and leaned his elbow over the door. "Good morning, madam. Someone wants to meet you."

A giant dark grey draft horse slowly brought its massive head over the stall door.

"Her and her brother Philippe do all our heavy lifting. Including pulling Santa's sleigh during the Christmas parade," Zach said, his voice filled with pride.

"How do you feel about Françoise?" she asked Jesse.

"Alright. She's been a respected employee of the ranch for some time now." His voice was still tight, but he'd relaxed a little.

"Can you saddle her?" Lily-Grave asked. "Or has she just been a working girl her whole life?"

"Oh yeah. Our foreman, Felix, loves taking her for quick solo rides around the property."

"Hmm, good to know. Okay, who would you suggest for my first outing? I'm confident, but rusty."

"Well, I'd say Bam Bam. Crowd favorite. Sweet as hell, but Evie's taken him today. May I suggest—" Zach slowly spun around, tapping his index finger against his lips. Lily-Grace leaned back against Jesse and felt him exhale a little. She wished he could join them, and more so when he dropped a soft kiss to the side of her neck.

"I think we're gonna have to go with the freshest MC this side of the Sierra Madre."

"Oh, good choice," Sam said from Fickle's stall.

Zach turned on his heels and motioned for them to follow. Two stalls down they stopped to be greeted by the ass end of a tall gelding. Sensing he had visitors, the horse turned around, revealing a black muzzle that blended seamlessly into its brown body. His black mane was pulled back in an impressive fishtail braid. Lily-Grace didn't hide the snort that slipped out of her.

"Why is this horse prettier than I am?"

"He knows how to find his light." Sam laughed.

"May I present DJ Clip Clop," Zach said. "He does very well with the teens. Big personality, but a bit of a human whisperer himself. He knows when to rein it in, and also takes direction from my noble steed, Steve, very well."

"Great, DJ Clip Clop it is." She glanced back at Jesse,

who was looking at her and not the horse. "Will you stay until we set out?"

"Yeah, I can do that."

"Great."

Zach slapped his thigh. "Alright. Let's get you set up."

Zach was very serious about getting a joke off at least every other minute, but he was a shockingly good teacher. He patiently walked Lily-Grace through each step of getting DJ Clip Clop ready for the trail, while Lilah helped Fetu get set up on a horse named Bert. Jesse posted up by the door, well out of the way, but every time she looked in his direction he had a little smile for her. Finally they were ready to go, seven horses and their riders. And two dogs.

She fell in line behind Zach and Evie, with the rest of the gang behind her, and Sam bringing up the rear. She waved goodbye to Jesse and decided to focus on what her horse was doing instead of watching him disappear as they rounded the side of the barn and headed for the trailhead.

She realized pretty quickly why Zach liked to head out this early. The cool morning air on her face and sky brightening over the mountains was something she couldn't describe. Good company welcoming her already, like she was family. Sam's demands for a sing-along rendition of "Can We Talk" as they crossed a small stream. Lily-Grace couldn't remember the last time she'd felt this free. She took a deep breath as the sun finally came into view, and all she could think of was Jesse.

All the things he'd said about his family, how alienated he felt, even though he was close with his brothers. She understood why now. He'd spent his whole life missing moments like this. She absolutely understood his fear, but couldn't believe this was a property he owned and he'd never gotten to experience it this way. She hated that they weren't experiencing this moment together now.

Dane's dumb ass entered her mind too, but in a way that made her realize how much of Charming she'd missed in the years that she'd been gone. How much time she'd wasted with him. Of course she came home for holidays, but even that ended when she made enough money to fly her father wherever he wanted to go. Her good memories of this hometown of hers involved Jenny, and her dad, and sometimes those thoughts were still clouded by the memories of all the people who had bullied her. She had to admit to herself, she'd never seen this side of Charming and she'd never experienced it with the Pleasants. Or Fetu.

They stopped at another wider stream and let the horses rest, when Sam turned to her.

"I'm gonna stay out of Jesse's business," he said.

"No it's fine. Get all in his business," she replied, laughing a bit.

"Nah. I was gonna say I'm glad you could come, because the way Miss Leona's been talking about your dad, you might be family sooner than we thought."

"Oh, I believe that. He is really into your grandmother. Like really into her." She didn't want to blow up his spot, just in case he hadn't dropped the L-word to Mrs. Lovell's face, but she'd never seen her father so in love. She was surprised that *he* hadn't gone horse shopping yet.

"I'll get in your business for a second," Evie said. Lily-Grace glanced up at Clip Clop before she looked back at Evie, who was rubbing her stomach in a very particular way.

"Go for it. I'm an open book until I'm not."

"See, I like you." Evie laughed before she grew serious. "Obviously this thing with you and Jesse is new, and it's clear that he really likes you, just from the fact that he actually set foot in the barn."

"Hey, he came in the barn with me," Fetu teased.

"He really likes you too, Doc. I'm sure."

"Thank God. He's so hot."

"As I was saying. I just—" Evie was definitely about to cry.

"I think what she means to say is thank you," Zach cut in. "You've brought Jesse out of his shell a lot. In a way none of us could. And you too, Fetu. You sexy man, you. It's nice to see Jesse happy and making new friends."

"I was ready to kickbox him in the throat after what happened with my father, but I'm seeing a change too. A huge change from when we were kids. I'm sad he didn't come with us," Lily-Grace said.

"That's right," Sam said. "I keep forgetting you guys did elementary and middle school together. Jesse's basically still the same height he was then so at least there's that. But yeah. He's *really* happy."

"So you're saying I have to marry him?" she joked. Kinda.

Zach's expression dropped suddenly. He dropped Steve's reins and marched right for her. She stood her ground just in case shit was about to get weird. She'd punch Zach Pleasant in the throat if she had to. Both his large palms dropped down to her shoulders. "If we could bind you to this family through means of marriage and make use of that financial genius of yours, I would propose to you on Jesse's behalf."

"Babe, stop!" Evie yelled. "Leave the woman alone."

"I'm trying to help you too, baby. Lily-Grace and that app of hers are the reason I was able to keep not-at-all-creepy tabs on you during college." Zach turned back to Lily-Grace. "We got a big acquisition coming up. Just think about it."

"Ooof, wife and business partner all at once. Let me think it over." She winked at Zach, which seemed to be all he needed to return to his horse. "And if that doesn't work out, as your maybe step-aunt? I think I can still slip you guys a few tips here and there. But it looks like you and Jesse have things well in hand."

"Yes, but your mind, I can't walk away from that time of financial brilliance."

DJ Clip Clop chose that moment to give her a little head butt in the shoulder, as though he agreed.

They stayed at the stream a little longer, then headed back to the ranch. Lily-Grace knew the experience would stick with her for a long time. She just hoped she and Jesse could do more things like that together.

Chapter 20

"I need some more eggs. Any for you?" Jesse asked his grandmother. He had plans for some soufflé omelets somewhat made-to-order. Miss Leona turned from what she was doing at the stove and looked over at the island. They were halfway through making breakfast, enough food to feed their family, their guests, and to get Jesse to at least one p.m.

"I am all set. Mind Goose when you go out there. She's been snippy all week."

"Got it." Jesse headed out back to his grandmother's garden and caught sight of the menacing hen in question. "I got no beef with you, Goose." He made a shooing noise, then his phone vibrated in his back pocket just as he opened the coop. He stepped back, closing the gate, and checked his phone. He felt lighter as soon as he saw the text from Lily-Grace.

On our way back!

Her text came with a selfie of Lily-Grace with DJ Clip Clop. He couldn't help but smile. She was glowing, genuine happiness written all over her face. Buying her something as extravagant as a horse didn't seem like an over-the-top idea anyway. Just as he was about to respond, a text from Zach slid across the top of his screen.

> Hey man, just a heads up. I think Lily-Grace is a little upset you didn't come.

Jesse read the text twice, trying to process what Lily-Grace had just sent him and what his brother was telling him at the same moment. He let out a deep sigh, feeling like his chest was about to cave in. He had a feeling he'd fucked up, sending her off to be the seventh wheel with three couples, even if the thing between Lilah and Fetu was just an act. He was sure she was having a good time, but he knew enough how it felt to be the odd one out, not having a partner. Even if she had a blast, it wasn't hard to imagine that she felt some way about having someone, and him choosing not to be there. Fuck.

He quickly responded to Lily-Grace's text, letting her know he'd be waiting for her outside of his place. Then he switched to his text conversation with his brother.

> Did she say anything?

> Hi, it's Evie. Zach's driving.
> She did mention she wished you'd been there,
> but she had that look on her face
> every time I looked back during our ride.
> Us ladies know that look.

> Thanks for letting me know.

Jesse quickly grabbed some eggs, free of injury from the demonic Goose, and then headed back inside.

"Gang's on their way. I'm gonna go meet them."

"Make sure Lily-Grace and the good doctor know my rules."

"Don't worry. They've been well instructed in post-trail-ride protocol and assigned a shower and a dressing room."

"That's excellent news." She smiled at Jesse and turned back to the sauce she was making. Jesse took off his apron and turned for the door. He stepped over Clementine before another heavy thought occurred to him.

"Miss Leona?" Jesse said.

"Yes, baby. What can I do for you?"

"Is there a reason you stopped riding with Granddad? Or why you don't ride now?"

She turned her burner down and turned to face him. "I don't ride now because if I fell off a horse, my body would immediately turn into dust. I still got it, but I don't got it like that."

"Fair." Jesse chuckled. If Zach was still jumping off horses when they were in their eighties, he'd stage an intervention.

"And as for your grandfather, I never stopped riding with him."

"You didn't?"

"No. At least once a week, we'd go out together. That was our favorite time together. We'd talk or just be silent together. It was those moments that reminded me why I fell in love with him. He's the one who taught me to ride."

"Right, okay."

"Is this about your young lady?" she asked.

"Possibly. I think I should have gone with her today."

"Well, you haven't been near a saddle since you were three years old, so I wouldn't recommend heading right out to the trail, but if you want to spend time with her, I don't know a woman who wouldn't love the idea of a man stepping outside of his comfort zone just so he could spend time with her," she said, but then she frowned a bit and gave him a hard look. "But only do it if you want to, Junior. You've made a lot of changes lately. Good changes. And I love Lily-Grace. She's a wonderful young woman. Just make sure there's a good balance there. Okay?"

"Yes, ma'am. I hear you." And he did. She didn't want his desire to please Lily-Grace to lead to resentment down the road. He'd keep that in mind, because he didn't want that either. "I'm going to go out and meet them."

"Tell Lilah to come see me before she scurries off to shower."

"Will do."

Jesse stepped outside just as Zach pulled into the cul-de-sac. He could see Lily-Grace's SUV and Fetu's truck still making their way up the lane. He walked right for Zach and Evie as they hopped out.

"I gotta ask you something," he said to his brother.

"Yeah, shoot."

"With the help of a licensed therapist to deal with the actual fear, do you think you have the patience to teach me to ride Françoise?"

Zach's eyes popped wide as he nodded. "I think you should learn on Bam Bam, 'cause Françoise is never going out on a trail, but yeah, I can do it if you have the patience to learn."

"Okay. Let's do it."

He ignored the way Zach and Evie were looking at each other, and walked over to his house. He waved Lily-Grace into the driveway, then directed Fetu to park his truck beside her SUV.

Lily-Grace hopped out, that same luminous smile still highlighting her beautiful face. Jesse took her overnight bag out of her hand and pulled her in close for a kiss.

"How was it?" he asked, his gaze still taking in every inch of her.

"Amazing! I'm going to be sore as hell tomorrow. But we had a great time. Your brothers are hilarious. Also, Zach proposed to me on your behalf for tips on the Golden Gulch deal."

"I'm gonna have follow-up questions, but okay."

"You got Fetu, Jesse?" Lilah called out from across the driveway. She was holding hands with the veterinarian in question, and Jesse remembered what Fetu had told him about his feelings for his baby cousin.

"Yeah. Fetu. Got the guest room shower all set up for you."

"You're gonna love it," Lily-Grace assured him.

"Dope. Let's do this." Fetu chuckled. Jesse tried not to cringe as Lilah hopped up on her tiptoes and kissed Fetu on the mouth, then turned and practically skipped back to Miss Leona's, faking that fresh, in-love glow. Fetu's eyes followed her, his cheeks turning dark red as he probably thought about how this situation wasn't getting any easier for him. Jesse might have to talk to Lilah about this genius plan of hers. Fetu was gonna get hurt.

"I desperately need to bathe." Lily-Grace's groan of disgust brought him back to the moment. "I might need a nap later too."

"I think we can manage both. Come, Doc!"

"Right behind you."

Jesse showed Fetu to the guest room and left him to it once he was all squared away. Then he led Lily-Grace down to his bedroom. He sat down on the bed, pulling her close between his spread thighs.

She set her Stetson on the nightstand, then pressed a light kiss to his lips. "Hi."

"How you doing?"

"Better now. Uh, I have something to tell you."

"Sure. Tell me."

She bit her lip, her gaze dipping down to his lips before she looked him in the eye. "I'm gonna stay. I'm gonna move back to Charming."

"Really?" Jesse didn't mean to sound like a kid on Christmas morning, but it was too late.

"I mean, my dad is here, and so is this super-hot guy I want to ask to be my boyfriend."

"The answer is yes, but go on."

Her expression grew serious as she ran her thumb over his shoulder. "I think I was looking at Charming through the lens of a thirteen-year-old with exactly two friends. I was convinced this was a place I would outgrow. Small-town life was too small for me, and I left. I saw the world, and I wouldn't change those experiences—well, the good ones, anyway. But none of those places were home."

"I know the feeling. I thought things would change in undergrad and in grad school, but I just wanted to come back and be on the ranch."

"I really convinced myself there was nothing here for me. But it never occurred to me that mornings like this one were a possibility. Your brothers are funny."

"Oh, so you're saying you're staying for my brothers. Great."

"No." She laughed. "Part of me was so Jesse-drunk, I wasn't thinking clearly, but when we were heading back to the stables this morning, I was thinking about stepping out of my place back in the city. Waiting for my car service, going to some annoying party, or sitting in some boardroom, and I'm just over it. I've been getting offers for meetings all week, and every single one just made my stomach curl, but being here with you and my father and your family? This feels right."

Jesse felt like his heart had just tripled in size. "I just want you to be happy."

"I know." She leaned forward and kissed him again. "I was thinking of maybe starting an animal sanctuary. I looked last night, and there are a bunch of rescues, but somehow there's not a single sanctuary around here. I could open one and give animals their own happily ever after."

"That's an amazing idea."

"Thanks. I have to get my own place in the meantime though. There are a few things I want to try with some nylon rope and a riding crop, but we can't do that under my father's roof. I think I'm gonna head back up north on Monday and settle things up with my place. Rent it out, figure out what things I want to ship back."

"I had some news of my own, but it's not as significant, I don't think."

"I'll be the judge of that. What is it?"

"Well, first I wanted to apologize for not coming with you this morning."

"Jess, it's okay."

"No, it's not. I might live to regret it one way or another"—Jesse winced—"but I asked Zach to teach me how to ride. I can go to Dr. Brooks for the crippling-fear part."

Lily-Grace's mouth popped open, then closed again. "Are you sure?"

"You almost drowned, and then you were willing to get back in the pool the next day. I'm holding on to a fear from a grudge with a horse that's been dead for years. Maybe, while I'm working on some of my issues when it comes to connecting with people, I can take a look at my issues with members of the animal kingdom. And maybe it would be a good idea for me to be comfortable in a barn if I'm going to be owning *another* ranch."

"I am one hundred percent on board. With personal growth, with the horse whispering, with the idea of you up in the saddle. God, I can just picture it. So hot." Lily-Grace paused, the tongue darting out over her bottom lip like she was really taking a moment to process the vision. She shook herself and looked back down at him. "Well, if you're sure, I definitely don't want to stop you. I want to go out with the whole gang again, and I'd love it if you were there too. It was me and *a lot* of couples."

"What's this about my brother proposing to you?"

"He just wants to book me into the family in some way, shape, or form so he can tap into my financial genius. I'll just give him my hourly rate and he can see if he thinks it's worth it. Speaking of your brother. And his wife. Is Evie pregnant?"

"Uh, I don't know," Jesse replied.

"Oh!?" She leaned back, her eyebrows shooting up. "What?"

"Nothing, just another interesting thing to know about you. You, sir, are a terrible liar."

"What? I don't know." They were going to tell the family today and then call their parents tomorrow, but it was still their news to tell.

"Sure. Whatever the truth is, her secret is safe with me."

"I have no idea what you're talking about."

"Uh-huh."

Jesse stood and kissed her on her cheek and then her forehead. "Get cleaned up and then we can eat. I'm gonna make you a soufflé omelet that'll blow your mind."

"Ugggh that sounds amazing. You sure you don't want to join me?"

"I do, but Dr. Kuaea is right down the hall, and I'm not sure if I'm ready for my grandmother to see either of our post-coital glows just yet."

"Uh, yeah. Okay. I'll be quick. And maybe you can, like, watch."

"I think I can work with that." Jesse swatted her on the butt, and followed her into the bathroom.

An hour later, the center leaf had been added to the dining room table and they all took their seats, glasses full and plates piled high with the delicious food, including soufflé omelets made to order. Jesse took his seat at the head of the table, opposite Miss Leona.

"So you take the king's chair," Lily-Grace teased as she took the seat beside him.

"I've mentioned that I've talked to my therapist about my issues with my father?"

"Nuff said." She gave his hand a squeeze. Jesse appreciated the comfort, but really the last thing he was thinking about was his dad. He was still thinking about being back in his bathroom, leaning against his sink, watching the curves of Lily-Grace's naked body through the fogged glass. He'd done the right thing not jumping in there with her. They would have definitely been late for breakfast. He'd have to hold on for what he had in mind later.

"Okay, my babies. Lily-Grace, who is practically my baby. And Dr. Fetu, I'm sure we'll get there."

"I hope so. I have to start seeing patients in a little over an hour. A meal like this is a great way to start the day."

"Well, you make sure you get seconds and a to-go plate. We have plenty. So. Who has news for me?"

"I do—we do," Evie said, taking Zach's hand. Jesse took a sip of his drink, trying to think of the most naturally surprised reaction for the news he knew was coming. He did his best to ignore the way Lily-Grace was tapping his foot under the table. "I think today was my last ride for a while. I'm pregnant."

Miss Leona gasped amid the various congratulations from around the room, her manicured fingers going to her chest. "Another great-grandbaby?"

"Yeah. I had a feeling before the wedding, but I went to the doctor when I was in the city this week. Definitely pregnant."

"That's wonderful news," Jesse said. "Congratulations, you guys."

"Sam, Jess—and Miss Leona, we'll definitely want to talk to you guys about the restaurant—"

Sam waved her off, his mouth still half full of pancakes. "Of course. It's *your* baby. Not your actual baby. You know what I mean. Whatever you decide."

"Whatever you decide," Jesse clarified. "It's your decision. We're here to support you. I'm just excited to be an uncle. The kid deserves someone in their life to teach them how to cook a steak properly."

"Here this mufucka go," Corie groaned from her seat next to Miss Leona, who didn't miss a beat flicking the back of her hand.

"Thanks, man." Zach chuckled. "We haven't told Mom and Senior yet."

"We're going to this weekend," Evie added. "I'm still in shock a little. Good shock. But still in shock. We've talked about it a lot though, and we want to raise the baby here."

"That is music to my ears," Miss Leona said, happy tears lining her eyes. She rose from her seat and planted a kiss on Evie's forehead.

"Please, please let me know when I can start shopping," Amanda said. "I love buying baby clothes."

"Knock yourself out. I've already ordered Baby Jordans," Zach replied.

"Excellent. I can't wait to blow all of Sam's money on this kid."

The ladies started in on their series of questions. Asking Evie how she felt, if she had ideas for names. Lily-Grace offered her own congratulations and words of support before she turned to Jesse and whispered, "If you think I'm not going to call you Uncle Jesse, you got another think coming."

"Pssht. Stamos wishes he looked this good." She managed to muffle her gleeful squeak as he squeezed her leg under the table.

The conversation about the baby dominated most of the meal. Even after they talked a bit about the possibilities with Golden Gulch and Amanda's new staff-writing gig, which she'd worked her ass off for, and the good news that Vega's grandmother was recovering just fine after her knee surgery, Jesse looked around the room, took in the smile on Lily-Grace's face, the love in his grandmother's eyes, and even he could feel another shift. The strange hollowness that had filled his grandmother's house in the last few months, the quiet, the stillness, the tension, was gone. They still had a lot to discuss, but he was glad Zach and Evie were coming home for good. No more traveling back and forth to New York for weeks at a time. He was glad their child would be close by, surrounded by love.

Still, he couldn't keep his mind off what it would be like if his granddad was around to see all this. He couldn't help but think about the fact that his parents should have been there to hear the news.

Chapter 21

The bar at the Charming Marriott was the perfect place to catch up with Jenny and Ned. Sam sent Jesse a text, saying they were heading over to Claim Jumpers, but hitting that place twice in one week would set a precedent that Jesse didn't want to be a part of. Besides, after the day he'd had, all he wanted was time with Lily-Grace and some adult conversation, and by adult conversation, he meant spending nearly an hour listening to Ned and Jenny catch Lily-Grace up on almost everything she missed by not attending Charming High. The conversation might have gone in another direction, if one of the old assistant football coaches hadn't spotted Jesse the second they walked in the door.

Jesse hadn't realized how well he usually scheduled his time around town to involve church, the senior center, and not much else. He was enjoying himself, but he was glad he'd made the decision to save himself from a lot the small talk that came with running into certain people around town.

Ned pulled his phone out of his pocket. "Shit, it's my

kid. I gotta take this—Hey, honey," he said as he got up from the table.

Jenny watched him until he walked out the front door and then she whipped her head back around. "Okay, so what do we think?"

"You know what I think," Lily-Grace said with a shrug. "I love Ned."

"Jesse?"

He shrugged too and took a sip of Coke. "I also love Ned."

"You're a big girl and you can make your own big girl decisions, I'm just gonna say you haven't called or texted me once this week complaining about Ned. By the way, I can still get Jesse to fire Vinny for being an ass," Lily-Grace added.

"No, she can't," Jesse replied with a shake of his head. Vinny may have been a shitty boyfriend, but he was great at his job. Jesse wasn't cutting him loose.

"Okay, no I can't, but you have to admit, just scheduling this date was easier."

"It was. Fuck. Now I see what you mean," Jenny said, and then she bit her lips like she'd just dropped a secret.

Lily-Grace nudged Jesse's shoulder, coming clean. "I told her how easy things are with you."

"I wasn't aware that good relationships were supposed to be hard, in a painful way."

Jenny peered at the door, then turned back around, lowering her voice, like Ned might hear her through two doors and over the music and the white noise of conversation and clinking glasses flowing through the space. "But I can date a guy with kids, right?"

"Is it a deal breaker?" Lily-Grace asked.

"No. I just never thought I'd date a guy with kids. But I am sliding firmly into the divorcé dating bracket, so I guess . . . huh." Jenny looked down at her drink like she'd just had the biggest revelation of her life. "Shit, you're both right. Okay. If he's good for another date, I'm gonna do it. Right after I use the ladies. Excuse me." She hopped up and rushed to the bathroom. Jesse stared after her, feeling his eyes glazing over. It was barely ten o'-clock and he was wrecked. No way he would have lasted twenty minutes in Claim Jumpers without sprouting a migraine.

"You okay?" Lily-Grace asked, giving his thigh a deep rub under the table.

Jesse blinked wide before he squeezed his eyes shut. He opened them again and looked over at her. "I'm so fucking tired."

"We did like four hundred things today and we were up before dawn."

She had a point. They should have napped after their more official swim lesson, which unfortunately didn't in-clude any dry humping, since his family decided to join them and offer support. Lilah and Vega were a big help, but the lesson eventually turned into a pool party/cookout that lasted until it was time to leave for their next en-gagement.

He could feel himself fading before they headed out to the senior center to help with bingo, but he rallied and got through it. Having Lily-Grace there helped. The usual bingo crew was a little too set in their ways to let her try out the monumental task of calling numbers. That was Lilah's job, but she helped Jesse hand out refreshments and prizes. Everyone knew her dad, of course, and a handful of people remembered her from when they were kids. It was another warm reception that he thought affirmed her decision to stay. That was definitely enough to keep him awake, seeing the smile on her face.

"I'm running on fumes and vibes right now," she said, giving in to her own deep yawn. "You want to go back to your place and I'll let you tuck me in?"

"No, I want to go to my place and then I want you to show me where to put my mouth."

"Mr. Pleasant!" she gasped.

"I thought you liked dirty talk."

"I do. Say something else nasty."

Jesse looked down at her lips, trying to think of where to start. He'd spent the whole week thinking of the things he wanted to do to her, all the things he wanted her to do to him, all the things she wanted to show him, and he knew that long list only scratched the surface of what they could get up to. Still, this was all new for him. He wasn't used to having someone to share these things with, someone who wanted every vulgar detail. He liked it.

"I'm surprised you behaved yourself today," he said.

"Oh, it was definitely touch-and-go there. If a member of your family hadn't been around at every possible moment, I definitely would have shown you a thing or two I can do with my mouth."

"The night's still young."

"I thought you were tired."

"I lied."

"Well good, 'cause we gotta make up for some lost time. It's one thing when I can't see you and I just have to deal with all of my fantasies of breaking into the ranch again, then finding my way to your office and finding a nice comfortable spot under your desk so I can—"

"You know I have an office back at the house."

A devious smile spread out over Lily-Grace's beautiful face. "Well, maybe we should let Jenny and Ned finish this night alone. It would probably be good for them to have some more one-on-one time."

"Agreed," Jesse replied just as Ned came walking through the door. Jenny emerged from the restroom and they stopped to talk by the bar. From the look on Ned's face, the call he'd received wasn't a good one.

"I gotta go. My babysitter has food poisoning and my nine-year-old thought she could play nurse," Ned said when they came back to the table.

"No problem. You take off, I got this covered," Jesse offered.

"You sure?"

"Yeah."

"I'll walk you out." Jenny grabbed her jacket and her purse, then walked with Ned out to the parking lot. Jesse settled the check and he and Lily-Grace followed. They walked out to Jesse's truck just as Jenny was waving goodbye to Ned.

"You get that second date?" Lily-Grace yelled across the parking lot.

"Shhh!" Jenny laughed as she power walked over to where they stood. "We're gonna try for next Friday night. Next time we're all together we gotta go to Claim Jumpers. I gotta move. I gotta dance."

"Ehhh," Jesse groaned.

"You were just there with Fetu," Lily-Grace pointed out.

"I thought you'd be eager to show off your sick dance

moves," Jenny added. "Vinny told me you're quite the legend on the dance floor."

"Vinny witnessed one lackluster dance-off between me and Chris at a birthday party. While the music at Claim Jumpers is good, I prefer to express myself in a more controlled environment, where less of my own employees might be in attendance to witness my greatness."

"Fair." Jenny laughed. They said their good-nights and waited until Jenny was safely in her Subaru.

"Am I ever gonna see these sick dance moves?" Lily-Grace asked once they were back in Jesse's truck.

He pulled out his phone and paused a moment, considering how badly he was willing to embarrass himself for this woman. He went to the video his cousin had sent him from the wedding, then handed over his phone. He stared out the windshield, as the words to "Crazy In Love" came through his phone speakers.

"Is that Amanda?" Lily-Grace squealed.

"Yeah. Only person who can match me on the dance floor."

"Please send this to me. I need it. I need this footage with me at all times."

Jesse held his hand out for his phone, and once she'd placed it back in his palm he pulled up the video of him doing the "WAP" choreography in Miss Leona's living room. The wedding footage was nothing. Lily-Grace needed to understand what she was really getting into here. She needed to understand him as a man. He handed the phone back and waited as the edited lyrics to the ode to juicy genitals filled the car. Lily-Grace replayed it three times before she put the phone back in sleep mode and stared at him.

"Your thoughts?" he said.

"Jesse. What do you expect me to say? I mean, I'm stuck on the fact that you landed that split, but even more puzzled on how all eight feet of your legs didn't kick a hole in Miss Leona's ceiling. But let's come back to the split."

Jesse started his truck and pulled out of the parking lot. "You can thank my football-playing days for that."

"I mean, I hope there's more where this came from. A lot more, and I hope I get to see it in person. It doesn't have to be at Claim Jumpers. I'll go full *Wedding Crashers* with you if it means I can witness this gloriousness for myself."

"I won't make you wait that long."

When they got back to Pleasant Lane, Jesse quickly checked in with Zach and attempted to collect Clementine but she refused, choosing to stay glued to Evie's side. Jesse felt the acute burn of betrayal; still, it was for the best. No dogs to interrupt what he had planned next. They walked into his house, where he asked Lily-Grace to follow him into the kitchen.

"Can you do splits in the kitchen?" she asked.

"I'm sure I can, but that'll have to wait for later." Jesse connected his phone to the house speakers, then watched her face as the opening notes of the "Thong Song" started to play.

"You have a choreography routine worked out for this?"

"Maybe." He held out his hand, and when their fingers touched, he pulled her into his arms. Effortlessly he began slowly swaying them both to the music.

"I've never slow-danced to Sisqo," Lily-Grace said quietly.

"One thing my granddad taught me, you can slow dance to anything if you're with the right partner."

"I'm seeing that." She swallowed, her gaze drifting down to his lips, and Jesse felt that shift in the air, the moment they'd both been waiting for all day. They were finally alone, finally free to dive back into the carnal desires they had for each other.

"So what do we do now?" Lily-Grace asked.

"You tell me."

"Well, I'm moving back home. If things go well, this time next week you'll be buying me a horse. What's next for you and me?"

"I think we'll just have to get married. Really lean into our own happily ever after."

"I don't hate that idea. We have to have like one real fight first though."

"Uh, excuse me, I think we've already had our first fight."

"That was a passionate, pre-relationship exchange of conflicting viewpoints."

"I don't want to fight with you."

"I see."

"I want to give you whatever you want, until the end of time," Jesse said.

"Is that so?"

"Mm-hmmm. I can argue with Corie. I don't want to argue with you."

"Wow. A man, this handsome, this skilled, this tall, with such good taste in music—" Lily-Grace sighed and shook her head as "We Like To Party!" started to play. "Jesse, what the hell is this playlist?"

"What, you don't work out to the Vengaboys?"

"Anyway. What am I supposed to do with a man who gives me everything I want?"

"Enjoy the hell out of him." Jesse wasn't done listening to Lily-Grace. He could listen to her talk all day. He wanted to learn everything about her, hear every word she had to say, but he'd been waiting for hours. He had to kiss her properly. He pressed his lips to hers, going hard almost instantly at the way she moaned against his mouth. She moved closer, putting their slow dancing to a stop as she slipped her tongue against his. Jesse responded in kind, letting their tongues move together until he needed to step back and take a breath.

"Tell me what you want, right now," he whispered.

"I want you to show me your office."

"And what's going to happen there? Tell me so I can make it good for you. And don't hold back because you think I can't handle it."

"Oh, I know you can. Come on. Show me the space so I can see what I'm working with."

Jesse took Lily-Grace's hand and led her through the house, the sound of Sean Paul's "Temperature" accompanying them. Jesse turned on the lights in his office and leaned against the doorjamb while Lily-Grace had a look around.

"Hmmm, this is nice." She walked along the bookshelves on the far wall, pausing to look at the few service awards he'd won over the years. She turned and looked at his desk, then walked around and swiveled his custom office chair on its base. "This is fairly sturdy?"

"I think so. What are you thinking?"

She walked back to the loveseat in the corner and leaned her thighs against the arm. Jesse didn't hide the way he was taking her in, letting his eyes roam over every inch of her body. Those tight jeans, her simple white top that made her breasts look amazing. Her lips.

"I'm thinking you should sit. Keep your clothes on, and then I should join you, on my knees, with my clothes off."

"Do you need help undressing?"

"No. I think I got it. Do you have condoms in here?"

"I'll go grab some."

"I'll be ready when you get back."

"Okay." Jesse slowly walked down to his room and took his time grabbing a few condoms and then lube from his bathroom. Lily-Grace clearly had a plan and he wanted to give her a few minutes to get things and herself just the way she wanted.

He waited in the doorway of his own bedroom for the entirety of "All The Stars," then headed back down to his office. What he saw when he entered the room had his jaw on the floor. Lily-Grace stood in the same position beside the loveseat, completely naked.

"I don't know which part of you to worship first," Jesse said, his voice thick with lust. His erection was nearly full, pressing hard against the seam of his pants.

"Let me have my turn while you figure it out." She came over to the doorway to meet him, then took his hand and brought him over to the desk. "Sit."

He tossed the condoms on the desktop and did as she directed. He watched her, giving in to the urge to brush his finger over her soft belly, then over the tightened tip of her nipple as she moved to her knees between his spread thighs. She peered up at him before her gaze went down to his crotch. "I like that," she said. "Keep touching me."

Jesse didn't need to be told twice. He traced a lazy circle over the soft skin of her shoulder, trailed the backs of his fingers over her neck. He realized then that he'd found a spot, a perfectly sensitive spot as goose bumps spread out over her skin as she swallowed a thick lump in her throat. He did it again, stroking over that same spot, and her eyes slipped closed, her tongue peeked out, and she licked her bottom lip. His cock twitched forward in his pants.

Lily-Grace's hands went to his lap. She looked up at him with those dark brown eyes, through her thick lashes, rubbing up and down his thigh, squeezing a little, right before she moved her fingers to his belt. He shifted a little to give her better access, spreading his legs even more as she splayed open the fabric of his pants and reached into the slit in his boxers. He held back a moan of his own when she pulled out his cock. He watched her hands, long slender fingers, pigment missing in small and larger patches, as she fondled him. She used her other hand to cup his balls through his pants, and something about that, Jesse couldn't explain it, but it was hot as fuck. A bead of moisture rushed to the tip of his erection as if to pass that message along to his partner.

She rose up on her knees, her tongue darting out to lick the drop away before she took the whole head with her lips. He was too big for her to take down to the root, but that didn't stop her from trying. One hand stroked up his shaft while her mouth slid down to meet it, her wet tongue swirling over every inch it could reach. It felt amazing, pinpricks of electricity bursting over his skin in reaction to the way she was expertly sucking him. She kept her eyes on him, watching his every minute reaction. It was sexy as hell, the way her gaze bore into him. He measured his breath, trying not to let the pleasure overtake him, but soon Jesse realized her plan. He looked forward to coming in her mouth, but not this time.

Jesse cupped her cheek, reaching for a condom on the desk with his other hand. She sat back again, frowning a bit as she wiped her mouth with her fingers.

"What's wrong?" Jesse asked before he rolled the condom into place.

"Nothing," she replied, her tone light. "I was just thinking."

Jesse took her by the elbow and encouraged her to stand up. He moved forward, sliding the chair closer to the desk, forcing her to rest her perfect ass on the edge. The same gentle way he touched her neck, he used the back of his index finger to lightly stroke over her delicate slit, which was visibly wet. He parted her lips with his knuckles, rubbing slow, deliberate circles over her clit. "What are you thinking about?"

She squirmed, swallowing again, jutting her hips out to give him better access or maybe to ease the ache between her legs. "I was—I was thinking about just how much I like having you in my mouth, but this is nice. This feels good."

Jesse leaned forward and took her left nipple between

his lips. He turned his hand between her legs and used two fingers to stroke and pet her, to tease her entrance. She moaned, gripped the back of his head as she bucked against him. He switched to her other breast, opening his mouth wide to lick and suck every inch.

"Jess." Lily-Grace's pained moan filled the room and he couldn't wait any longer.

"Come here." He gathered her close, an arm around her waist and around her leg. Sitting back he pulled her into his lap with one smooth motion, glad he'd selected a wide-model chair with extra sturdy padded arms, plenty of room for her to straddle him. He gripped his erection and carefully guided it to her entrance. She couldn't wait either. No teasing touch, she sat right down on his dick, taking every inch of him all at once. The cry she let out went right through him. Gripping his shoulders, she pressed her forehead to his. It was the closeness they both needed so they could adjust to finally getting what they wanted, after waiting all day long.

"Babe," she said, her breath coming out in a harsh pant against his mouth. "You feel so fucking good."

"You remember the way you felt, earlier tonight. When you realized I could do a split? That's how good you feel." Jesse smiled at the sputtering laugh that came out of her. Just as quickly it melted into another moan. She rocked her hips forward, clamping down around him and every thought, every joke left his head. All he could think about was the woman on his lap and the way she felt in his arms.

Lily-Grace cupped his face and kissed him. Jesse kissed her back, wrapping his arm around her waist to give him the leverage he needed to rock his hips up against the perfect cradle of her body. She rode him hard and slow, grinding her hips like she was searching for something only he could give her. Jesse kissed every inch of her skin he could reach. Her cheeks, her soft full lips, her smooth shoulders. She cried out when he used his tongue to tease that spot on her neck. Even louder, when he scraped that spot with his teeth before he used his mouth to lightly suck on it. That was all it took and she came apart in his arms, soaking his lap with the evidence of her orgasm. She collapsed against him, arms gripped tight around his shoulders like she didn't want to let go.

Jesse lifted her and set her down on the desk, still deep inside her as he moved. She wrapped her legs around him as he pumped into her in deep, punishing strokes. The curses that slipped from her lips spurred him on and soon he filled the condom, eyes squeezed shut against an eruption of stars. He came back down to Earth with the feeling of her fingertips creeping under the hem of his shirt. His ab muscles twitched as she drew her nails over his skin.

"Round two," she panted, her eyes barely open. "Let's take this off."

Chapter 22

Lily-Grace tried to open her eyes, but she was still mostly asleep. The urgency in Jesse's whisper had penetrated her REM sleep cycle though. After the amazing time they'd had in his office, they'd taken a quick water break and moved things to his bedroom, where she gave Jesse another lesson in oral sex. He was a quick study, of course, and by the end, she had to beg him to stop. Another orgasm might actually kill her. She had every intention of convincing him to skip church so they could spend the whole morning in bed together.

Even though she was extremely out of it, she knew this was not that kind of wake-up call. She rolled toward him, then froze when he gripped her upper arm, holding her in place. Her eyes sprang open and that's when she heard it. Dogs barking in the distance. She blinked hard and looked up at Jesse in the near dark.

"What's wrong?" she breathed.

"Someone's outside my house. Keep quiet, grab your phone, follow me," he whispered back. As soon as she'd reached for her cell off the nightstand on her side of the bed, he took her hand and tugged her out of bed, rushing her to the closet. He put his finger to his lips, then threw her a T-shirt. He stepped into a pair of gym shorts.

"Should we call the police?" she asked, her adrenaline already pumping up to her eyeballs. She tried to take a slow breath but it was useless.

Jesse held up his own phone, before he set it silently on his watch case. "Family panic button. Corie's on it. Tuck yourself behind there and wait for me to come back." Jesse motioned to his dressing table, which was plenty big, but there was no way she was just gonna tuck herself anywhere and hide.

"Are you crazy? I'm coming with you."

"And what if this someone has a gun?" he hissed.

"And that means you should go alone? This isn't a horror movie. We're not splitting up," Lily-Grace hissed back. She looked around until she spotted Jesse's pristine golf clubs. She grabbed the driver out of the bag and shoved it in his hand, then grabbed the nine iron for herself. She nodded toward the door.

He looked her straight in the face, a different kind of hard edge hitting his voice this time. "Stay behind me." She nodded in agreement and followed him out of the bedroom. They made it down the dark hallway, every sound, the air conditioning, her breathing, his, the sounds of the dogs barking getting louder and louder, all of it pounding in her ears and somehow all she could feel was the eerie stillness that only came in the middle of the night.

And then the pounding.

Jesse stopped. He stuck out his hand to stop Lily-Grace from running into him. The pounding got louder. They inched forward until they got to the end of the hall.

Jesse peeked around the corner into the kitchen and Lily-Grace peeked around him, but only for a split second. That was all she needed to see two men in the backyard. One seemed to be standing watch. The other was trying to break the glass of the patio doors with the lawn chair.

Another loud thud and Lily-Grace sucked in a tight breath. She was about to tell Jesse they should make a run for the garage when the glass shattered.

"Fuck man! Shit!" she heard one of the men yell.

"Come on, man! This way! This fucking way!"

There was the crunching of glass and then a second later the alarm started blaring. Alarms usually scared people away, but the intruders were inside the house, screaming and swearing, crashing into Jesse's living room furniture.

Jesse pressed himself back against the wall and pinned Lily-Grace back with one arm. She braced herself, gripping her golf club, ready for what was going to happen next. She was going to have to help Jesse fight them. She closed her eyes for a second, then opened them, realizing the inevitable. They were gonna have to kill her if they thought she would make this easy. She listened, though, and it sounded like they'd run the other way. Jesse waited a beat, probably hearing the same thing, before he tapped her arm and started moving forward.

They made their way through the house, golf clubs raised, the alarm still blaring, the dogs still barking, when they found the two intruders by the front door.

"It won't fucking open!" one of them said.

"Don't fucking move!" Lily-Grace thought she might

be hearing things for a moment, but it was definitely Lilah's voice coming from the driveway. The robbers kept scrambling, completely unaware that they were two seconds away from getting their heads bashed in, Arnold Palmer style.

"Man, open the fucking door. He didn't pay us enough for this!"

Suddenly Jesse reached over and turned on the light. Both men jumped and turned around. One of them screamed as a metal baseball bat clinked loudly against the polished concrete floor. They were wearing hoodies and ski masks, but Lily-Grace could see that one of them was Black and the other was white.

"What are you doing in my house?" Jesse asked, his voice deep and menacing.

"Nothing, man. Nothing! This was a mistake!"

"Jesse!?" Lilah yelled.

"We're okay!" he called back. "Stay where you are!"

"I got him!" she replied. Lily-Grace felt herself frowning. What the hell was going on?

"Kick me the bat." The Black guy fumbled twice, but managed to get the toe of his sneakers under it and finally kicked it toward Jesse's feet. Jesse bent over slowly and picked it up, then handed it back to her. Lily-Grace kept her eyes on both men as Jesse stepped closer, then pressed the four necessary numbers into the keypad on the wall, silencing the alarm. Then he nodded toward the larger of the two men, the white guy. "There's the top lock there. Flip that, then walk outside nice and slowly."

"Listen man! I said this was a mistake. We're cool. Everything's cool. We're going. We have no problem here."

"Yeah. I'm sure. Open the door and walk out slowly."

The white guy did as he said, but as soon as he stepped on the porch he jumped back, crashing into his buddy. Lily-Grace looked around and spotted Lilah in the middle of the cul-de-sac holding a shotgun.

"Lilah, we're all coming out!" Jesse yelled.

"Yeah, okay." She swung the gun back around and pointed at someone she couldn't see. Lily-Grace couldn't see the dogs, but she could hear them barking wildly.

Jesse jabbed the white guy in the back with his golf club. "Go." Then he turned his head a bit, his eyes still forward. Lily-Grace knew better than to take her eyes off the men too, but she could just feel the way Jesse's body was trying to check in with hers. They both needed a split second of grounding. "You okay?" he asked.

"No. You?"

"No. Come on."

Lily-Grace didn't take his hand, but followed with fingers on the small of his back. They slowly walked outside, keeping a golf club's length between themselves and the intruders. She saw the dogs then as they came around the edge of the garage. The dogs' shockingly vicious barking focused on the two men, who stuttered to a stop, caught between a club, two dogs, and a shotgun. She followed Jesse's lead, coming around the cars to edge closer to Lilah, who had a third man on the ground at gunpoint. What in the whole fuck was going on?

"This one was snooping around the front. You think there's more?"

"This it, or do you have any more buddies?" he asked.

"It's just us, man! Call the dogs off."

Instead, Jesse glanced back at Lilah. "Where's Miss Leona?"

"Corie's with her. I told Zach to stay with Evie. I had it handled."

Almost on cue, Zach stepped out on his porch. The fact that he was in his boxers absently reminded Lily-Grace that she wasn't wearing pants, but it didn't seem important at the moment.

"Stay inside, Zach!" The booming baritone of Jesse's voice made Lily-Grace jump. He whipped back around to the three assholes cowering as Euca and Clementine growled at them. She would never want to be on the receiving end of the murderous look in his eye.

"What the fuck are you doing here?" Jesse said, his hands flexing on the handle of the golf club. "Talk, or I'll tell her to shoot you. It won't be fatal, but I don't think recovering from a shotgun blast to the nuts is fun. Talk!"

"Okay, okay! We were just supposed to come scare you," the white guy who'd been inside the house said.

"Scare who?"

"You, man! You're Jesse Pleasant, right?"

Lily-Grace looked up as she saw lights and heard their accompanying sirens in the distance. They were still a long way off, but it looked like at least three cruisers were making the near mile-long drive down Pleasant Lane.

"Keep talking!"

"We just came to scare you. He didn't tell us you were seven fucking feet tall and jacked as shit."

"Who?"

"Shut up, man!" the Black guy said.

"There's still time to shoot you and claim self-defense. Answer him," Lilah said. "Who?"

"Dane. Dane Locklear."

Lily-Grace knew she was hearing things. There was no way she'd heard that name correctly. "Say that again?" she said.

"Dane Locklear. This hedge fund douchebag. Something about you taking what was his. He told us to come scare you. That's it."

"Who the hell—"

"My ex." Lily-Grace felt like her chest was caving in. Jesse looked over at her, that homicidal look now focused in her direction.

"What?"

"Dane Locklear is my ex-partner—boyfriend, whatever."

"We were just supposed to come here and rough you up a bit. Nothing serious. He didn't say shit about dogs and you being a fucking beast. We fucked up, okay!"

The sounds of the sirens became too much to compete with. A few moments later they were surrounded by sheriff's cruisers. Jesse called the dogs to him and they finally settled between him and Lily-Grace as one of the officers climbed out of his car. Even though it had been years, Lily-Grace immediately recognized Ned's older brother Mike.

He calmly took stock of the situation. "We have some unexpected guests?"

"Looks that way," Jesse said.

"Miss Pleasant, if you could, put the gun down."

"Yeah, sure." Lilah slowly lowered the gun and set it on the ground to her left.

"How did you guys get here so fast?" Jesse asked.

"Park and Miller were driving by. Saw a car parked out on the road over there just as the call came in. Lots of Giants stickers, which we don't get much around these parts. Thought we'd check it out," he said.

There was a flurry of activity; still, by the time the geniuses were unmasked and handcuffed and the property searched as a precaution, Lily-Grace still had a hard time processing how Dane could do this. Lilah graciously gave her some shorts and a blanket when they gathered in Miss Leona's kitchen to give Mike a thorough rundown of what had happened. Miss Leona had hot tea handed out before they could even sit down. Mike had questions for everyone, Corie, Zach, and Evie included. Sam and Amanda were spending the night up at the ranch. They were in for one hell of a story in the morning.

Lilah was explaining what she saw when she stepped out her front door, when one of the deputies came in to join them.

"What you got, Coop?"

"They're spilling everything," she said. "This Dane Locklear hired one of their cousins, who passed the job on to them. Luckily they didn't do much in the way of recon. They didn't even know there were three houses out here."

"More like lucky they are bush-league amateurs."

Lily-Grace was going to be sick. Jesse's whole family was in danger because of Dane. Because of her.

"Can you tell us more about this Dane?" Mike asked her.

"Yeah. I—" She tried to speak, but her voice was

trapped in her throat. She caught the look Jesse shot over his shoulder, and next thing she knew Zach was herding everyone but Miss Leona and Jesse out.

Lily-Grace looked between the two of them, Miss Leona where she was sitting, and Jesse where he was leaning against the counter, arms folded tight across his chest. He was almost as tense as he'd been the moment he'd woken up. There was a rage simmering in him and she was wondering when it would break. She didn't think an apology would be enough but she tried anyway. "I am so sorry."

"Don't apologize, sweetheart," Miss Leona said. "Just tell Michael what happened with this Dane person."

"We were together for five years. He was possessive . . . but that was a part of our dynamic." Mike nodded for her to go on. "I was sexually harassed at work and he basically told me I should be flattered and it wasn't a big deal. He knows the guy who harassed me."

Mike sighed, sounding annoyed on her behalf. "Okay. Then what happened?"

"I left my job and I broke up with Dane. I came home to—regroup. I think he thought we were just fighting at first. No." She stopped herself. She was being a little too fucking charitable. "We broke up. I told him it was over before I left. But he called me and texted me and emailed me pretty much every day." She glanced at Jesse. He was looking at the floor.

"When was the last time you heard from him?"

"Last week. I told him not to contact me anymore or I was going to go to the police if he didn't stop. I emailed him because I wanted there to be something in writing, and I know how he can be on the phone."

"How's that?"

"Pushy."

"So you felt like it had gotten to that point, that you should go to the police?"

She swallowed, forcing herself to nod. "Yeah, yes. I blocked his number and he just kept calling me from different unknown numbers. He replied to the email with a link to the article about the date auction and said he hoped Jesse and I would be happy together. That was a week ago. Same day."

"And you haven't heard from him since then?"

"No. No calls from weird numbers, no voicemails—beyond actual spam—and no emails."

"Jesse, have you heard from this man?"

He shook his head. "I didn't know his name until thirty minutes ago."

"Toxic masculinity, folks. It's a hell of a drug. Okay. Well, I think the next person we need to talk to is Dane Locklear."

Mike had a few more questions and they spent more time checking things out at Jesse's. Eventually the police packed things up and assured them they'd be in touch, probably with more questions soon.

"I should—I should call my father," Lily-Grace said once they were gone.

"Let's wait until the morning, okay?" Miss Leona said. "We have everything under control now, and waking him up will just be added to the list of people with the two a.m. jitters. You and Jesse sleep here."

"Okay."

"The sunshine room is all ready. We'll clean up the glass and board things up and maybe file a restraining order in the morning. Okay?" The smile Miss Leona gave them was the exact comfort Lily-Grace needed for now. She was right. They needed sleep. There would be plenty of time to stress over all this in the morning. They said good night and she followed Jesse down to the west end of the house. He held her hand, but something was off in his touch, like he was just cupping her fingers to make sure she was with him, not because he wanted to touch her the way she *needed* to touch him in that moment.

He showed her into a large guest room with white furniture and bright yellow linens and accents. Jesse flopped down in the side armchair across the room, which wasn't really big enough for his large frame. Lily-Grace headed toward the window seat, when they heard a knock at the door.

"It's Lilah."

"Yeah, come in," Jesse said.

His cousin poked her head in, then stepped all the way inside. "I just wanted to see if you guys are okay? My hands are still shaking."

"Here, come sit down." Lily-Grace grabbed the white and yellow throw blanket off the end of the bed and wrapped Lilah in it. She sat down beside her on the bed and gave her shoulders a good rub.

"Thanks. I didn't want to be alone in my room while I was crashing off adrenaline."

"You're good," Jesse said quietly.

"Yeah. Hang out with us. I'm wired too." Lily-Grace climbed under the covers and tried to warm up her bare toes.

"How long have you had a gun?" Jesse asked.

"Since I was twelve? Daddy taught us all how to

shoot. I think I've exhibited I'm a responsible gun owner by now."

Jesse just grunted in reply, dropping his gaze to the floor.

"Babe, are you okay?" she asked. He nodded but didn't say anything else. Luckily Lilah filled the awkward silence. She groaned, then flopped on her side and moved up the bed.

"Ugh, I wish Fetu was here. He gives really good hugs."

"First thing tomorrow, I'm sure he'll be more than happy to give you a big-ass hug."

Lilah yawned. "I'm so screwed."

Lily-Grace almost asked what she meant, but Lilah closed her eyes, and if sleep was finally calling to her, Lily-Grace didn't want to screw that up, not after the night they'd had. She didn't think she could sleep. She wanted to talk to Jesse, but she could tell—by the look on his face, the tense way he was still holding his body, the way he was staring at the floor—now was not the time. She looked over at Lilah again, then settled into the covers. She didn't mean to, but a few minutes later she fell asleep.

The sun was just coming up when Lily-Grace opened her eyes again. She could see why they called it the sunshine room. Even though the curtains were closed, she could feel a thousand watts of early morning sunlight coming through the large bay window. Jesse was still awake in the chair, looking at the floor. She checked behind her, and the spot where Lilah had been was now empty.

"She went back to her room," Jesse said.

"Oh. Have you slept at all?"

Jesse shook his head, and swallowed deeply. He was trying not to look at her.

"Come lie down for a bit," she said, making room for him, but he didn't move. She didn't know why she was surprised. Her own words echoed in her head. *This is so easy, so easy.* Of course it was too good to be true. Attempted assault was reason enough to take a step back from something so fresh. It hurt, the way he was icing her out, but she didn't blame him. There was baggage and then there was what Dane had tried to do, and might try to do again. "I understand if you're pissed. I should—"

"That's not—no." He leaned forward and scrubbed his face. "I was sitting here all night because my hands wouldn't stop shaking. I didn't want to touch you like that. I don't—I was so angry. I don't ever want to do anything to make you feel like you need to run away from me and hide like that."

"No, I wasn't hiding. I'm not."

"But you were scared of him, weren't you?"

"Yes," she finally admitted. She hated to say it out loud. Dane didn't deserve that kind of power, but it was true. He let her down, but when he kept pushing her to come back, something shifted and she didn't know how to describe how it made her feel. It was fear. "I thought he was just full of shit. I mean—I didn't think he actually cared. I thought he just thought he missed having access to me or my body. He cares about *you* being close to me."

Lily-Grace fought the sudden urge to sprint out of the room and drive full speed back to her father's house. She tried to blink them back, but tears rose to her eyes. She wasn't sad or even upset. She was angry. So fucking pissed that Dane would even think that sending people after *Jesse* was something that made sense. That he would hurt people she cared about just because he didn't get his way—his way that told her that her feelings, her life, her career, anything she wanted for herself didn't matter.

Jesse looked up at her suddenly and she knew she should go. He was doing such a great job working out his own shit. He didn't need her stuff to pile on.

"I love you," he said, his voice so clear it shocked Lily-Grace right back to the present. Miles away from the last year, from a few hours before. He said it again. "I love you, and if Lilah hadn't been there, if she hadn't been armed, I was ready to rip three men apart with my bare hands. And I would have done it. You, Evie, the *baby*—I've been sitting here considering if I need to get dressed and drive up north and put my fist through Dane Lock-lear's face. Fuck his whole shit up. I—" He looked down at his hands, opening and closing his fists. They were still trembling.

Lily-Grace knew he was serious. She'd managed to cross into that group of people Jesse truly cared about, that he loved. People he'd kill for, in a very literal sense, the same way she was willing to burn a whole bitch down for her father. But Jesse wasn't proud of it, the literal part. The part where he was really considering getting behind the wheel with the express purpose of beating the living shit out of Dane. He didn't like that he was so close to losing control. But he hadn't. He was still there with her. Talking to her, thinking things through before he did anything he'd regret. He'd come a hell of a long way. She was so proud of him.

A strangled laugh bubbled from Lily-Grace's throat, the tears spilling over. "Did you miss the part where I was ready to go full Tiger Woods on whatever was waiting for us in the dark? You, your family? You mean so much to me. I would have bitten ears and poked out eyeballs, kicked some serious shins if any of them had gone near Zach's house, or Evie. Or Miss Leona. But I still should have told you that he was . . . harassing me. I should have told you and I should have told my father. He doesn't know any of it."

"Is there anything you left out?"

"That night, when we had our little picnic in my car? It was him who kept calling. It wasn't spam."

Jesse stared back at her. She didn't know how to read the look on his face. The anger was still there, but there was pain too, and something close to helplessness. "You know you can tell me anything, right? And I'm positive the same goes for your father."

"I do and I can. I was . . . trying to ignore it. I was done with him and I thought if I just pretended it wasn't happening when I was with you, he would just go away. Guess who was wrong?" she said with a mirthless laugh.

Jesse stood and pulled her into his arms. She could feel how cold his hands were through the fabric of her T-shirt, but all she could think of was how badly she wanted to warm them. She didn't want him to let go. "I'm just glad you're okay," he said against her temple.

Then he leaned down and kissed her. For the first time in hours Lily-Grace felt like she could exhale.

"I thought you were about to dump me."

"No. Hell no. We're getting married. We just survived a B and E together. We can get through anything." She laughed at the lightness that had returned to his voice. Dane was lucky his plan had failed. She'd be on her way up to San Francisco to do some tearing limb from limb of her own if anything bad had happened to Jesse Pleasant.

Chapter 23

Jesse pulled the trigger on the nail gun, securing the final board to the frame that formerly held up his back door.

"That looks good," Zach said from the other end. They both stepped back and examined their handiwork. He'd have a new patio door installed by the time they got back from their quick trip up to Golden Gulch.

"Yeah, it'll hold," Jesse grumbled in response. He couldn't shake the cloud that had settled over his brow. Lily-Grace was back home with her father. They'd managed to get a few hours of sleep, together in the bed. Holding her helped, but even after she'd called him to let him know she'd gotten back home okay, he was still tight as hell.

He'd spoken to Mike again and the police were already in the process of getting everything in place to scoop up Dane Locklear. The rest of Jesse's family was fine, and Clementine was knocked out, happily lying in the sun on the other side of the pool deck. Everything was fine, except it wasn't.

He thought cleaning up broken glass, taking a drive

into town for plywood, even doing a little manual labor, would help ease the tension rolling off his body, but nothing worked. If he was still carrying it all around by Tuesday, he could at least talk to his therapist about it.

Sam came around the side of the house, shoving his phone in the back pocket of his jeans.

"Amanda and I are gonna stick around a few extra days. She doesn't need to be back to LA for work until Wednesday."

"You guys are more than welcome to stay here," Jesse replied.

"Thanks, man, but we'll stay up at the ranch. Things— uh—it can get loud. We appreciate it though."

"Say no more."

Zach finished stacking the few pieces of leftover wood, then looked hard at Jesse, squinting under the brim of his Stetson. "You alright?"

"Senior should be here." As soon as the words were out, Jesse felt that telltale tingle in his chest. His palms started itching, like things wouldn't be right if he didn't punch something. The instinct kicked in, to hold his breath, or worse, start yelling at Sam or Zach, but luckily he had a new voice of reason, one that sounded a little like Dr. Brooks and a little like Lily-Grace. He looked over at Zach. There was no judgment on his face, he was just waiting for Jesse to go on. He rubbed the center of his chest through his shirt, like that would help make sense of what he was feeling. He had to get it out.

"He should be here," was all he could say. The words were filled with bitterness because that's all he had in him. Bitterness and irrational fear. "I can't explain it, I just—I'm pissed he's not here right now. Like, as our father."

"No, I'm with you," Zach said. "The thing with the Gulch, I told Evie I was pissed about what he put in the email, but I was more pissed about him being all up in our shit, but refusing to be *here*. I didn't know how to act with him at our wedding."

"Shit, me too!," Sam said. "Amanda said I was acting a little strange all night and it was because I didn't know how to deal with Mom and Dad, 'cause I knew they weren't staying. She told me to talk to you guys about it, but I just didn't."

"We have a father," Jesse replied, thinking of the conversation he'd already had with Dr. Brooks about Senior. What he was feeling and the whole reality of the situation. "And it's not like he's locked up or dead or even a bad man."

"Yeah, I think we all have our issues, but my grown-man issues with him all have to do with the fact that he isn't here," Zach said. He looked at his brothers, and he knew they were thinking the same thing, the words left unsaid. Senior had left the job of showing them how to be men unfinished.

"I was sitting up last night trying to pull it together and I'm looking at my girlfriend and my grandmother," Jesse said. "I—he should be here."

"Have you called them yet today, told them what happened?" Sam asked.

"No. I haven't told them yet."

Zach glanced at his watch. "It's nine o'clock there now, and I think Dad has to shoot tomorrow. They should be back at their place. I say we call them."

"And say what?"

"We want them to come back. It's the same issue with Mom. Evie was walking on eggshells with her 'cause during the wedding Mom's not here for them to establish their own adult relationship."

"Do you know how fucked up it is we're talking about our own parents like this?" Sam said with a dry chuckle.

"It is," Jesse said with a painful sigh. "Okay. Let's call them. Come on." His brothers followed him inside and gathered around as he set up the laptop on the kitchen island.

"You want me to start?" Zach asked as Jesse sat down. It was not a secret that Zach was their dad's favorite. They'd spent the most time together, had a deep bond, even if it was strained now.

"No, I need to do this," Jesse replied. He had it in him to say what he was feeling now. If he didn't get it off his chest, he didn't know when he would, or how explosive that eventual revelation would be. He had to deal with it now. He brought up the video chat app and hit his father's contact. The bubbling ringtone was like a jackhammer to his temples.

A few moments later, his father popped up on the screen. He was wearing a vintage *42* sweatshirt. He could see all three of them in his father's features: Sam favored Senior the most, but Jesse had his high cheekbones and the same set of his mouth; Zach had his nose and the shape of his jaw. Jesse blinked, looking at all four of them, the Pleasant men reflected back on the screen.

"Oh. It's all of my sons at once," he said, even though he was walking through their flat and not looking at the screen.

"You got a moment, Dad? We need to talk to you."

"One moment, please." Their dad groaned as he made himself comfortable in his home office in their London apartment. "I always have time for my sons."

Yeah, Jesse definitely needed to speak up. They couldn't go on acting like this shit was okay anymore.

"Um—we think you and Mom should come back. You should move back to Charming. You should be here." His throat went tight at the end there, but he had to see this through. If his dad blew them off, then he could do the more permanent hard work of putting him in a different sort of box, with a label reserved for someone who he couldn't actually rely on.

Jesse went on though, filling his father in on the situation with Dane Locklear and the men who'd broken into his house.

"Everyone's okay, though?" Senior asked. "Your grandmother's okay?"

"Everyone is fine, but the dust was settling and I felt like I'm the man of this whole family, and that doesn't sit right with me. I'm trying to figure out my own shit—stuff. Sorry, sir. I'm trying to be a better person and a better man, and it's hard when I feel like I have to pretend I don't have a father to turn to for anything. You should be here." Fuck it all, but tears rushed to Jesse's eyes, blocking his throat. Years of hurt and frustration, rejection finally spilled over. This was what he'd been carrying around all day, and for the last however many years.

Zach squeezed Jesse's shoulder and went on, probably sensing Jesse couldn't. "Yeah, Dad. We have his back, but Jesse really has been the glue keeping this all together. Making it so Sam and Evie and I can do what we want. Looking after Lilah and Miss Leona. Dealing with Corie. I'm surprised he had time to even start something with Lily-Grace. We didn't make it easy on him." Zach let out another deep breath of his own. Jesse looked up from where he was staring at the corner of his screen and saw the look of determination on Zach's face. He'd reached his limit for holding things in, too. "Dad, Evie and I are about to have this baby, and I want you and Mom around. *We* do. I don't want to think about you guys only seeing your grandchild in person twice a year."

"That's not what I want at all." Senior sighed and Jesse could see where he got it from. His dad was trying to hold all kinds of thoughts and emotions inside. "Your mother and I discussed this after the wedding; we didn't know if you wanted us to come back, but I'm the parent here and I should have just asked."

"We want you to come back," Sam piped up, his status as the baby of the family showing. As it should. Senior had taken off, the second the ink on Sam's GED certificate dried. They'd had the least amount of time together. "But only if you want to be here. We understand that you left to pursue your career, but I don't think any of us thought it would be like this. Barely seeing you, barely talking to you, like there's some beef when there isn't. At least that I know about."

"There is no beef." Senior chuckled. "I left because of a disagreement I had with your grandmother. I also needed to put some space between myself and your grandmother and your mother, but that's all water under the bridge now, and has been for some time. Zachariah, Sammy, give me a moment to speak to Junior, please."

"Yes, sir." They both gave Jesse a pat on the back and

walked toward the front door. Jesse looked back at the monitor when he heard it click closed.

"I owe you an apology," Senior said. "You are absolutely right. My brothers and I had our own struggles with your grandparents and with each other, and when I saw how capable you were of handling things and how you and Miss Leona saw eye to eye on the Big Rock, I thought I was doing the right thing, but there's a difference between stepping aside and me skipping town."

"I'm glad to hear you say that. I think each of us had our own theory as to why you didn't want to really be our father anymore."

"No. Never. That's never been the case, but it's my fault you feel that way. Your mother is just here to support me. I know she misses you. I was angry with my mother and my brothers and I didn't see how that had affected you and your brothers. Thank you for stepping up, but you're right; you shouldn't have had to."

Jesse didn't know how to trust in the relief he felt. Of all the possible outcomes of one day confronting his father, he never saw it going this way. He never thought his dad would be open to talking like this. He definitely never thought he'd agree or apologize. Clearly his therapist had been on to something.

"Miss Leona is getting older and Zach is gonna have this baby, and Sam and Amanda, and Lily-Grace and I—"

"Your mother and I should be there."

"Should be where?" Jesse heard his mom say in the background.

"I'm talking to your oldest."

His mom popped into the frame. Her hair was wrapped

up, but she was wearing a fur coat. "My handsome baby. What's wrong? Are you upset?"

"No, yes. The therapy is working, I guess."

"Our boys want us to come home," Senior said. "For good."

"Well, let's go. I have a nursery to help decorate. It's my time to level up to grandma status."

Jesse managed not to roll his eyes. His mom and Evie would definitely have spirited discussions about cribs and strollers, but that's what family was all about.

"Let me finish up here with Junior, and then you can speak to them."

"Oops, okay. Father-son talk. I love you, baby."

"I love you too, Mom." She blew him a kiss before she popped out of the frame.

He spoke to Senior more about what had been going on, the date auction, things with Lilah and his uncle, and most importantly, the way Senior handled business emails about the ranch, since they were airing things out. "I think it makes Zach feel like you don't take his role seriously, when we are partners, fifty-fifty."

"I see," Senior said. "I can be better about that. I didn't realize you or Zachariah were taking my emails that way, which was not my intention at all."

"I appreciate that," Jesse replied. After he told his dad about the way things were going with Lily-Grace and the impending horse purchase, with his dad fully supportive, Senior talked to Sam and Zach privately before they said their goodbyes. Senior had six weeks left on his current project, but after that he and their mother would come back to Southern California. He wasn't going to give up acting, so there were some logistics to work out about whether they would set up shop in LA or Charming, but Jesse and his brothers agreed a two-hour drive with traffic was much better than an international flight across the Atlantic.

"Shit, I'm glad we had that talk, but damn, we should have done that sooner," Zach said as he collapsed onto the couch.

"But we did it now, and that's what matters, right?" Sam replied.

Jesse could just nod. His tears were dried, but he still felt raw as hell. Better, but still a little messed up.

"You okay?"

"Yeah, I'll be alright."

"Alright." Zach hopped up again, like he hadn't just made himself nice and comfortable. "I'm gonna go check on my wife and maybe cry some thug tears of my own. You know where to find me." He dapped Jesse up and then grabbed his Stetson and headed out the door. Sam looked like was about to follow.

"You want to come over to Miss Leona's? Amanda and I are gonna chill over there for a while. Probably stay through dinner."

"Yeah. I'll come by in a bit. Just gonna, ya know, jot down some notes for my therapist. Do breathing exercises. Then see what Lily-Grace is up to."

Sam walked over to him and wrapped his arms around him, pinning Jesse's arms to his side. "I'm really proud of you, man. I don't want you to step in for Dad, but you're a good-ass brother."

"Thanks, man."

"It's the rock!" Sam threw his hands in the air as he walked out of the kitchen.

When he was finally alone, Jesse called Clementine back inside, then went down to his room to collapse on his bed. Another thing he was working on, recognizing what he was feeling in the moment, and in that moment he was bone tired. He rolled on his back and pulled up his conversation with Lily-Grace.

> Can I see you tonight?

Wanna come over for pizza
and a movie with me and my papa?
Come at like 6.

Jesse thought about it for a moment, and that sounded like the perfect way to spend a Sunday night.

> I'll be there.

Great, bring Clementine.
And some ice cream.
And your hot hot ass.

> I'll make sure I have all 3 on hand.

At 5:50, Jesse pulled up to the LeRoux house on Wildwood Canyon Road. He wasn't expecting Mr. LeRoux to be standing in the driveway. Jesse parked his truck behind Lily-Grace's SUV, then let Clementine out of the back of the cab. Jesse grabbed the bag with the scotch for Mr. LeRoux and the ice cream for his daughter.

"She's trying to convince me to get a dog, but you

have a dog right here. Hello, Clementine," Mr. LeRoux said.

Clem wagged her tail, knowing she'd made a new friend. The older man looked up at Jesse, the smile dropping from his face. "I wanted to thank you for looking out for my daughter. She'd kill me if she knew that's what I was out here saying to you, but it's true."

"What does she think we're out here talking about?"

"Miss Leona."

"Oh. Do you have anything to share on that front?"

"No." He shook his head. "We're on a different terrestrial plane than you young people when it comes to relationships. She said she'll tell me when she's ready for a ring, so I'm just gonna wait."

"Okay." Jesse chuckled.

"But I did speak with Dane Locklear this afternoon." That, Jesse wasn't expecting.

"You did?"

Mr. LeRoux nodded. "I'd never met him. She said it wasn't serious, even after five years or so, but you know. I give her space. I regret that with this one though."

"What did he have to say for himself?"

"Oh, he played dumb. Maybe that's for the best for him right now, legally speaking, but I told him if he ever messes with my daughter or you again, I'll kill him myself."

The man was seventy-five years old, but Jesse believed him. "I thought about driving up to see him today," he admitted. "Just to talk, maybe break a finger or two."

"I understand the inclination. But for you, your future, your career. It's not worth it. You belong here, with her. Not in Folsom on an assault charge."

"You have a very good point."

"Send him the bill for your patio door though. He can definitely pay for that."

"I will. Uh—" Jesse cleared his throat. This day was filled with stark honesty, and while his emotional door was open he might as well keep his hot streak going. "Sir, I wanted to let you know, especially after everything that happened, I'm falling in love with your daughter."

The bright smile returned to Mr. LeRoux's face. He held out his hand and met Jesse's with a solid shake. "I think she'd like that. Just be good to her, Jesse."

"I will, sir."

"That's what I like to hear. Why don't you come on inside? You and your prize puppy."

They headed up the front porch and spotted Lily-Grace watching through the side window. "Oh hey," she said when they opened the door. "Wasn't expecting you."

"I'm gonna go call Roma's," Mr. LeRoux said, leaving them alone in the entryway.

"Hey, Clem. Hello, Mr. Pleasant," she said, waggling her right eyebrow. "Hiya doing? You should kiss me."

Jesse didn't hesitate to pull her into his arms. He tipped back his hat, and leaned down to kiss her long and hard. It had only been half a day, but he started to miss her whenever she wasn't around. From the way she was kissing him back, he knew she felt the same way too.

"I talked to my dad," he blurted out.

"Oh yeah?"

"Yeah, about everything. It went really well. My parents are going to move back to Charming."

"Babe, that's great. Like, damn. It's hard to have those

kinds of talks with people, especially our parents. I'm really happy for you."

"Thank you. How was your day?" he asked quietly before he kissed her again. Finally she stepped back a bit, but not too much. She was still close, her hands splayed on his pecs, awakening every inch of his body. It was gonna be a special kind of torture making it through PG movie night with a chaperone.

"You know, I told my father everything. Finally. Cried most of the afternoon. Contacted my lawyer, see how to handle this situation, cried some more, but I feel better now. I thought about everything I could do to make Dane's life a living hell, but I'd rather focus on you. On us."

"Well that's good, 'cause you're my woman now, and if he has a problem with it, he's going to have to deal with me."

"Ugh, why is it so hot when you say it?"

"It might have something to do with my rugged good looks and said sick dance moves, but it might be because I love you."

"I'm gonna say it back soon, okay?" she replied quietly, her gaze drifting over every feature of his face. "I just—I want there to be no ex-related static in my head when I do. I want it to just be me and you up in my brain. I want my mind to be clear so I can process this good thing the right way. And maybe we're in like a really nice hotel in Greece. We bring the dogs, of course."

"I'll wait as long as you need."

Jesse reached up and stroked his thumb over her soft cheek. He remembered all the times in middle school he thought about getting up the courage to talk to her, what it would be like to hold her hand, and now she was in his arms. Lily-Grace had opened his eyes to what it could be like to be with someone who respected him and cared for him. He'd give her anything and everything she wanted, and Jesse knew he would get that kind of love right back.

Epilogue

"Miss Leona. Please. Go sit," Lily-Grace pled. The woman had been running around nonstop since October. All the presents had been opened, everyone had been fed, and Miss Leona had been the most gracious of hosts throughout. She deserved at least five seconds of rest before they moved on to the next Christmas Day activity.

"Girl, don't tell me what to do in my own kitchen. That dish goes right down there." The mac and cheese Jesse had made didn't stand a chance. She smiled to herself as she scrubbed the hand-painted baking pan, thinking about how Sam and Zach had had a standoff over the last helping; the last helping that had eventually gone to Evie. She was breast-feeding times two these days. She deserved all the mac and cheese she could handle.

"Leona, where would you like this?" Mrs. McQueen asked. Lily-Grace glanced over and caught sight of the crystal pitcher Amanda's mom was holding.

"Just leave it right there on the counter. Thank you, sweetie."

Every woman in the general orbit of the Pleasant

family was buzzing around Miss Leona's house, helping with cleanup. This division of labor of the sexes was not commonplace, and hadn't been nearly an hour ago, but all of the menfolk had gone up to the ranch to help Jesse prepare for his final part of Lily-Grace's gift. It wasn't a surprise. He'd spent months and months working with Zach and Senior, learning how to ride Bam Bam, and today was the big unveiling of his skills in the saddle.

Lily-Grace looked around the kitchen, trying to see what else needed to be wrapped up and put away, and what else needed to be scrubbed. Christmas brunch for fourteen was no small undertaking, and neither was the cleanup. But they were actually close to finished. Teamwork makes the dream work.

She genuinely didn't know it was possible to be this happy. The last eight months had been more than she could imagine. The plans she'd made for herself were going off without a hitch. Especially after the Royal Fuckface Whose Name She No Longer Mentioned had been dealt with. She hadn't taken out a hit on him or anything, but she had filed a proper restraining order, and while that was being processed, someone involved in his none-too-bright scheme took issue with a missing payment and paid a visit to Dane outside of his office.

He'd walked away with just a broken wrist, but that brush with actual violence seemed to put some things in perspective for him. He'd emailed her eventually to apologize, and though she ignored it, she had a feeling he'd finally figured out it was time to let her go and leave her alone. She hadn't heard from him since, and she knew she wouldn't ever again.

Which suited her just fine. She was too busy living her best life.

Two months after she'd settled things up in the Bay Area, she'd moved in with Jesse. She'd looked for her own place, but nothing seemed to fit, mostly because she knew in her heart where she belonged. They'd spent so much time driving back and forth from Pleasant Lane, it just made more sense for them to wake up next to each other every morning. Over the summer she found the perfect farm to serve as the spot for her animal sanctuary. The Rollins family was retiring and moving to Lake Tahoe. They loved the idea of a hometown girl like Lily-Grace giving their farm a second life that would help so many animals in need.

After a few long talks with Evie and Jesse, she realized she didn't want to run it herself full time, but she wanted to be the money behind it all, and thanks to her and all the Pleasants' connections drumming up support and publicity, she knew Sunshine Animal Sanctuary would be a success. They were still hiring staff and completing renovations on the barn and the main house, but they were on track to receive two cows and three elderly horses who'd arrive the first of March.

There had still been the matter of Ulway and what to do about Aaron Genicks. She'd talked to Jesse and her father, and decided to link up with her own therapist. Dr. Lydia was amazing and she'd given Lily-Grace all the time and space she needed to work through her lingering feelings about the harassment and what she needed for herself moving forward. Thinking back on all the hard work she'd put in and all the young women who'd come behind her and were still to walk through Ulway's doors looking to build their career, she wanted to do something. In the summer, after she got the sanctuary up and running, she was going to go public with her story and let as many people as would listen know exactly what Aaron had done.

Lily-Grace knew at best, Aaron might lose his job, but at least there would be something on record. Something out in the world that might protect the next woman who came in contact with him. She knew there would be fall out, but she'd do her best to take it day by day. She had a plan. She had good people around her, and a soft place to land.

For years, she'd convinced herself Charming was just too dull for her, but maybe she needed the chance to see what else was out there. To see what she needed for herself, what she really wanted, and the classic saying turned out to be true. There was no place like home. There was always something to do and also someone to spend her time with, now twin babies to help out with. Lily-Grace never thought she would enjoy babysitting this much, but she loved any time she got to spend time with little Seraphina and her brother Justice, younger by exactly three minutes.

She had a real girl crew now, fleshed out with Jenny, Evie, Lilah, Vega, and Corie. Brit and Delfi popped in and out often too, and Amanda whenever she was in town. Always someone to talk to and thank God for Mrs. Pleasant and Miss Leona, always someone ready to go to LA at the drop of a hat to go shopping. Things were going great between her father and Miss Leona. She didn't think Miss Leona was in the market to remarry, but that suited her father just fine. It was clear they couldn't get enough of each other.

And then there was Jesse.

"Okay. We're ready," Evie said as she and Mrs. Pleasant walked back into the kitchen, carrying a baby each. "If we go now, I might be able to get away without a backseat diaper change."

"Come on, come on. We'll clean up the rest when we get back," Miss Leona said, waving everyone out of the kitchen.

"Let's do it." Lily-Grace dried the last dish, then rushed to the bathroom to touch up her makeup. When she came back out, Lilah handed her her coat and her Stetson. A few minutes later Evie, Mrs. Pleasant, Lilah, and the twins piled into Mrs. Pleasant's Escalade. Lily-Grace, Miss Leona, Mrs. McQueen, Amanda, and Corie climbed into Lily-Grace's Tahoe, and they all headed over to Big Rock Ranch. Vega had spent the morning opening presents with her family, but she was going to meet them over there. No way she was going to miss Jesse's big reveal.

Lily-Grace and her father both finished their swimming certifications down at the rec center, which she was grateful for considering how much time she spent in Jesse's pool. And now, finally, they'd be able to ride together. She was happy for selfish reasons, but she knew this was important to Jesse in his role as the owner of one, and soon to be two, ranches, when the Golden Gulch deal closed in a few weeks' time. He could finally say he was a rancher who knew his way around a horse.

"Mom, we have to get you in the saddle," Amanda said to her mother in the back seat.

"My Black ass will be staying right on the ground, thank you very much."

"You can join all us old folks who no longer defy gravity," Miss Leona said. "Climbing in the saddle is not a requirement for spending time with us."

"Why am I nervous?" Lily-Grace laughed. She gripped the wheel like it was the only thing holding her down.

"Secondhand nerves, honey."

"Secondhand embarrassment is real," Corie added.

"Listen." Lily-Grace glanced up and caught Corie's eye in the rearview mirror. They had a good relationship now, but shit-talking was definitely a part of Corie's DNA. "However this goes, do not give him a hard time."

"I won't! You notice I can't ride either."

"I'm just saying."

"You have my word. Besides, I'ma find fifty other things to clown him about before dinnertime."

"Yeah, I'm sure you will."

Miss Leona fielded Mrs. McQueen's questions about the ranch and Charming for the rest of the ride, giving Lily-Grace's mind the space it needed to focus on the only thing that mattered right now. Jesse. She was so proud of him, and not just for working on his fears and learning to ride, but for how much time he'd spent trying to be a better man.

He was right, they never fought. Even when they disagreed and he would get a little grouchy, they always gave each other space, then talked things through. And he wasn't just using that constructive approach when it came to her. Zach and Sam had told her on more than one occasion that the three of them were closer than ever, that they knew they could really talk to Jess and he felt more free to come to them. He'd even asked his parents to join him in therapy a handful of times and it had really paid off. He and Senior were moving forward in a way that made Lily-Grace all the more grateful for the relationship she'd always had with her father.

They pulled through the iron gates of Big Rock Ranch and followed the Escalade back to the stables. A few guests were milling around the property, taking in the bright sun and the cool winter air, but she was sure the rest were enjoying their warm fireplaces and Brit's fantastic holiday menu.

When they reached the barn, she waved to Vega, who was standing with her cousin Donie, who they'd hung out with a few times. Donie was a photographer and Jesse probably wanted to properly document his progress.

Right as she climbed out of her car, Lilah rushed over and took her hand. "If you'll follow me."

"Whooop, doesn't look like I have a choice." She laughed as Lilah tugged her over to the paddock fence and opened the gate. As they walked toward the middle, she could spot a metric ton of rose petals scattered in the shape of a heart.

"Don't worry. The roses are horsey safe," Lilah said.

"Oh good."

"Okay, you stand right there. And we'll be good to go in just a minute."

She followed directions and waited as Lilah rushed around and tried to get everyone in place for Jesse's maiden voyage around the property.

"Okay, we're ready!" Lilah yelled. A few seconds later the barn door cracked open and Jenny and Amanda's dad, Mr. McQueen, slipped out, carrying a portable speaker. They were both wearing tuxes.

"What in the! Jenny?!"

"Aren't you glad I dragged you to that date auction?"

She and Mr. McQueen got the table and the speaker set up and then rushed back and pulled open the barn doors. Lily-Grace realized what was happening then. The only reason her best friend would ditch her parents on Christmas Day and put on literal fancy pants.

"Oh, fuck," she muttered to herself. "This negro is gonna propose to me." She took a deep breath and made sure to unlock her knees. The last thing she needed was to faint before Jesse was able to pop the question.

Out came Sam first, riding Majesty, his white cowboy hat in perfect contrast to the horse's beautiful black coat. They carefully made their way to where Lily-Grace was standing. Then Sam leaned down and held out a fresh long-stemmed red rose.

"Lily-Grace Leroux."

"Yes, Sam."

"Will you accept this rose, on behalf of my brother Jesse?"

"Of course I will." Sam handed her the rose and turned Majesty, who just barely missed whipping Lily-Grace in the face with her tail as they trotted off.

Next came Zach and Steve. They approached, and then in the most Zach-like way ever, Steve made a dramatic show of getting on his horsey knees right in front of her. Lily-Grace didn't know whether to laugh or roll her eyes.

"Miss LeRoux."

"Zach."

"I had a whole speech planned, but Jesse told me to hurry the hell up. Would you accept this rose on behalf of my amazing brother, Jesse?"

"Absolutely," she said, taking the rose.

Zach clicked his teeth and Steve popped up, but made sure to plant one of his trademark horse kisses on her cheek before they trotted to the side to join Sam.

Senior came out next, riding DJ Clip Clop. No fancy tricks, but Lily-Grace was overwhelmed by the serious but sincere expression on his face when he handed her the next rose.

"As the kids say, no spoilers, but if your answer is yes, Junior's mother and I would be overjoyed to consider you and your father a part of our family, us a part of yours."

"I think I better say yes then." She smiled back at him as she took the rose.

Next came her father, walking with her horse Margot Thee Stallion's reins in his hands. The deal for Monty had fallen through, but a few weeks later Jesse had tracked down the most stunning blue roan mare. She was the best riding companion Lily-Grace could ask for, and currently on her best behavior as she picked her away across the grass beside her father.

"Oh hell." The tears came then, happy tears of course, but they spontaneously spilled over her cheeks as they got closer. Her dad had been her whole world for so long, just the two of them, and she was so happy he was there to experience this moment with her. He brought Margot to a stop, then handed Lily-Grace another rose.

"I know you don't need my blessing—"

"Of course, I do. You know I wouldn't be standing here if you thought he was no good."

"Well then, I don't think you could have picked a better man. You should see him back there now. Sweating bullets because all he wants is to spend the rest of his life with you."

"The feeling's mutual."

"I love you, LilyBug."

"Love you too, Dad."

He handed her the rose, then moved just to the side to keep a grip on Margot's reins.

A moment later, from where she stood she could hear the opening notes to Luther's "Here and Now," the song that was playing when they shared their first proper slow dance. She let out another shaky breath, then dabbed her eyes. Thank God for a good setting spray.

Bam Bam came strolling out of the barn with Jesse high astride his back. She could see his intense dark eyes and that handsome face under his black Stetson and thought she might faint after all.

"Jaysus!" she called out. "My man looks good in the saddle."

Jesse smiled for just a second before it faltered, as their family and friends laughed at her little outburst. She could tell he was concentrating so hard on not falling off the horse. She realized as he got closer there was something in this lap. He made his way over to her and Lily-Grace couldn't stop herself from out-and-out weeping. He'd worked on his fear, for her, and was now confidently riding a horse. Even without all the fanfare and the question that, she was sure, was to come, she couldn't have been more proud of him.

He stopped Bam Bam just a few feet away, then carefully swung his leg over, those thick thighs looking amazing in his jeans, before he carefully slid to the ground. He was still clutching the bundle that had been in his lap, now close to his chest. He closed the distance between them and it was like everything fell away—the music, their families and friends and various horses. It was just the two of them.

"Hi," he whispered.

"Hello, Mr. Pleasant."

"Did you see me riding that horse?"

"I sure did. That's going right in the spank bank for sure," she said so her dad couldn't hear.

"Oh good. That's my favorite place to make appearances. So, I had two questions I wanted to ask you. First—" He unwrapped the little bundle and the cutest black, gray, and brown puppy looked up at her, sleepy eyes blinking. "What are we gonna name this little guy?"

"Jess, oh my God."

"He's a blue heeler–rottie mix."

"You mean the cutest dog ever." She went to take the puppy, but the flowers got in the way.

"I'm holding too many things. Can someone come take these roses?" Amanda appeared and took them with quickness. Lily-Grace cradled the puppy in her arms and looked back up at her man. "Oh, we have to think of the best name for you. What was the other thing you wanted to ask me?"

"I was saying—" Jesse dropped down on one knee and opened the ring box. A peach sapphire with diamond leaf side stone sat nestled in the white cushion. "Lily-Grace LeRoux. I want to spend the rest of my life with you, making you smile, making you pancakes and finely crafted steaks, and buying things you say you don't need but clearly want. More horses, more puppies, and maybe a couple of chubby babies, but one at a time."

"Would recommend. Two at a time is harder than it looks," Evie shouted.

More tears poured out as Lily-Grace nodded. "Yes. I want to marry you, absolutely yes."

Jesse sprung to his feet, careful not to squish the puppy, as he cupped Lily-Grace's face and kissed her softly, perfectly, on her lips. She could hear muffled sounds of their family and friends cheering all around them, but there was just Jesse in that moment. The absolute man of her dreams.

"I wanted to get a string quartet to play the "Thong Song" for you, but my grandmother is here," he said when he pulled back. "And it's Christmas Day."

"You made this plenty special. Trust me. I love you so much, Jesse Pleasant."

"I love you too."

She switched the puppy to her other arm, then held out her trembling hand so Jesse could slide the ring on her finger. They were swarmed with congratulations and at some point someone produced many bottles of champagne. And then it was time for their real ride. Lilah took the puppy so Lily-Grace could climb in Margot's saddle.

"My dad and Sam are gonna join us, if that's okay, at a distance." Jesse had really outdone himself, and having experienced riders out on the trail for their first time was a very smart idea.

"Of course." They set out on the trail, with Senior leading and Sam bringing up the rear. Sam kept his singing to himself this time. As she glanced back at Jesse, at her fiancé, the sun disappeared behind the clouds. She could feel that crisp bite in the air. Snow was coming, but there was no way it would dampen their afternoon.

They stopped at the stream where Sam and Senior rode ahead a bit to give them some privacy. As soon as they were alone, Jesse dismounted and pulled her close. He kissed her like he'd never kissed her before. Deep and sweet, like he was never going to let her go. Lily-Grace melted into his arms, kissing him back with every ounce of love and appreciation she had for her man, her charming prince. She still couldn't believe how easy he made things for her, being so kind. So loving, so giving and open, and all she had to do was sit back and enjoy their happily ever after.

Can't get enough of these cowboys?

Don't miss the full series

A Cowboy to Remember

If the Boot Fits

A Thorn in the Saddle

Available now
Wherever books are sold

Connect with

Us

Visit us online at
KensingtonBooks.com
to read more from your favorite authors, see books
by series, view reading group guides, and more.

Join us on social media

for sneak peeks, chances to win books and prize packs,
and to share your thoughts with other readers.

facebook.com/kensingtonpublishing
twitter.com/kensingtonbooks

Tell us what you think!

To share your thoughts, submit a review,
or sign up for our eNewsletters, please visit:
KensingtonBooks.com/TellUs.